THE
OLD
PLACE

THE
OLD
PLACE

a novel

BOBBY FINGER

G. P. PUTNAM'S SONS
NEW YORK

PUTNAM
— EST. 1838 —

G. P. Putnam's Sons
Publishers Since 1838
An imprint of Penguin Random House LLC
penguinrandomhouse.com

Library of Congress Cataloging-in-Publication Data

Names: Finger, Bobby, author.
Title: The old place: a novel / Bobby Finger.
Description: New York: G. P. Putnam's Sons, [2022] | Identifiers:
LCCN 2022019072 (print) | LCCN 2022019073 (ebook) |
ISBN 9780593422342 (hardcover) | ISBN 9780593422359 (ebook)
Subjects: LCGFT: Pastoral fiction. | Novels.
Classification: LCC PS3606.I53378 O43 2022 (print) |
LCC PS3606.I53378 (ebook) | DDC 813/.6—dc23/eng/20220422
LC record available at https://lccn.loc.gov/2022019072
LC ebook record available at https://lccn.loc.gov/2022019073

Printed in the United States of America
1 3 5 7 9 10 8 6 4 2

Title page art: Linen background © Limolida Design Studio / Shutterstock
Book design by Alison Cnockaert

For Joshua

THE
OLD
PLACE

1

MARY ALICE ROTH WOKE UP AND STARED AT THE BIG OLD trunk, which may as well have been a reflection. Unmoved for years, the hunk of carved, glossy hardwood sat under the window in her bedroom because she'd lost the only people strong enough to lift it somewhere else. At her age, the number of able bodies in a household doesn't tend to change, and neither does the way you sleep, which meant Mary Alice—the sole inhabitant of 4 County Road 1818 for over ten years and a left-side sleeper since she was in a crib—knew that for the rest of her life, the first thing she'd see in the morning would be a hideous antique trunk she hated more than just about anything else in the world. And now she couldn't get rid of it even if she tried, unless she wanted to throw out her back and spend hours moaning on the floor hoping someone would knock on the door and check on her. It was that sort of terrible, bottomless pit of a fact that made her wish she were dead. But she wasn't, not today at least. So she silenced the buzzing clock and began another week of living. What else was there for her to do, anyhow?

For most of her sixty-three years, Mary Alice held a grudging respect for mornings and the way they provided a solid foundation to the structure of her busy days, but lately they'd felt absurd. Starting a new day knowing you had nothing to make or do was utterly ridiculous, maybe even sinful. Monotony was only acceptable if imbued with some sort of greater purpose—like providing for a family or teaching math to the bright-eyed youth of small-town America—and Mary Alice hadn't figured out her new one yet. But a tiny, if fading, speck of hope that she would eventually sort out this stage of her life remained, so she flipped off the covers with a grunt and twisted her tall, bony body out of the four-poster. Seated, feet on the floor, she kept her eyes on that trunk as she offered the house a single droning sigh, a reminder that she was still here, and stood. Her joints were old, but they didn't creak. Her body was tired, but it didn't ache. Frailty would have been a welcome excuse to let herself wallow horizontally a little longer, but like all the women in her family, who had been growing old in this part of Texas since arriving from Germany some 150 years ago, she was cursed with good health and a revulsion to wasted time.

Today was the first day of classes at Billington Independent School District, a sprawling complex of small-to-smallish redbrick buildings and rusty tin just off the old highway, which itself was just off the new highway—the past butt up against the present. Had this been a normal year, Mary Alice Roth would have been among the scores of other employees, getting there early to memorize a handwritten seating chart she hid in the locked top drawer of her matte green metal desk, drinking warm coffee out of a thick mug stamped with a faded BHS logo, and basking in the light from the wall of windows she refused to obscure with decorations. But today, Mary Alice was exactly where she'd been for the past three months. She was home.

Earlier that summer, a few weeks into her district-mandated exile—or compulsory leave, or forced retirement, or whatever flowery term they ultimately chose to call it once that Josie Kerr swooped in and took over her old classroom—Mary Alice confronted two fundamental things about herself. The first was that she hated doing nothing. The second was that, without a job, she had nothing to do. That her next-door neighbor, Ellie Hall, happened to call at the very moment of her epiphany one June morning was lucky for the both of them, as the friendly check-in—one of their long-standing regular chats that was comforting, if superficial and always the same— quickly became an even friendlier standing invitation.

Here's how it happened: Ellie asked about Mary Alice's summer plans now that she was unemployed, and Mary Alice laughed. Mary Alice asked about Ellie's work, knowing full well that she hated talking about work, and Ellie laughed. So they did what Texans always loved to do, though they may deny it if asked: they complained about the heat. This led to complaining about the new priest, which eventually transitioned into gossiping about the family who moved into Margaret Rose's old house. He was a former Billington High School prom king, she was a city girl he dragged back home along with their son, and they must have gotten a great deal because Margaret Rose smoked at least a pack a day in that living room for eighty years. That place didn't just need a coat of paint, they decided. It needed new walls. Every old house comes with ghostly memories of its former inhabitants, but Margaret Rose's walls were a sickly yellow with tar caked onto every surface. Billington got noticeably quieter the day she died, they agreed just before their chatter began to wane. They'd never expected to miss the sound of her wheezing cough.

After even considerable time spent apart, the best of friends can usually start back up again as though only seconds have passed, but there was more than just time between Mary Alice and Ellie's last long chat. There was loss, too much of it. But this morning meant something, Ellie decided, so she tried her best to regain momentum, and there was no better way to do so than with gossip. She asked if Mary Alice had heard the news about the wife. No, Mary Alice had *not* heard that the wife had been hired at BHS; she'd deliberately avoided all news about that den of cowards and thieves masquerading as educators, and her casual acquaintances knew better than to say anything that might cause her ruffle-hungry feathers to as much as twitch. Ellie didn't need to explicitly mention that the wife was given Mary Alice's old job; it was obvious in her anxious delivery and confirmed by the silence that followed. And Mary Alice knew in that empty moment that Ellie regretted bringing it up and was about to say goodbye, so she blurted out, "Would you want to come over for coffee tomorrow morning?"

"You know the last time I had coffee at your place?"

"No, I don't."

"That's 'cause it's never happened before," Ellie said with a hearty laugh that made Mary Alice smile so big she got nervous someone might see. When was the last time anyone else had been in her house?

"Well, I'm sorry for being such a crummy neighbor all these years. How about I make it up to you tomorrow morning. All you have to do is show up."

"Well," Ellie said, with a hesitation that made Mary Alice's smile fade.

"Does seven-thirty work?"

Ellie said it did, surprising both of them.

THE NEXT MORNING, Ellie pushed open the gate on the south side of Mary Alice's house, its rusty hinge casting out a piercing squeak, and followed a short trail through the bushes onto her back patio, a covered, polished concrete rectangle with tiers of potted plants on wrought iron shelves in every corner and two large white Adirondack chairs in the center, facing the fenced backyard. A plastic side table was between them, with just enough room for the hot plate and coasters Mary Alice brought out from the kitchen. She removed her glasses and started filling two mugs as soon as the hinge squeaked.

"What, no eggs and bacon?" Ellie said as she stepped into the shade.

"Coffee's enough breakfast for me," Mary Alice said.

"I'm only pickin' on you." She sat and faced the pale yellow cornfields that began just past the fence and stretched all the way to the horizon. Mesquite trees dotted the edges of their view, jagged reminders of the land's fraught history. The tinkling from the wind chime came to an abrupt stop, as if the wind realized it was interrupting something momentous.

Mary Alice's mind raced. Another person on her patio! Was Ellie here out of pity or loneliness? Would it happen again or was it just going to be today? She used her own voice to drown out her thoughts. "You don't take milk, do you?"

"Heavens no."

"It's 'hell no' in this house, you know that," Mary Alice said. "So the coffee's good then? Tastes fine?"

"Better than what they've got at the hospital," Ellie said. "And even if it weren't, I'd drink every drop anyway."

And with that, after twelve years of awkward pleasantries, they were friends again. Not just neighbors, but actual friends. Friends who met face-to-face, who made each other laugh, and who could be happier than they'd been in years simply by sitting side by side in silence. All it took was a phone call and a pot of caffeine. Mary Alice turned her gaze to Ellie, eager to change the subject. She looked her friend up and down and squinted, craning her neck over the hot plate as she examined the pattern covering Ellie's body. "I never see you in your scrubs. What's all over those? Kittens?"

"Puppies."

Mary Alice's eyes narrowed even further, then popped wide open. "Oh, I see now."

"Kittens are Tuesdays."

They laughed a gentle, early-morning laugh and looked back to the sky, which had gotten a little brighter, as the dawn sky always manages to do. Thirty minutes later, Ellie was gone. Three hours after that, Mary Alice finished her book—a meandering experimental novel about a beloved radio host preparing for his final shows—wrapped the cord around the hot plate, and went back inside. Every time this new version of their friendship began to excite her and feel like something that could become permanent, Mary Alice snuffed out all flickers of optimism from her mind. She would enjoy their moments together as she was in them but would not yearn for more than Ellie was willing to give. She would distract herself from intrusive thoughts with another book, something propulsive and surprising.

She would keep tabs on her neighbors, which was easier than keeping tabs on herself. Avoiding disappointment was a full-time job, and her schedule had just opened up.

Two beams of light burst through the living room window that night as Mary Alice stabbed her fork into the final piece of steamed broccoli resting on her plate. Ellie was home from work. Not ten minutes later she phoned Mary Alice to tell her about a child with a broken arm who thought her scrubs were kittens, too, isn't that funny? And then, to suggest that they have coffee again tomorrow.

A week of mornings later, Ellie said she'd bring the coffee the following day; all Mary Alice needed to do was turn on the hot plate and bring out the mugs. At some point, an egalitarian schedule just sorted itself out without too much talking, the sort of thing that marks a friendship as true, even if it took a decade or more to get there. Mary Alice would make the coffee on Mondays, Wednesdays, and Fridays; Ellie would take Tuesdays and Thursdays, transporting her own carafe the two hundred feet or so from her back door to her neighbor's. "It takes thirty days to create a habit," Mary Alice often told her son, Michael, when confronted by his unmet potential. Turns out she'd been wrong. Sometimes it took just under ten.

Every morning since their meetups began some two months ago, Mary Alice walked downstairs into the kitchen, removed the hot plate from a drawer beneath her old coffee maker—whose once white plastic had aged into a pale sepia—and grabbed two mugs from the cabinet above it. Then, as she walked to the sliding door, the saying came to her as it always did. *Every morning I wake up alive,* she thought. *I celebrate with coffee.*

Twenty-four years earlier, she and her husband, Samuel, had driven two hours, plus a miserable hour-long detour, to take Michael to SeaWorld, which he didn't enjoy as much as they wanted—or needed—him to. In his defense, though, the park *was* a little awful. Overcrowded, overpriced, and impossible to navigate without overheating. Lines for its few rides, if you could call them that, were an hour long apiece; all three of them got sunburned. And the main attraction—the show with the poor, imprisoned orca who seemed thrilled in all the commercials—was cut short when an employee tripped on the stage, knocked his head on a fake rock, and rolled into the tank. They soon found out that the giant cloud of blood made his injury seem worse than it was, but the show was still canceled for the remainder of the day for draining and cleaning. "Blood," Samuel said, covering his own eyes along with Michael's. "I can't look at the blood."

They stopped for a late lunch on the way home at a Cracker Barrel near the park. Every other Shamu fan must have had the same idea because the line for a table was endless and the waiting area-cum-gift shop smelled like chlorine and SPF 50. Mary Alice didn't even want to bother putting their name on the list, but Michael was hungry and Samuel very sternly reminded her that they wouldn't be home for at least two more hours anyway. "We're not going to get him addicted to chicken nuggets and French fries," he said as a closer. Mary Alice almost argued that a place like this was just as unhealthy as fast food, only more expensive, but knew it would only make things worse. Plus, Michael was more excited by the kitschiness of the restaurant than any of the animals at SeaWorld, and she liked seeing him happy. Seeing him happy was the whole point.

She and Samuel ambled through the crowded aisles behind Michael without saying a word to each other as he darted from display to display, first zoning in on the cheaply made plastic toys in one corner, then transitioning to home decor. He picked up one sign and stammered through its factory-printed message word by word. "'If . . . Momma . . . a . . . uh . . . a-neet . . .'"

"'Ain't,'" Mary Alice said. "That's OK, it's a new word. A confusing word, too. 'Ain't' means 'is not.'"

"'If Momma ain't hap . . . py . . . ain't no . . . body happy.'" He lowered the sign and looked up at his mother, searching her eyes for praise.

"What do you think that means?"

His face dropped. The excitement, gone in a poof. "It means," he said, lingering on the thought for a few more seconds, "if you're happy, then me and Daddy are happy."

"That's right," she said, hoping that would be the end of it. But Michael was an inquisitive child, his head permanently swimming with questions, and Mary Alice knew one was liable to jump out and bite the silence between them at any moment.

"Are you happy?"

It was one of the most dreadful things she could think of, being asked that question by her own child, even if he didn't mean to upset her. The hum of despair she'd felt all day—no, longer—calcified in that moment, and she imagined herself scooping Michael up into her arms and running out of the restaurant, running all the way back home, running for a hundred miles and not stopping until she was lying beside him in his bed, making sure he was asleep, and hoping he'd forget he'd ever asked her such a dreary, unanswerable thing. But then again, maybe she was overthinking it, as usual. Maybe nothing was as awful as it seemed—not his question, not the park, not this godforsaken gift shop. She remembered the blood of that

SeaWorld employee, and how it looked so much worse than the injury itself. He was probably at home by now, touching the bandage on his forehead and feeling like a fool for slipping in front of all those people.

"Of course I'm happy," she said before pointing at a sign beside it. "Now, can you read me this one?"

"'Every morning I . . . wake up . . . alive,'" he said, sounding out each word before committing to it, "'I celebrate with coffee.'"

"What do you think that means?"

"It means," he said, fingering the words once more as if scanning them for clues, "you don't drink coffee if you're dead."

Mary Alice laughed for the first time that day and wrapped her arm around Michael, who beamed at her delight. "Can we buy it?" he asked.

"I don't think so."

"Why not?"

"I don't think we're the kind of people who put that sort of thing on their walls."

A woman to her left, who was just about her age, overheard and snipped back, "And what kind of person is?"

Mary Alice looked down and noticed the woman was holding the sign about dead people not drinking coffee, along with plenty of other items with similar sentiments. "Oh, I didn't mean anything by it."

"If you didn't mean what you said," the woman growled, "you shouldn't have said it so damn loudly." She marched off toward the cash register.

Mary Alice yearned to tell her to wait, so she could explain herself. But what would she have said? How could she have convinced this angry stranger of how embarrassed she would be if people could read all the tchotchkes filling up the walls in her head? The ones she'd never dream of hanging in her home, where everyone could see them? She couldn't. So she just shouted back, "Just so you know, I love coffee!" People turned their heads at the noise, and then turned back. The incident had lasted mere seconds, but Mary Alice knew her whimpering retort would haunt her for years. Or maybe she just decided that it ought to.

"Why are you fighting with that lady?" Michael asked.

"We weren't fighting," Mary Alice said. "She just wanted to remind me that sometimes people think things that they shouldn't say out loud. Have you ever thought a thing and not said it out loud?"

Michael nodded, clearly out of confusion. Mary Alice could see him unpacking the entire confrontation inside that still-growing brain. At this age, he seemed to be getting smarter by the minute. He wasn't just noticing things, he was processing them—taking them apart, examining the pieces, and reassembling them. She wondered how long he would have to process this moment with the stranger in a Cracker Barrel. She wondered whether it would affect the way he communicated, or even *felt*, long-term. She wondered whether it would be a story he'd tell in therapy twenty years from now. But maybe, she tried to hope, he'd forget it by tomorrow. Maybe! Maybe. Oh God, but maybe not. She was spiraling now, debating between the value of saying one more thing and just shutting up. She had to stop; he was still looking at her. So she picked him up and said the first thing that came to her. "But you should *never* be ashamed by something that you feel." That must be the right lesson, she thought. How could it be the wrong one?

Over time she came to appreciate that moment of public embarrassment and private existential panic as a piece of herself that would never go away. So many things had left her over the years, almost all of them by choice, but those memories were hers forever. She would respect them, even if they brought her pain. And remembering that moment in the gift shop was part of her morning routine, just like showering or getting dressed or plugging the hot plate into the extension cord that snaked across the patio or reading as much as she could before Ellie arrived.

That morning, the heat radiating from the plate had only begun hitting her shoulders when she heard the familiar squeak from her left. She dog-eared the paperback in her hand, placed it on her lap, and turned to the bushes as Ellie shuffled toward her. Ellie tripped after stepping up on the patio, catching herself in time to prevent a fall but not before a few splashes of coffee sloshed out of the carafe and onto her scrubs, turning a few of the taxis and pedestrians on the cartoon cityscape pattern brown. Mary Alice bolted up.

"Are you OK?"

"I'm fine, I'm fine. Just clumsy and in a hurry."

"I only read seven pages. That must be a record or something."

"Sorry, I just need to be out of here by seven-forty-five today."

Ellie filled the two mugs and gently placed the carafe on the hot plate before inhaling deeply, smoothing out her scrubs, and landing on the chair with a slow, forceful exhale. Her eyes were closed. Ellie was Mary Alice's age, down to the Libra sign, but looked at least a decade younger. Her hair, which had eased into a warm gray after a lifetime on the dirtier side of blond, was pulled back in her work-mandated ponytail, which kept her face taut and knocked off another five years. Everything about her face was kind, but in a practiced way. That was one of Mary Alice's favorite things about her: there was an edge to Ellie's charm that made you know she worked at it. Ellie's very presence usually tended to lower a person's blood pressure; Mary Alice knew this for a fact. But not today. Today there was something missing. Or maybe there was an extra piece. Ellie was the only person in town Mary Alice could never quite figure out, even now, with their friendship finally rekindled. Ellie was an "only" kind of woman in a lot of ways. The only person in her family to move away from Houston, which made her the only city slicker in Billington, where she was the only person in town who worked in healthcare— such an interesting, metropolitan job—not to mention the only woman who'd ever been divorced—which was the only "only" that Ellie ever had a hard time believing. "It's true," Mary Alice had assured her so long ago. "You'd be surprised by how many people are happy to choose misery over divorce. Especially here."

And now, as the only person invited to sit on this porch in at least twenty years, she was the only thing on Mary Alice's mind. "You sure you're OK?"

"I said I'm OK." She opened her right eye and pointed it at her friend. "Are you?"

Mary Alice scoffed. "I'm not the one who nearly fell into scalding-hot coffee and shattered glass."

"But you *are* the one who's home on the first day of school for the first time in, what? A hundred and two, a hundred and three years?"

"Forty," Mary Alice interrupted. "And yes, I'm OK. Thank you for your concern." She took another sip of the coffee.

"Bull."

"Fine, I'm miserable. No, I'm furious. You know she's putting in a pool?"

"Who?"

The muscles in Mary Alice's shoulders went limp. "You know who."

"Josie Kerr? You have to leave that poor woman alone. Haven't you done enough to her already?"

"Her stomach issues are not my fault," Mary Alice said with a sly smile.

Ellie's head shook with disapproval, but her smile suggested otherwise. The wind chime took its cue and played a few delicate chords as Ellie processed this information. "So is Miss Queasy's pool aboveground?"

Mary Alice smiled. *"In."*

Ellie snapped back into sternness and raised her hands up, palms toward the rising sun. "You know what, I don't want to be involved in your gossip. Not about her, anyhow. If she wants to sink money into digging a hole in that yard, that's none of your business and it sure as hell isn't any of mine. That pool's for Josie and Josie's family to swim in, so it should be between Josie and Josie's family to worry about."

"Josie's family and their bank. You know how expensive it is to break through limestone?"

"Is that a question or a statement?"

"Tommy said it's costing her near forty-one thousand for the whole damn thing. It's why Samuel and I never put one in."

"Forty-one?" Ellie nearly wretched, then composed herself. "I said I don't want to get involved! And more importantly, I don't want to know how you or Tommy Lutz got that number so easily. She can spend her money however she wants. You know Travis probably does well for himself anyway; smart, handsome thing like that. Maybe Faye even chipped in."

"Travis's doing more than fine, but I still think she comes from it."

"Comes from what?"

"What do you think? Money."

"Ha! You don't know anything about that woman. You've spoken to her, what? Once? And I wouldn't exactly call those circumstances fair."

"Fair? She stole my classroom. Though I guess rich people don't steal, they just take."

"She was *given* your classroom because she's a bright young woman. And she took it because she's a bright young woman with a family to take care of and a brain to use," Ellie said. "This wasn't a conspiracy, Mary Alice. And you're not gonna find peace until you acknowledge that as the truth, because that's what it is. The truth."

Mary Alice wanted nothing more than to soak this into her pores, to accept it as the obvious truth that she knew it was, but she couldn't. "I don't have to be happy."

"You're crazy not to be," Ellie said, shaking her head as she looked back at the cornstalks in the distance, swaying left and right as if listening and unable to pick a side to agree with.

"I'm what?!"

"You are crazy for not being happy."

"You don't know what you're talking about," Mary Alice snipped with a near-laugh. "Never did."

Ellie scooted her chair to face Mary Alice directly. "No more phone calls or unscheduled house visits with angry moms and dads? Not to mention phone calls with the stupid ones. No more conversations with Will and Gina and Laurie and all those other fools you used to spend all your time arguing with in the teacher's lounge? No more filling in for a sick bus driver because you were dumb enough to get certification?" She took a breath, and then another sip, but she wasn't finished. Something lit up inside her. This was no longer one of Mary Alice's silly complaints, it was an affront to her own life. "You think I'd still be working if I could help it?"

"I know you wouldn't."

She pointed at an old oil drum in the far corner of Mary Alice's yard, to the right of her woodshed. "You think I wouldn't throw these scrubs in that burn barrel and light them on fire if someone told me I'd have a pension and benefits until I'm dust in the wind?"

Mary Alice turned away and pursed her lips. "OK, I get it."

"Good." She laughed, knowing one push was enough. "Now, will you enjoy this gift you've been given? Because that's exactly what it is. A gift. Don't you forget that."

"I will *try* to enjoy my time as a"—she stopped and shuddered—"retiree . . . But I will never refer to it as a gift. You hear me? Not now and not ever. Is that good enough for you?"

"I guess." They both took another sip of coffee, despite neither of them wanting more. "What're you getting into today while I'm out saving lives?"

"Nothing."

"Nothing?"

They sat in silence for a moment, until a thought hit Ellie like an arrow. She darted her eyes toward Mary Alice, who immediately felt her gaze. "You're planning on going to that school again, aren't you."

"No," Mary Alice said. "I mean, I'd considered it. But no."

"What would you do there? Think about it. What would you actually accomplish besides killing your own time and getting on everyone else's nerves?"

"Isn't killing time enough when you're retired?"

"I'm serious."

"It's certainly better than killing myself," Mary Alice said, regretting the words even before she could hear them.

Ellie turned cold. "Don't," she said, the word piercing the air as her mug slammed down on the table. "Don't you do that."

Mary Alice flinched at her own bad joke, some combination of the sound and the memory roiling inside her, but straightened her back and put the moment behind her. "To answer your question, I'd let them all know that I'm still here," she said. "I'd let them know that I will not—no—that I *refuse* to be forgotten." She had had the thought countless times that summer, but she'd never said it out loud. And it felt different now. As a thought it was empowering. As a confession to a friend, it felt self-aggrandizing and pathetic, and she cowered in her chair immediately after saying it.

"No one could forget you," Ellie said. If Ellie was a church mouse, Mary Alice was the cracked bell roaring over her head. "How could they? You're too damn loud."

Ellie was right. But so was Mary Alice. This was one of the keys to their friendship: they were never wrong together. So many people in this town had a way of bringing Mary Alice down, letting her wallow in her wrongness, but never Ellie. She refused to let commiseration become a hobby. Arguments, she thought, were key to making friendships work, which is why theirs had lasted so long—to varying degrees—since Ellie arrived in town. Ellie had surprised both Billington and herself by moving in. There was no family connection. No husband who dragged her kicking and screaming from the city. There was only a good job in Trevino, and an affordable house fifteen miles away in Billington. That she happened to move in next to another single mother with an eleven-year-old boy was pure luck, though she took it as a sign that she'd made the right choice.

Though the Halls proudly inserted themselves headfirst into the community—attending mass even though Ellie despised the church, signing Kenny up for all the sports but football so he'd have a shot at making friends, and volunteering at the modest senior center in the middle of town—few expected the two Halls to stay long. Billington wasn't a place you arrived in, it was a place you never left. But against all odds they sprouted roots on Mary Alice's whisper of a county road, and Kenneth and Michael's instant and overwhelming friendship nourished the one between their mothers.

"I'll call you tonight," Ellie said, empty carafe in hand. "Hope you're not too miserable today."

"So you'd be fine if I were only a little miserable?"

Ellie was already in the bushes, but she turned back. "Everyone's a *little* miserable," she said. "Bye now."

Mary Alice waved, missing her already.

With no coffee left, she had nothing else to do but think. Staring out at the horizon, where the sun was high enough to make her feel like she ought to be busy, she went over the beats of their friendship. Ellie and Kenny moved in. Kenny and Michael became friends. In time, so did she and Ellie. And when they lost the boys, one right after the other, of course their friendship changed. Whose wouldn't? An acute understanding of the other's misery prevented either of them from resenting their sudden estrangement, but over time their grief transferred itself from their sons to their friendship. They'd lost the boys, but why did that mean they had to lose each other? Now, more than ten years after the accident, Mary Alice was glad she had finally decided to try a little harder. And every morning she watched Ellie step up onto the patio, she was certain, absolutely certain, that it wasn't only because she had nothing better to do.

2

THE MILE-LONG DRIVE FROM MARY ALICE'S HOUSE TO THE school took about four minutes on a normal day, five if she hit the town's only light, six if there was a train, and anywhere from seven to thirty if she needed to get a little lost in her head beforehand. Today's drive took thirteen, but she regretted not making it a few minutes longer by the time she parked under the big climbing tree in the teacher's lot. She felt an unpleasant sensation in her chest when the motor stopped running, a reverberating tightness she could actually hear. A racing heart was unfamiliar to her. She put her hand over her chest, after pulling the keys out of the ignition, to figure out what exactly it was she was feeling. It couldn't be a heart attack, she thought at first. Heart attacks hurt, didn't they? And this didn't hurt, it was just uncomfortable. But isn't that what most pain was, really? Discomfort. No, pain is *painful*. She took a few deep breaths and convinced herself it was just nerves or low-grade panic, and she'd never let something as trivial as that stop her before.

More or less convinced that she wouldn't drop dead in the teacher's lot, Mary Alice stepped out of her car, a twelve-year-old Buick bought eight years ago, and marched toward the entrance. The muted crunching of blue gravel felt familiar, and the dull edges comfortable under her feet. She considered returning to the car to check on some invisible issue with the door handle just to maintain the sensation a little longer, to do one more lap, but her watch read 8:03, twelve minutes to the first-period bell. There just wasn't enough time. She pulled open the front door and let her eyes adjust to the relative darkness inside. The ominous echoes of her footsteps bouncing off the painted cinder blocks had no business making anyone feel even remotely comfortable, Mary Alice knew this, and yet the walk down the hall did exactly that. Every time she saw photos of a new school built in a nearby city, she'd laugh at the progressive openness of their design. There was always some press-hungry vice principal who'd tell the local news that students need to feel "invited," which Mary Alice thought was a gross and potentially dangerous misunderstanding of the public school experience. School had no business being a prison, but being there *was* compulsory. A school isn't supposed to feel comfortable, she thought. Life isn't comfortable, and isn't that one of the most important lessons a teacher can share with her students? That nothing worth doing is easy? She would have continued developing her theory about the emotional implications of school design, but the muffled voices coming from the other side of the teacher's lounge door brought her panic-driven mental tangent to a halt.

She twisted the knob and held the cold metal in her fist for a moment. This would not go well, she knew that, but she had to look confident. Two more deep breaths, and she pushed. For the tiniest of moments, it looked like her old life was waiting for her on the other side. Teachers drinking coffee, grading papers, talking about whatever television show they'd watched the night before. But then one of them spotted her, and she felt something new. Shame? Fear? Whatever it was, it was awful, but there was no going back, so she took two commanding steps in and let the heavy purple door slam behind her.

If Louis Ortiz had been holding a mug of coffee, he would have dropped it. The principal was a child's drawing of an adult, disproportionate and wobbly, but with the pure face of someone you could always trust. "Mrs. Roth," he said, stammering. "Did you forget something?" He realized how stupid the question sounded as soon as he asked it, but Mary Alice's overwhelming presence prevented him from finding any other words.

"I didn't, but thanks for your concern," she said before marching to the coffee maker and pouring some into a paper cup. "Happy first day of school, everyone." Coffee probably wasn't the best idea, given her episode in the car, but she didn't have to drink it. The pour was the thing. Holding it. Standing with it. Looking like she belonged.

Louis, dressed in his trademark vest and poorly matched tie, inched his way toward Mary Alice, who looked taller than he remembered. He checked her shoes and was surprised to see a pair of flats. "You know you retired, right? We had a party and everything."

"Oh, was that what that was?"

"You know we didn't intend for the cake to say, 'Surprise!'"

"'Sorry We Forced You Out for No Good Reason' didn't fit, I know. I just wanted to check in and make sure the place hasn't fallen apart without me."

"Well," Louis said hesitantly. "It hasn't. Sturdy as ever." He banged on the wall, and a mildewed corner of drop ceiling crumbled onto the floor. "Ignore that."

"Nice to know everything's the same as it was. Well, minus one thing."

"A very special, very important thing we miss dearly. But as you know, we removed that thing from the roster. And the payroll."

"You didn't get rid of my mug." She pointed at Coach Martin, who was flipping through his phone on the squishy plaid couch against the far wall. He'd been at BHS almost as long as Mary Alice had, and never took off his coach jacket while on school grounds, even on a hot August day in a room with nothing but a sputtering window AC unit. All eyes in the room bolted to him, but he just kept mindlessly scrolling until someone cleared their throat. Coach Martin's eyes darted up, and he suddenly realized he was the center of attention.

"Mary Alice? The hell are you doing here?"

"The hell are you doing with my mug?"

He looked down at the piece of faded yellow ceramic in his hand. "This thing's yours?"

"I drank out of it every morning as long as you've known me, didn't I?"

Coach Martin scoffed, then coughed. "I don't pay attention to that crap. And you didn't answer my question—the hell are you doing here?"

"My name's on the bottom, Judd."

He flipped the mug over, spilling black coffee all over his pants and most of the couch's right cushion. "Son of a bitch in a god-damned basket," he said, scowling. "Will someone get me a goddamned towel?"

A few nervous bodies scurried to the sink to help him out, but Mary Alice wasn't among them. She turned back to Louis. "So how's the new me?"

"The new you?"

Mary Alice took another sip. It tasted worse than she remembered.

"Oh, you mean Mrs. Kerr."

"The great Josie Kerr, yes. How's she working out?"

"Well, this is her first day," he said, looking up at the ancient, synchronized clock above the door. "So I can't say for certain, but I think we made a good choice hiring her."

"So she might end up being terrible . . ."

"I doubt it," Louis said, momentarily forgetting his audience. "She's no *you*, of course."

"I'm not a dummy, Louis."

As Louis and Mary Alice stared each other down, more teachers than necessary helped Coach Martin sop up the coffee. "Get your goddamned hands off my legs and focus on the damn couch," he told them. The bell rang, making the whole room vibrate, and the teachers scattered like ants. In seconds, Coach Martin, Mary Alice, and Louis were the only people left in the room.

"I suppose I should check on her," Mary Alice said. "See how she's doing." She set her cup on the counter and started for the door.

"Uhh, M-M-Mrs. Roth, I don't think that's a good idea," Louis said. "In fact, I'm going to have to ask you to leave the premises."

"Ortiz," Coach Martin grunted. "Get your ass back here and get me a towel from the bathroom. These paper towels ain't soakin' up a goddamned thing. It's like they don't even exist." Louis's gaze bounced back and forth between Mary Alice's shrinking back and Coach Martin's growing scowl. He was torn, but rather incapable of change, so he let her win.

"Hold on, Coach," Louis said, lumbering toward the bathroom.

Mary Alice emerged from the hallway into the covered path surrounding the high school's main courtyard. The tables and benches and planters and walkways surrounding the broad, sprawling live oak in the center must have been beautiful back when it was built, but in the harsh Texas light and heat looked like they'd all crumble if you so much as tapped them with a fingernail. She watched one student, a freshman most likely, bolt from one of the six classrooms lining the courtyard to another. It shouldn't be easy to get lost on a campus this small, but it happened more than one would think.

Her autopilot insisted she cut through the courtyard and follow a more direct path to her old room, but she felt like having an audience, so she took the long way, past the walls of glass filled with minds young and old. She walked slowly and made as much noise with each step as her soft soles would allow. Though it was tough to know for certain, she felt eyes on her, and imagined what those watching her could have been thinking. *I thought that witch retired.* Or maybe, *Didn't she die?* Or what about something nice, like . . . She drew a blank. All she really wanted was to be seen, anyway. The accompanying thoughts didn't matter. Once she reached the fifth door on the right, she didn't knock or even pause. She just opened the door and walked right in.

The students saw her before their teacher did. Mary Alice closed the door gently behind her and took in the sight of her replacement. Josie was taller than Mary Alice in heels but her stance was inauthentic. From a visual perspective, authority fit her like a glove, but was clearly not her style. She faced the class but kept her eyes on the floor, weakly gesticulating in front of the chalkboard like she'd somehow just been switched on. Her outfit, a mid-length skirt and silk blouse, had clearly never been worn before, and Mary Alice gathered the whole thing cost around, oh, three hundred dollars, give or take. She wasn't sure if she should be surprised or disappointed.

"What's Mrs. Roth doing here?" a voice from the back asked. The room erupted in gasps and laughter, and Josie finally turned her head and noticed her guest.

"Oh! Mrs. Roth!" She nearly toppled over. "Nice to see you again."

"Don't stop on account of me."

"Stop what?"

"Your lesson! This is an algebra II class, right? Or is it precalculus today?"

"Precalculus."

"Then by all means!"

Mary Alice waved Josie on and moved to the bookshelf along the windows. She set her coffee on the windowsill, crossed her arms, and leaned back and watched as Josie stumbled through what sounded like a rehearsed introduction.

"As I was saying, I know you all remember doing radical equations in your algebra II class last year, and for the first few weeks you're probably going to feel like you've learned all of these things before, but every math class builds on the one before it," she said, rolling her fists over one another in a circular motion. She was

25

picking up steam. She was growing more comfortable and confident, despite the ghostly intruder. "You rarely learn a skill in an earlier level that you won't find yourself needing later on."

"Long division," Mary Alice said sternly. The students turned their heads, eyes wide as they sensed a confrontation.

"What was that, Mrs. Roth?" Josie asked, deflated once again.

"Long division is utterly useless."

A few students chuckled, but Josie maintained her composure.

"To be fair, Mrs. Roth, understanding the concept of division is essential to getting through our daily lives. We divide things all the time."

"Well, I said 'long division,' which is explicitly by hand and, allow me to repeat myself, utterly useless if a calculator is within reach."

"Well," she said, forcing a smile, "what I'm saying is that it isn't."

The sound of yipping dogs came from the back of the class, breaking the tension and leading to more laughter from the students. One of them, a floppy-headed thing in the last row, was maniacally rifling through his bag.

"Mr. Jenkins," Mary Alice said. "Does that barking phone of yours have a calculator on it?"

"I'm sorry?" he stammered.

"I didn't ask you to apologize, this isn't my classroom anymore, I asked if it has a calculator on it."

At last, he pulled the phone out from the bottom of his bag and stopped the noise. "Yeah. All phones do. You just swipe it up like this and—"

"That answers my question, thank you."

Josie gave her a bigger smile than she deserved and straightened her back. "Mrs. Roth, can we speak outside for a second?"

"And leave these hormonal teens unattended?"

"Outside, Mrs. Roth."

A chorus of "ooohs" wafted from the desks. Mary Alice followed Josie outside to the center of the courtyard, where she hoped their voices would be muffled by the wind.

"May I ask, with the utmost respect, what you're doing here?"

"You may. And with the utmost respect myself, I'm simply checking up on my classroom. Making sure it's in good hands."

"Well, it is," Josie said, holding her hands out—palms up—in front of her, like she was offering Mary Alice some kind of blessing.

Once it became clear Mary Alice would not be leaving without force or an act of God, Josie took a slow, deep, silent breath and exhaled. Her aura changed. Her body seemed calmer. "Well," she said in a near whisper, "I'd appreciate it if you wouldn't drop by unannounced and interrupt my class. It was bad enough that you came to the parent-teacher open house last week. Now you've undermined my expertise and authority in front of impressionable teenagers on the first day. You've set the tone for the entire year."

Before Mary Alice could respond with what she'd been rehearsing during her thirteen-minute drive, Louis burst through the hallway door behind them and she recalculated. "Will I see you at the planning meeting tomorrow?"

"What?"

"For the picnic?"

Josie cowered. "Oh. I completely forgot. Seven o'clock? At the church?"

"Eight o'clock. My house. You know which one it is, right? You know everything."

Louis's gasping breaths interrupted them. "Is everything OK here? Mrs. Kerr, are you hurt? Do I need to call the police?"

"The *police*?" Mary Alice asked.

"Everything's fine, Louis," Josie said.

Louis gave Mary Alice a nasty once-over. "You sure?"

"Mary Alice was just here to remind me about the picnic planning meeting tomorrow night," Josie said. "I would have missed it had she not dropped by."

Louis's eyes stayed on Mary Alice. "Is that so?"

"Are you deaf, Mr. Ortiz? I always said you needed to start listening to women," Mary Alice said. "Oh, and, Mrs. Kerr, I hope your stomach's feeling a little better. Coach Martin usually keeps a few bottles of Pepto-Bismol in the teacher's lounge if you, you know, have the urge again." She smiled at both of them and walked back to the main hallway. It wasn't her finest moment, though at least it was far from her worst. But as she approached the exit, a glint of silver caught her eye and her satisfaction waned. The trophy cabinet. She could have kept walking, but her legs came to a stop right in front of the glass. It was dusty, and nothing inside had been updated for at least nine years. Old class photos, trophies for state championships, assorted statues of bucking broncos, and in the middle, somewhere near the bottom, a photo of a young man with the brightest smile you can imagine. A modern, full-color graduation portrait dominating a row of vintage black-and-white. On the bottom of the frame, a small plaque: IN LOVING MEMORY OF KENNETH HALL. AUGUST 25, 1984–MAY 28, 2002. With a sinking feeling, she pulled her phone out of her pocket and the lock screen lit up. There, obscuring a stock background photo of Earth taken from the moon, was today's date. August 25, 2014. Kenneth would have been thirty. "Well, shit."

3

WHEN TRAVIS KERR MOVED BACK TO BILLINGTON, EVERYONE was surprised that he didn't build a house on the family property. The ranch, as it was known to the Kerrs—or the Kerr Compound, as it was known to those who had the misfortune of not being a Kerr— was a lush and secluded five-hundred-acre patch of grass and ponds and live oaks that appeared like a mirage after driving through the miles of wheat and sorghum north of town. Travis's grandparents Patrick and Louise were early landowners in town and built the big farmhouse at its center after the birth of their one and only child, Leonard. Years later, Leonard and his wife, Faye, started construction on *their* house the week after returning from their honeymoon, a two-day affair held ninety miles away in San Antonio. Then, Travis's older sister, Mae, and her husband, Freddy, broke ground just after their own engagement so they could be wed in their new backyard. (The reception was held in Grandma and Grandpa Kerr's farmhouse.)

Not only did each new house seem to come a little sooner in the lives of its owners than the ones before it, they kept getting bigger. So it was expected by everyone, even a preteen Travis, that he'd follow suit by inching his major life decisions up even further, breaking ground on the Compound's biggest house in the summer after high school graduation, just a stone's throw away from his sister's. But this was a family that was so busy either looking backward or planning ahead that they often missed out on the present, which is why it shocked the Kerrs—and no one else—when Nora Kellogg broke Travis's heart.

Nora Kellogg had famously been looking for a husband ever since her mother showed her her wedding dress. She was only twelve years old, but the dress was so beautiful, so well-preserved in its plastic zip-up sleeve, that becoming the third woman in her family to wear it down the aisle suddenly became the most important thing in the world. The dress wasn't just a dress or even a tradition, it was a stark white, lace-covered finish line. The Kelloggs weren't all that sentimental, but they were driven. So from the moment Nora grabbed Travis's hand in the eighth grade, it was assumed they would get married. It was also assumed that one of them would eventually start sleeping around, but only because everyone felt like the Kerrs were due a spell of bad luck. So when word got around that Nora was fooling around with someone named Cody who played for the basketball team in Trevino, those closest to Travis couldn't help but feel like they were partly responsible. Nora was wrecked with a load of guilt so heavy, it was as if she had disappointed not just her boyfriend, but every single person she'd ever met. And she probably had. Oh, how she begged for his forgiveness. She called every phone and banged on every door at the Compound. She stopped maintaining the curls she religiously preserved every night, making her hive of thick brown hair fall flat just like her hopes. The other Kerrs begged Travis to forgive her, if only to put an end to the pitiful sight of her, but he was unwavering. She'd set fire to the story of his life, he told them, and would have no role in its future.

Travis removed her photos from his wallet and flushed them down the toilet, knowing full well they would strain the septic tank. He threw letters she wrote him into the shredder in his father's study. And once the time came to apply to colleges, he ripped up the application to Texas A&M (with grades like his it was just a formality, anyway) and sent the scraps to Nora in the mail. When she called him, sobbing, pleading one last time for him to take her back, he sobbed right back and said she'd never have to see or even think about him again. He'd applied to NYU and Columbia, he stuttered through his tears. As a backup plan, he'd even applied to a few of those liberal arts schools that were only a train ride away from Manhattan. One of them would accept him, Travis assured her as proudly as he could muster mid-meltdown. There may have only been seventeen people in his graduating class, but a valedictorian was a valedictorian no matter where you came from. She hung up, and he decided he would never speak to her again. It wasn't the lowest moment of his life, Travis decided. It was the first one.

The Old Travis was confident, but you never really saw it on his face. To the smart and beautiful and well-to-do Kerrs, modesty was the virtue one clung to most tightly. It would have been unseemly to come across as proud. But New Travis wore pride like a well-tailored navy suit. He was unstoppable. So when the acceptance letters poured in and his parents said they wouldn't pay for a place like Columbia, he called them on their bluff. Pay they did—in full, and largely without complaint. What was there for them to complain about, anyway? He was a perfect kid, or at least one who'd never caused them any real heartache. His grades had been impeccable since kindergarten, he took the high school baseball team to the state championships for the first time in generations, his social life was robust yet responsible, and the college girl he fell in love with in the big city? Well, they fell in love with her, too.

But the Kerrs' excitement always came with the unspoken understanding that Travis would return home after four years of school and take over Leonard's land surveying business, which was as lucrative as it was boring. Certainly more boring than anything he could do with a degree from Columbia. Still, Travis was able to hold out in his metropolitan escape for ten years doing project management for a handful of startups that paid him so much for his unshakable charms that he felt guilty every time a new check was deposited. He and Josie spent the whole of their twenties in the greatest city in the world. They were married at the courthouse in Manhattan. They bought a condo in Brooklyn, thanks to the "gift" of a down payment from Josie's parents, just blocks from the public school where they planned to send their son, Henry. (A sort of penance, they thought, for his mother teaching at a private academy in the city.) It was a full decade of times so great that when his mother called one morning to say his father hadn't woken up, he felt like the town he'd been running from had finally caught up with him. He and Josie put the apartment on the market the following week, and it was sold the next day. All cash. Tech millionaires, the broker said. They planned to flip it. A decade of their lives, erased.

Once the shock of Leonard's death wore off, Josie was actually excited by the idea of moving to Billington. The only thing she drew a line at was living on the Compound. If she was going to be in a small town, she wanted to be *in* a small town, not outside its limits. They'd already traveled eighteen hundred miles from New York City to Billington, so what was another twelve miles to his family's house? Finding a home for her family would be her first task as a small-town woman, and she approached it with the same pride and gusto with which she approached everything else. But like most decisions in Billington, this one was rendered quick and painless due to a lack of options. A new build would have been ideal, but it was also time-consuming and impractical. As for the two houses for sale in town, only one was big enough for a family of three. Margaret Rose's house, a long and short ranch built in the fifties, had been on the market since her death six months before, and they bought it for a song.

Josie had spent enough time ironically watching HGTV to know a non-load-bearing wall when she saw one, and soon found herself fantasizing about all the big, inviting spaces where her family and friends could gather once she started knocking all those walls down. Space was the one thing they lacked back home, and she rarely yearned for it. To a city girl like her, space meant distance or, worse, settling. But the moment she had a surplus of it, space meant possibility. Every time Travis watched her leaf through paint swatches and furniture catalogs and pool pamphlets, a sliver of guilt was shaved off. He couldn't believe it when Josie, born and raised in Manhattan, moved to Brooklyn for him. And now she'd gone and moved to Texas.

But in Texas she had a house. And she had family nearby. She even got a job at a school where teachers never left unless they were forced out or dead. Her New York City friends couldn't believe how happy she seemed in a town so small it didn't even have a Wikipedia entry. The only problem with Billington, she told them, was that her new house didn't have a pool. But that was an easy fix, she assured them. That was just a hole that needed to be dug. Margaret Rose's house sat smack-dab in the center of a plot that could fit more than three pools, and she only needed one. It all seemed so easy, she thought. But then again, when hadn't it?

The pool wasn't the source of every problem that arose after they moved in, it was just big enough to hold all of them, even unfinished. So that's where Josie let them sit and fester. It began before the surveyor came to examine the land. She could tell something was wrong by the way he sighed into the phone after repeating, "Billington?" How was Josie to know that the entire town, like so many towns in this part of central Texas, was sitting on a bed of topsoil so thin that the first settlers called it a "trap"? Or that the only reason wheat grew as far as she could see was because nothing else would take root? Or that most people have aboveground pools not because they find them aesthetically pleasing but because you can't dig more than two feet without hitting limestone? "It won't be cheap." That's how the man answered her over the phone. For the next few weeks, she didn't hear him say much else.

Josie understood why they had to make holes in the fence to move the backhoes in and out but couldn't for the life of her understand why it was taking so long to do the actual digging. A machine that big and loud, something that actually *smoked* at times, seemed like it would dig a pool-sized hole in a matter of minutes, but Blue Getaway's crew, professionals that they were, assured her this pace was perfectly normal. So she let them pulverize the backyard in peace and focused on the other problems bubbling up to the surface of her new life, or at least the most pressing ones.

It had initially struck her as a little funny that she would be teaching three different math classes to three different grades and that the grand total of students was somehow under fifty, but her first parent-teacher conferences quickly revealed the bigger issue at hand. The parents who showed up were either completely silent, as if they just wanted a reason to leave their homes, or disarmingly curious about her family background. She rarely encountered adults who didn't show at least a glimmer of surprise or veneration for her alma mater, but it appeared to mean nothing to any of them. She was asked about her husband, and her son, and what church they planned on attending. She was told about Margaret Rose's alcoholism, and how rare in-ground pools were in the area. But more than anything, she was reminded of Mary Alice, even if the parent didn't mention her by name. "You've got big shoes to fill," Barry Watkins's mother said in a tone Josie had trouble reading, but which made bile bubble up into her throat nonetheless. "And I mean that. Mary Alice wears an eleven."

"You plan on staying here long or are you just here for a visit?" said Laura Gonzalez's mother, in a tone she understood immediately.

Kelly Cruz's mother went straight to the point, asking, "What's Mary Alice have to say about all this?"

"I don't actually know," Josie said.

"You mean you haven't met her?"

"We haven't had the opportunity."

"All she does is sit in that house. I'm sure you could swing by and ring the doorbell."

Before Josie could express how mortified she was at the very thought of ringing a stranger's doorbell, Mary Alice strolled into the classroom and took a seat right in the front row. She pressed her knees together and pulled her seat under the desk, the grinding noise putting a scowl on every face but hers. Looking back, Josie admired the move.

Before anyone in the room could acknowledge her presence, Mary Alice turned on her teacher voice and addressed the room. "Don't mind me. I just came to see who the sniveling bastards at this fine institution replaced me with."

"Mrs. Roth, I'm pleased to meet you, but—"

"This is not a social call, Mrs. Kerr. *This* is a defining moment of this school year. Don't talk to me, talk to the parents."

And that's when Josie threw up on her desk, which had been, up until very recently, Mary Alice's desk.

Hours later, after the parents brought paper towels from the bathrooms and pretended to ignore the splatters on the top of her blouse, and after Principal Ortiz yelled at a stoic Mary Alice in the courtyard, and after giving herself one hour alone in her empty room to come to terms with the fact that she would begin her first day as a math teacher at BHS knowing that every child in the room would know that at least some of her vomit had been flung onto at least some of their parents, Josie went home to have dinner with her family.

THE FOLLOWING WEEK, she arrived home after her first day of school. She hadn't expected to get home after Henry went to sleep—being home early was the most appealing part of the job—and the silence of the house broke her heart. "How was it?" Travis said from the barstool, lit by a pendant light and the blue of his phone. When she didn't respond, he turned and saw it in her eyes. "Oh no. What happened?" Another silence, and he knew. "Mary Alice."

"She hates me."

"She doesn't know you. More importantly, she doesn't matter.

You're the one employed there. She isn't! It just hasn't gotten through her head yet."

"Do you think it ever will?"

Travis stood and walked to the door. He held her tightly, just like she'd hoped he would, and whispered in her ear, "You didn't barf, did you?"

She hid her smile and pushed him off of her. "I'm serious. Any chance I had at impressing any semblance of authority on these kids has just, I don't know, disintegrated. They think I'm just some idiot from New York City who throws up like a child when she's nervous and can't keep it together around menacing old women in blue jeans and orthopedic sneakers."

"Why'd you need to stay so late?"

"I rearranged the room. Moved all the desks, then moved them back. Then moved them again. I have to make it my own somehow. I have to get *her* out of there."

"Today was always going to be bad," Travis said gently, but with just enough pity for Josie to notice.

"Was it?"

"Yes, and you know it."

He was right. She hated him sometimes.

"I know you said no drinks on weekdays, but there's a small glass of red in the fridge if you want to go . . . do whatever it is you do out there," he said. "I'm gonna go shower."

She kissed the back of his neck and went straight to the refrigerator, which was covered in some of Henry's most stunning works of art: a Manhattan-sized plane over Brooklyn, a demented snowman holding carrots as weapons, and a wildly inaccurate but still very much recognizable abstraction of the state of Texas. She pulled out the glass of cold red wine, her favorite, and walked out the back door. Careful not to spill any of her drink, she took the fifteen or so steps to the center of the mud-covered yard, where she'd set two chairs on the edge of her theoretical pool.

Travis may have brought her here, but everything that happened since? Her idea. It was her idea to put deck chairs on the edge of the hole in their backyard. It was her idea to dig the hole in the first place, on the day they moved in. It was her idea to send the backhoes through a new hole in their fence even after Travis told her how much all the holes would end up costing them. But Josie remained committed to all of this even after her husband warned her of the full extent to which people would talk. "No one whispers in this town," he said with that gentle bluntness she always respected and resented. "They just wait until you're far enough away and talk normal."

The hole was big, but it still left plenty of yard for a garden and a swing set and a shed. As Josie sat in the quiet, she imagined the ghost-shaped hole growing to fill their property, ten feet of ground crumbling in all directions, swallowing everything but her and her chair until being stopped by fences and foundation. She floated above, watching the sharp corners of brown and gray earth get covered in a slick coating of concrete, then filled just under the brim with water so cold you could smell it.

But a voice from behind snapped her back to reality. "Sweetie," Travis said, his head poking out of the cracked back door. "You coming to bed? It's late."

"Just a minute," she said, looking down at the hole in her yard. Even in the moonlight she could tell it was bone dry.

4

"YOU'RE DOING BEANS AGAIN, BY THE WAY," MARY ALICE TOLD
Ellie when she arrived for coffee Tuesday morning.

"Of course I am."

"Don't get too comfortable. You never know when I might switch
it up."

"After all these years, when have I not been beans?"

"That's exactly what I'm saying."

Ellie always had the easiest job for the picnic—beans—because
Mary Alice handled the assignments. And everyone in town knew
Mary Alice and Ellie were best friends, because everyone in town
knew what had happened to their sons, or at least they were convinced they did. Kenny's death had been a big, loud, violent thing.
There was a crushed car and a body and a scene and an obituary and
a drunk driver in jail. Michael's death wasn't just unspeakable but
unspoken, at least by Mary Alice. When they had framed photos of

both boys added to the school's trophy case, Mary Alice swiped the key from Louis Ortiz's desk drawer and took Michael's out wordlessly, in plain view of teachers and students as they shuffled to their next classes. She was in mourning, they thought as she locked the case back up. And mourning people behave in ways that shouldn't be questioned. *Thank the Lord*, they thought, *that she and Ellie have each other*—which was just a polite way of thinking, *At least they don't need me.* Maybe that rationale is why no one else tried to step in and be a better friend after it happened. You could see it in their eyes, even now. A worry about saying the wrong thing. A hesitation to get close. So that's why later today Mary Alice would tell Ellie she was responsible for beans, and none of the other women would bat an eye, even though she'd been beans for as long as they could remember. But that was still hours away. This morning, like all the others, was just for the two of them.

"I had a patient who reminded me of Michael," Ellie said.

Mary Alice felt a twitch in her chest. Ellie rarely mentioned the boys, and if she did, it was never as casual as that. It was never done over morning coffee.

"Oh," she said, trying to hide her surprise. "How do you mean?"

"Well, he was the spitting image of Michael the day I first met y'all. And he was so scared it would have broken your heart," she said. "Even though he was convinced he was on death's door, he was as polite as can be. Yes, ma'am. No, ma'am. Thank you, ma'am." She paused and tilted her head softly, as if trying to conjure images of the two boys in the space just beyond the porch. "You don't hear that much these days."

"What was he in for?"

"Well, that's the main thing. That's the Mikey Roth of it all," Ellie said, her mouth turning upward into a smile. She set her mug on her knee and turned to Mary Alice. "It was a baseball injury."

Mary Alice shook her head. "Black eye?"

Ellie nodded. "Can you believe it? Looked just like Michael, sounded just like Michael . . ."

"Terrible at baseball as Michael?"

Ellie laughed. "Exactly. Nothing was broken, thank God, but I tell you it was the ugliest black eye I've seen in twenty-five years. Poor thing thought he had brain damage. To be honest, I did, too, till I checked his eyes. Only thing missing was the laces."

"The laces!" Mary Alice was laughing now. She'd almost forgotten about those damn laces. When a pitcher threw a fastball right at Michael's face, the injury not only left him with a shiner the size of Ohio, it also left the delicate crisscross imprint of the laces just below his left eyelid. Damn near looked like his skin had taken on the red dye, but it was just his own blood.

"He cried and cried," Ellie said. "His mother kept apologizing, too. I hate that."

"Hate what?"

"When they apologize for their kids being scared. 'I'm sorry he's such a worrier,' she told me. 'When he gets started with those tears you can't turn off the spigot.' And right next to him, too! I swear some parents think their kids don't have ears. Brains, even. Don't they remember their own childhoods?" She turned to her left and looked at her house, remembering.

"So what was the prognosis, Nurse Hall?"

"He'll be fine," Ellie said, seamlessly stepping back into the present. "Told him to take some Tylenol and stay home from practice for the next two weeks. When I said that, Mary Alice, you should have seen him. He was thrilled."

"Thrilled over skipping baseball practice? Now, *that's* Michael." She noticed a squint of Ellie's eyes. "He didn't need to stay home from practice, did he?"

"The boy?"

Mary Alice nodded conspiratorially.

"Of course not. I could just tell he needed a break, and his momma wasn't about to give him one."

The two of them laughed for a few wonderful seconds, and the sensation that they were talking indirectly about their own boys fell on them like a sheet falling onto a bed. It's not a memory that ever goes away, but sometimes it takes a break. As usual, the laughter stopped, and the smiles faded. Life always clocks back in.

"I realized too late about yesterday, I'm sorry," Mary Alice said.

"Oh, you didn't need to say anything."

"I know, but it's just that—" Mary Alice stopped to find the right words. "I don't like that I forgot."

"It's fine to forget every once in a while. Forgetting means other stuff is happening. Forgetting means you've got distractions. I could use some."

"Oh, could you now?" Mary Alice raised an eyebrow and waited for Ellie to notice. After a few seconds of silence, she got what she wanted.

"What's that supposed to mean?"

"What do you think it means?"

"I'm not sure I know!"

"Aren't you?"

"Can we stop being so cryptic?"

"I don't know, can we? Fine. Are you sleeping with Gerald Harbison?"

Ellie gasped. "You damn little spy! Have you been watching me?"

"No! I just tend to notice when the view out my window looks a little different than it has since the nineties."

Ellie laughed haughtily. "Well, I hate to disappoint you, but no. I am *not* sleeping with Gerald Harbison. He said he'd help me streamline my finances, maybe save money on taxes next year."

Mary Alice said nothing. She just refilled the mugs and waited.

"I'm not lying to you, if that's what you're thinking right now. The man's an accountant. It's what he does."

Mary Alice set the pot back on the burner and took a loud sip.

"He made sense out of all of it and told me what to do with our new 401(k). I would've been lost without him."

"And now you're what? Found?"

Ellie nearly spit out her coffee, then lowered her chin to touch her chest. "Would it be so bad if I were?"

"Ellie Hall! You are smitten, aren't you?"

"What I *am* is running late."

"Mmm-hmm."

"You, too. See you tonight."

"You were blind, but now you can see."

"I don't know why I tell you anything."

As soon as Ellie left, Mary Alice began preparing for the meeting, not that there was much to do. She'd pull out the folding chairs and place them in a semicircle around the couch. She'd put a tablecloth on the dining room table to catch the inevitable spills. She'd dust a little more than usual for a Tuesday. And then she'd be done, with just over eleven hours to spare. Every other year she'd been at work before everyone came over. Today she was in the living room, alone, staring at her wristwatch despite knowing the time. "Cookies," she said to the minute hand before bolting up and grabbing her keys and purse in a single, graceful scoop.

Billington was a town passersby didn't really see until the fifth or sixth time they drove through it, a blip on a blip that existed mostly in retrospect. Its one and only grocery store, Carlye's, was smack in the center of Main Street, a glorified parking lot that ran parallel to Highway 90 and spanned the length of six 150-year-old buildings built behind a towering live oak that once provided year-round shade to travelers waiting outside the town's long-demolished train station. From west to east: the Longhorn Saloon and Steak House (famous for their housemade blue cheese dressing), Carlye's (famous for their expired canned goods), the post office (famous for closing early), Billington Savings and Loan (famous for being robbed by a duo inspired by Bonnie and Clyde but not Bonnie and Clyde themselves), the multiuse community center (famous for being haunted by the town's founder), and Kerr's Hotel (famous for never operating more than five consecutive years in a row since 1869). Over a century ago, when the town was made a stage stop on the route to San Antonio, it had all the bells and whistles you needed from a village: a place of worship, a school, a store, and houses. Then came the railroad, which led to the development of the brick and tile company, giving it an industry, a worthy place in the Texas economy. It's such a small little town in the fabric of the country that it's difficult to imagine a time when it could have been anything smaller, but even the tiniest of towns take generations to be built. Even a town in decline never really stops growing. People may leave, but their stories remain, re-verberating in the bones of all those left behind.

Trevino, a proper town about ten times the size of Billington, had cheaper and more reliable alternatives for all of Billington's businesses, but sometimes you didn't feel like making the drive, or maybe you felt like spending your time and money on someone you knew. Had this been a normal Tuesday, Mary Alice might have run into Carlye's for a pound of ground beef, a bag of buns, and a head of iceberg lettuce. But today she would be feeding a small army of loud, ravenous women, and Carlye's unreliable supply and inflated prices would never be able to match the price and selection of the super-center in Trevino. Even Eric Carlye himself shopped there, so why wouldn't everyone else? So off she went, a list folded neatly in the taupe handbag she'd had since her tenth anniversary. Eight miles may seem like a long way to drive for groceries to people in the big city, but with seven miles of that being open road, with green and brown cornfields in all directions, a speed limit of seventy, and not a single state trooper in sight outside of holidays, it's only a ten-minute drive. A reassuringly small amount of time. No one cares about ten minutes late. No one cares about ten minutes early. It's three songs on the radio or just enough silence before silence gets uncomfortable. And today, on the AM dial, it's five callers ranting about using tax-payer funds to build a new central library in nearby San Antonio. Listening to talk radio always made Mary Alice angry, but the alternatives—dead air or oldies—didn't make her feel much of any-thing at all, and she rarely turned down the opportunity to assert her own superiority.

"Sure, what on God's green earth would you possibly want a

library for," Mary Alice sneered while pulling into the sparsely filled H-E-B parking lot. If there was one good thing about retirement, she realized then, it was missing the crowds. The grocery story was always nice and empty during the day. There was never a line at the post office. And, as much as she hated to admit, doctor's appointments were a breeze to schedule these days. She'd been going more the past couple of years, not because she was sick, but because she was old. And it helped her heart to hear a doctor say she was doing OK.

As she pulled a cart from the stack near the store entrance, its automatic doors slid open and a *whoosh* of impossibly cold air pummeled her body, nearly knocking her sideways. Having lived all her life in Texas, she understood the importance of air-conditioning, but a similar appreciation for the value of a dollar meant the unit in her home was never set below seventy-eight. Anything lower, especially the low sixties of a grocery store, made her feel uneasy. She wished she'd brought a sweater, but that would have made her feel older than she already did.

The store was filled with area blue-hairs slowly pushing their carts or using battery-operated chairs to weave through every single aisle despite only needing a handful of things. The only thing keeping her from being too annoyed by their molasses-like pace was the fear that she was slowly becoming one of them. Mary Alice adjusted her speed to make herself seem like she didn't belong. She pulled out her list and began darting from section to section, tossing things in her cart with the confidence and energy of someone who normally shopped at 6:30 a.m. This wasn't her typical shopping time; she was just passing through.

In the produce aisle she grabbed a premade snack tray filled with freshly chopped broccoli and carrots and tomatoes and cauliflower, not caring too much about the produce quality because she knew people would only grab handfuls out of anxiety, virtue signaling but not actually taking any bites. In the bakery aisle she examined the cookies and chose a clamshell of blue ones as well as a carton of "one-bite" brownies that always seemed more like three or four bites to her. She grabbed chips and a box of Velveeta and a can of Ro*Tel. She bought a bag of pita chips and the largest available tub of pimento cheese spread made in-store. And then she zigzagged her way to the beverage aisle.

Should she buy beer and wine? Just one or the other? And how much of any of it? No one drank as much as they used to, but the base level in Billington must have been above the national average. Like most of the other women coming tonight, Mary Alice wasn't a drinker, she just liked to drink. There was a difference, she would assure you. All of them would. She put a twenty-four-pack of light beer and a magnum each of red and white in the bottom rack of her cart.

"Mrs. Roth," a bright, soft voice said behind her as she rose, knees creaking, from the alcohol. Startled, she jolted her head to the right and worried for a moment she had been mumbling out loud. She was fairly certain she hadn't.

"Emily Fineman?" The name jumped to her tongue like it always did with old students, reanimated with a jolt after years spent unsaid or even thought about. Emily Fineman. Pretty. Clever. Let Matthew Zerr cheat off her tests.

"Yes! It's so nice to see you! How've you been?"

Mary Alice wasn't sure whether she should lie or say she was miserable. That's the thing about seeing former students: it was hard to know how to approach that delicate balance of wanting to remain an authority figure while also wanting to finally shed the armor of the profession and remind grown students that she was just like them. Every time she saw one, especially after a decade or more, she was confronted by the same anxiety. Should she be Mrs. Roth, or should she be Mary Alice? And now, was there even a difference?

"I'm doing well," she finally said. "And yourself?"

"I heard you retired," said Emily.

How could she have known? was the first question that came to mind. The second was, *How could she not?* News travels quickly when there isn't much else to talk about. A parched gossip landscape is desperate to be kindled, and any kind of whisper, scandalous or otherwise, will do.

"Sure did, in May. Had a nice little party and everything. And how are you? Any babies?"

She regretted the question the moment she asked it, but Emily didn't seem to mind.

"Three! They're all in school by now," she said. "Zachary's nine, Mallory's six, and the little one, Riley, is four, just started pre-K. So I'm home alone for the first time ever. You caught me on my first time out of the house by myself since I honestly don't know when."

"Well, you deserve a little time to yourself."

"Maybe so. I already miss them. But there's plenty to do. There's always plenty to do," Emily said, her eyes breaking contact with Mary Alice's for a second or two before darting back to attention.

"Who did you end up marrying?"

Again, the question seemed callous as it rolled off her tongue, but, again, Emily answered as though she'd just been asked about the weather.

"Clay Wools! Just celebrated our tenth year in June."

Mary Alice remembered. They got married right after graduation, in a church filled with believers. They believed in the sacrament, and they believed this one was rushed for reasons that had little to do with love. It was funny how such a scandalous turn of events had evolved into something so perfectly normal, Mary Alice thought. Maybe even lovely. Only then did she realize another bottle of red wine was still in her hands. One of those fat bottles with a tiny handle on the neck, much too small for any adult's finger to fit inside.

She looked down at the bottle and nervously tossed it into the top of her cart, crushing her purse. "Oh mercy, I must look like some kind of lush."

"Ha! Don't be embarrassed. I'm in this aisle, too. Having a party?"

"Yes! Oh my, I hope you don't think there was any chance I wouldn't be. Having some people over tonight to talk about the picnic this weekend."

"Is that this weekend?" Emily said, suddenly seeming like a schoolgirl. "It was always my favorite day of the year. Still having the same old rides and everything?"

"Same old rides. Same old food. Same old me."

"Well, I don't believe we'll be able to make it this year; we're driving up to Fort Worth to see Clay's family, but I hope all goes well. I'll let you get to your shopping. Great to see you. Enjoy retired life!"

Mary Alice waved and watched as Emily strolled through to the end of the aisle, not grabbing a single thing.

She drove home and heard three more callers complain about the library. She unpacked the groceries. She made a BLT for lunch, her favorite. Normally she would cook the bacon on the stove, but with her newfound abundance of time, she put it in the oven. Every few minutes she cracked open the door to listen to it crackling and take in the scent. She was a healthy eater overall, but red meat was her weakness, and her doctor didn't seem to think it would be too harmful in moderation. As the bacon continued baking, she hiked outside to the small garden in the backyard to pick a tomato. Five tomato plants, the only fruit or vegetable she'd ever managed to care enough about to grow with any success, were inside the sturdy, oak-lined planter. She fumbled through their coarse leaves and lightly pressed down on the skin of three contenders before choosing the fourth. A perfect size; enough for four large rounds.

Toast. Mayonnaise. A layer of iceberg lettuce. Bacon. The glorious fruit she grew herself. After morning coffee, lunchtime was her favorite time of day. She'd never known how much she loved leisurely preparing a small but indulgent midday meal until finally having the opportunity to do so, and when she sat down to take her first bite, being retired suddenly didn't feel so miserable. A tiny weight was lifted as she picked up the sandwich, but as she opened her mouth, the tinny blare of her cell phone interrupted. "Son of a bitch," she said, matching the ringtone's brutal volume.

She slammed her napkin on the counter, rose from the stool with a huff, and marched to the side door to dig her phone out of her purse, resting on the small table beside an old jade bowl for her keys and loose change. It stopped ringing before she could get it out. She sighed as the notification faded into view. *MISSED CALL*, it read. No name, just a number, but one with a familiar area code: Atlanta. A city just far enough away to be far enough away. Her eyes stayed on the screen as she waited for the second notification to appear. *VOICEMAIL*, it finally said, just as she expected. The thin skin under her right eyelid twitched, and she instinctively raised a finger to touch it, a habit since childhood. Maybe she'd be able to feel it when it twitched again—catch it in the act—but once she'd touched the skin, the twitching always stopped, as if it was expecting her. She tossed the phone in her bag without locking the screen, shoving it under the rubble in her purse, and squeezed the clasp shut, snuffing out the screen's aggressive light.

5

THE CALL WAS ON HER MIND FOR THE REST OF THE DAY. SHE hoped at least one women on the planning committee would break her rule and show up early, but knew no one would dare. They would all arrive between 8:01 and 8:15, not a minute before or later. They did this not because she ever told them to, but because they knew what she'd do if they didn't. This is how a teacher must often teach, not by explicit lessons but by conditioning, and Mary Alice had decades of experience. Scolding wasn't an act reserved for children, at least not in the Roth house. Whether sixteen or sixty-seven, sometimes a person needs to be told when they've gone and messed up.

It wasn't exactly necessary for a dozen fussy ladies to fill Mary Alice's living room in order to receive their assignments for Saturday's annual church picnic, but like most traditions, it had developed too much momentum to be replaced with something as efficient, and boring, as a single well-composed email. Even so, complaining about the planning meeting was as essential to the process as the planning itself. Complaints aren't necessarily shameful acts of malice; they can be a kind of conversational awl that pokes right through even the toughest personality. You complain when the important stuff feels invasive or out of reach. You complain because complaining is easy. You complain about an event knowing you will attend it anyway, in part because attending the event will give you something new to complain about. You complain because you like complaining. No one pretended the planning meeting was anything but a social affair, one the women looked forward to every year. It was a time for Billington's women elders—plus a few token under-forties—to have an evening together under a roof that wasn't owned by the archdiocese or occupied by anyone's husband. They drank beer and wine, they ate chips and queso and those crumbly store-bought cookies from right out of the creaky plastic clamshell, they gossiped about the women who weren't there (not to mention the ones who were), they groaned about their children, and, eventually, they listened politely as Mary Alice told them what they would be cooking that weekend.

The picnic was part tradition and part self-fulfilling prophecy. Typically held the Saturday before Labor Day, its explicit purpose was to raise money for Billington's only religious organization within the town limits, the Holy Cross Catholic Church. It was effectively nondenominational, despite taking place underneath the town's largest crucifix. That people of all faiths were invited was less an act of open-mindedness than one of financial desperation.

Funds raised went straight to the Holy Cross Catholic Church's Altar Society, and were used for, among other things, repairs for the aging church building, a brick structure that even Billington's most devout believers found hideous, built in record time after the more imposing and elegant original building burned down in a blaze of hellfire in the sixties due to faulty wiring. The pews needed to be refinished. The songbooks needed to be replaced. Cracks in the floor needed to be filled in. And then there was the next year's picnic, which had always been financed by the picnic the year before. But despite the explicitly Catholic nature of the event, everyone in the town found the time to come, even the misers who rarely left home for more than Marlboro Reds and a twelve-pack of Keystone Light. All the money spent there, whether on raffles or games or rides or food, went to Him whether you believed or not.

The rides, a collection of three rickety old tetanus factories owned and operated by the same family for several decades, were dirty but reliable. And though they weren't the friendliest or most talkative bunch, the Saathoffs always presented their yearly inspection certificates, and the family of three—which had slowly whittled down from an all-time high of seven—were always on time, and never bent the rules regarding the height requirements. They were getting paid the same regardless, and the job of traveling from town to town twenty-five weekends out of the year was far too lucrative to risk losing over some brat who made empty threats over the horror of being an inch below the red line.

Mary Alice was in charge of the food, which is to say she decided who cooked what. The "what" wasn't complicated, as the menu was an unchanging array of barbecue and potato salad and coleslaw and beans and pie, but the "who" required ruthless strategizing. Mary Alice doled out responsibilities based on seniority, skill, and her own personal vendettas. Beans, for example, were easy to prepare, but they were also the most important of the three sides. As such, they were always assigned to people she trusted: Ellie. Wanda Moffet.

Maybe even Debbie Bergman, if she hadn't recently said something nasty to her at a football game or in line for the butcher at Carlye's. But because one should never be lulled into a false sense of security, she might want to surprise someone who'd cooked beans three years in a row with an assignment for pie, which required not cooking but time and space, as it was discovered a decade prior that buying fifty pies from the Alsatian bakery in Castroville was a more economical decision than having everyone on the committee bake three to five on their own. Next was coleslaw, a dreaded task, but one that required no cooking, just hours of chopping and a little bit of stirring— meaning arthritis-stricken Gloria Pflüger was in the clear. The most feared assignment was potato salad, the heaviest, hottest, and most labor intensive of all the sides. To be one of the three women assigned to prepare potato salad meant you had done something wrong in the eyes of Mary Alice over the past year. People who prepared potato salad for the picnic missed mass on a Holy Day of Obligation and didn't have a good excuse. They let their cell phone ring during the junior high school's borderline-offensive production of *The Sound of Music*. They gave their foulmouthed C-minus-student daughter a Mustang for her sixteenth birthday and, after it was totaled, replaced it with a second. A career spent in the public school system had made her a master at feigning diplomacy, so Mary Alice was sure to never directly explain her reasoning, and, in fact, did her best to hide any sense that her potato salad assignment was anything resembling an act of culinary penance. Every year, the women assigned with that most miserable task simply had to accept that it was their turn to boil forty pounds of potatoes. It was their turn to burn their fingers while chopping them. It was their turn to find space in their fridges to cool them down before drowning them in mayonnaise the next morning. But maybe, deep down, they knew what they had done, and told themselves this lie because attempting to figure out why Mary Alice looked down on them was not a fate they wished on their worst enemy, let alone themselves. Perhaps she was even doing them a favor by calling it out in her own subtle way.

The planning meeting had taken place in her house for decades, but it wasn't always just for the wives. When Samuel was still alive, couples came to the Roths' home as a sturdy unit, and the barbecue was discussed right alongside the sides that would eventually surround it. The husbands were responsible for the meat, and Samuel was their coach. For them, there was no real difference to any of the assignments, as everything was cooked on-site at the church, in the same pit, on the day of the picnic. But they took their jobs seriously and responded to Samuel's declarations with the same wordless machismo they performed in their high school football days. They'd nod and grunt, and he'd nod and grunt back, imitating the others as he often did. He was never a convincing brute, try as he might, but maybe that's what Mary Alice fell in love with.

Once the meat had been assigned, the men excused themselves to drink and smoke on the back porch, leaving the women to their own devices. To them, sides were distractions from the main event. Wanting more beans was somehow feminine, somehow lesser, and ʼn't get them *started* on the coleslaw. That a dish requiring almost ʒical-grade knife skills and perfect proportions of fat and acid and ʼnings was considered easy confused the women, but they were ʼo be left alone. The complicated nature of their preparations ʼer left as their little secret. What the wives knew that the either lacked the capacity to understand or refused to ac- was that there was no real skill or danger to barbecuing meat. Everyone who bought a plate knew this, but rarely would they say it aloud.

Once Samuel was gone, though, no attempt was made to keep the two halves of the planning meeting together. The husbands met at Willie Landry's place, which got dustier and more welcoming after the death of his wife, Greta, and the wives kept going to Mary Alice's, either out of stubbornness or because they needed an escape. And she was happy to provide one, for them and for herself.

The first to arrive that evening was Debbie Bergman, a tall, gray-blond woman about Mary Alice's age. She was an intimidating presence, tall and always sharply dressed in blue jeans and tucked-in shirt, but her voice quickly negated all suggestions of her physicality. Even though she was six foot three, people still described her as mouselike. She leaned over and gave Mary Alice the gentlest of hugs. "Sorry," she said. "I might be a little sweaty."

"Did you walk?" Mary Alice asked.

"Can't you tell by my breath? I'm in terrible shape."

"Well, you don't look it."

"Wouldn't that be nice," Debbie said. "When my doctor said he was worried about my heart, I said, 'But, Doctor, I feel fine! And I look better than I have in years!' He said, 'Debbie, if you could tell how sick a person was just by looking at them, I'd give everyone in the magazines in my waiting room a clean bill a health, and we all know how Hollywood is.'"

Mary Alice didn't quite understand this, and neither, she thought, did Debbie. But she laughed anyway, because it was polite, and anything was easier than thinking about the fifteen-second silent voicemail she'd listened to six times that afternoon.

Maria Aguilar showed up next, a solid-gray snowman in head-to-

toe sweats. She lived even closer than Debbie, just a quarter-mile down the road, but drove her big F-250 anyway. *At least she parked on the street and not in the driveway,* Mary Alice thought. Men in Billington fancied trucks as extensions, or perhaps steel and fiberglass mirrors, of their bodies. The bigger the truck, the bigger their egos. This was irritating to Mary Alice—also wasteful, given how few, if any, men who owned a truck that big ever actually took advantage of its capabilities and performance—but mostly it was funny. Small men. Big trucks. How could she not laugh? The women who drove these four-wheeled behemoths, though, bothered her less. At least women like Maria, who had her own sedan but occasionally swiped her husband's keys, seemed acutely aware of their obscene size, the utter ridiculousness of their very existence. For Maria, driving the big gray rig was fun. For Ignacio, it was a validation of his manliness. *"Pinche viejo,"* Maria had grumbled when he came home with it, just before swiping the keys so she could take it out for a spin. She gave Mary Alice a bear hug and then pushed her away, still clutching her shoulders. "Is Travis Kerr's wife here yet?"

Mary Alice laughed. "She's running late. Probably not coming at all."

"Damn," Maria said, removing her hands and starting off toward the snack-covered table. "I was hoping to ask her about that big-ass pool."

Margaret Meyers and Gloria Pflüger arrived at the same time, each holding a bottle of Yellow Tail. Then Jackie Salazar. Wilma Hueber. Betty Flores. Ellie. Linda Kerrigan. Linda Attaway. Lucy Lutz. Wanda Moffet. Monica Mondoza. Then it was 8:15, and there was no sign of Josie.

"So how's retired life treating you?" Maria asked as she sunk another chip into the marbled orange mound of pimento cheese dip. "You look like you're glowing."

"Glowing's when you're pregnant, and I wouldn't call retirement anything like pregnancy," Mary Alice said, wiping away the piles of crumbs that had already appeared on the kitchen counter. "What's the opposite of having something growing inside you? What's it mean when all you've got here is a black hole?" She patted her stomach and waited for a response.

Maria paused to think, but quickly gave up. "Jesus H, Mary Alice, I was just trying to be nice. Fine. You look exactly the damn same as you always look."

Mary Alice scoffed and addressed the room. "Y'all didn't come here to talk about me. Y'all came here to talk about this godforsaken picnic. Now, everyone come on over to the living room so we can get this over with. And don't let any of this food go to waste. Make a plate and eat up. I don't want it in my fridge or it'll just go bad."

A few of the ladies stood to load up on seconds and thirds as Mary Alice grabbed a legal pad from the breakfast table. She unfurled a few pages to the list she'd made the week before, noting everyone's roles. The roomful of eyes followed her as she stepped toward the fireplace and took an awkward seat on its low edge.

Wilma cleared her throat. "Aren't we gonna wait for little Mrs. Travis Kerr?"

"Absolutely not. I'm not changing up the schedule on account of one inconsiderate person."

"What if she doesn't show? I for one ain't cooking double anything."

"Nobody's cooking double. I'll send her a text."

"Why don't you send us all texts?" Linda scoffed. She continued as if a spotlight had fallen on her. "*There's* a question no one ever wants to ask. Why make us come all the way up here when we're just waiting for a single-word assignment? Beans. Slaw. Pie. Who needs to socialize?"

"I can't make anyone do anything, Linda. And if you didn't want to come tonight, I would have been happy to tell you about potato salad duty over the phone."

The room erupted in laughter, and a few childish *ooohs*. Linda sunk into her seat. "I should have known," she said, nearly breaking into a chuckle herself. "I've been pies for two years straight." Mary Alice flipped through her legal pad and did a little slashing and scribbling. That outburst may have ruined Linda's weekend, but it saved Monica's.

Over the next five minutes, which was really all it took, Mary Alice doled out responsibilities for the coming weekend. People protested, but only in jest. Mostly, they accepted their roles as law. *So it is written,* they all thought. *So it shall be cooked.*

As Mary Alice wrapped the crinkled top pages back over her pad, the doorbell rang. She shook her head. More *ooohs*. More *ahhhs*. "Someone's about to get a hundred lines to write after class," Maria said, refilling her glass with the dregs of wine left on the table. The wine had turned every woman here into a sanctimonious seventh grader.

Mary Alice set down the pad and walked to the door. Beyond the lace curtain and the leaded glass, she could see a distorted, blurry abstraction of Josie, fixing her hair and smoothing out her blouse. When the door opened, Josie's posture became nervously erect. "Sorry I'm late," she said before Mary Alice could get a word in. "Travis couldn't get home from work, I had to drive Henry to his grandma's, then

Travis ended up coming home anyway, so I had to go pick Henry up; it was a lot of back-and-forth that—"

Mary Alice swung the door wide open and waved her inside. "It's all right," she said. "You missed the most important part, though."

"I'm so sorry. Can you just tell me what I'll be cooking?"

The living room may as well have been a middle school. "Go on. Tell her, Mary Alice," Betty said.

"Yeah," said Linda. "Give her the good news."

"What good news?" Josie asked, suddenly filled with dread.

Mary Alice grabbed her pad again, but only for effect. "Do you have a big pot?" she asked. "Or better yet, do you have three?"

"We have a stockpot, sure. Why? Am I beans?"

"You're with me, darlin'," Linda said, half sunk into the couch like a corpse in quicksand. "Potato salad duty."

This seemed easy enough to Josie, and for a brief, wonderful moment, she felt like she'd dodged a bullet. How complicated could potato salad be, anyway? There were boiled potatoes, mayonnaise, a little bit of relish or chopped onions, and what—salt and pepper? Dill? Parsley? But the stares and snickers made her reconsider.

"Mary Alice," Josie said, her voice only a few degrees away from trembling. "What exactly does potato salad duty entail?"

"I thought you might ask that," Mary Alice said, turning back to her legal pad. She pulled a sheet of paper out from between some of the back pages. It was stiff, glistening, and Josie quickly realized it was laminated. "So I prepared instructions."

"You mean a recipe?"

Lucy guffawed. "Honey, recipes are for a nice dinner at home. These are *definitely* instructions."

The sheet was double-sided, with the bulk of it printed from a word processor, and a few choice reminders added by hand in ink. Beside the ingredient list, for example, it read: *10 large yellow onions,* with *finely minced* in 12-point font, and *yellow* highlighted in yellow. Above that, the words *finely minced* in Mary Alice's nauseatingly perfect cursive. Josie's eyes glazed over as they ran down the page. She felt like she had been handed nuclear codes, but instead of entering a 128-character alphanumeric string and turning a key at the same time as an ally, she would be peeling and boiling forty pounds of potatoes entirely alone, waiting for them to cool overnight, and then mixing them with enough onion and pickle and mayonnaise to start an artisanal salad dressing business.

"It's all technically *important*, but the *most* important bits have been highlighted," Mary Alice said, pointing at a note underneath the section on boiling. "Like here, take note that it says *be sure to refrigerate the boiled potatoes at least overnight before mixing them with the dressing.* If you do it when the potatoes are hot, they'll get mushy and won't hold up well throughout the day."

"We learned *that* from trial and error," Debbie said from the back of the room, her eyes on the ceiling as though accessing a traumatic mayonnaise-based memory. "Mostly error."

"I'm not sure if we have the fridge space," Josie said, exhaling what little energy she had out of her body.

"You'll find a way, a smart young woman like yourself," Mary Alice said. "Anyway, you're late, but there's still plenty to eat. Can't say there's much left to drink, though. You'll find that happens with this crew."

Josie wanted to fold the paper into square after square after square until it was so small that she could swallow it and forget potato salad even existed. But, she remembered, it was laminated, and far too big even for her purse. So she held on to it like her own scarlet letter while crossing the living room to the kitchen.

She pulled a paper plate from the stack and added a few carrots, some broccoli florets, a handful of chips, and a little bit of ranch dressing. After she took a bite of the broccoli, which was limp and an unpleasant room temperature, Maria noticed her eyeing the dwindling mound of pimento cheese. "They have pimento cheese in New York City?"

"They do in Bushwick."

Maria was surprised by the snap in her answer, and had no idea what Bushwick was, but didn't let that stop her from a little gentle ribbing. "Well, I'm sure whatever you've had at some fancy restaurant wasn't as good as this stuff. Better have at it before someone finishes the rest with a spoon."

Josie dipped a chip in the squishy concoction of cheeses (real and processed), mayonnaise, and chopped peppers and took a bite. Her eyes widened at its rich, fatty tang. Growing up in Manhattan, she'd spent a lifetime expanding her culinary palette, and had had her share of Southern and Tex-Mex dishes, but never in context, when the food had a home-court advantage. She smiled, to Maria's visible delight, and remembered one evening in Brooklyn shortly before moving, when a friend asked how Josie would "get by" in such a small town. The question chipped away at her those first few weeks in Billington. How would she get by? With her confidence and excitement and love for her family, of course! But she had been thinking too hard and, after moving, quickly realized what one significant coping mechanism would be: the food.

Ellie watched all of this from an armchair in the back of the room, where she sat next to Betty Flores (pie) and Debbie Bergman

(coleslaw), two of the quieter women in the bunch. When she noticed Josie had been cornered by Maria, she decided to do a good
deed and save her from what could easily be thirty-five minutes of
conversational misery. On her way over she and Mary Alice made
enough eye contact for Ellie to mouth, "You're a bully."

Mary Alice cupped her hand to her ear and mouthed back, "I
can't hear you," then returned to Betty's enthralling story about her
grandson getting a citation for underage drinking during his first
week at Texas A&M.

Maria was in the middle of a rant when Ellie approached. "Me
personally? I don't eat out unless it's a special occasion, but you and
Travis seem like the type, so take a word of advice," she said, holding
up a finger as if preparing Josie for something life-altering. "If you're
not in the mood for steak, stay away from the Buckhorn. Fact is,
you're gonna have to drive into Trevino if restaurants are what you're
after."

"Well, I like to cook, so . . ." Josie said after a pause, unsure anymore if she was telling the truth or just speaking out of discomfort.
A hand on her shoulder brought her back to life.

"Josie?" Ellie asked.

"Yes, hi, yes, I'm Josie," she said, startled, but mostly thrilled.

"Ellie Hall. Mary Alice's neighbor. Just wanted to introduce myself. Heard you and Travis moved into Margaret Rose's old place."

"We did! We did. Yes." Josie winced as her sudden bout with
social anxiety manifested in the singsong-iest of ways, where five
words were chirped when a response only required one.

"And you took Mary Alice's old job. How's that going?"

"Oh, well, I didn't mean to take it. I didn't know I was taking
anything. I thought I was just filling an opening, and there was no

animosity at all. I didn't even know who Mary Alice was until they hired me, so—"

"Hey, hey, it's all right. You don't have to explain yourself, and allow me to apologize for my friend. She's, um, how can I put this gently?"

"She's an old bitch," Maria said. "But we love her."

"I heard that," Mary Alice said from the other side of the room.

"I wanted you to," Maria shot back, scooting back over to the others and leaving Ellie and Josie to themselves.

"So," Ellie said. "Potato salad!"

"What do you have?"

"Beans."

"That sounds easy."

"The easiest," Ellie said. "Not to brag. All you need is heat and time. Not an ounce of skill."

Josie smiled uncomfortably and darted her eyes from left to right while searching for a question. "So how long have you, uh, lived in Billington?"

"What would you say if I said I was born and raised here?"

"I'd say, *congratulations?*"

Ellie laughed. "Well, I wasn't. I moved here about twenty-five years ago. Thereabouts."

"Where from?"

"Houston. You're from New York City?"

"Yes, I guess word gets around."

"It does."

"Well, I lived there my whole life. Born and raised and went to school and met a man and had our son there. Now I'm here."

"You sound delighted."

"I am! Oh, I am. Believe me. But it's just like any new place, I guess."

"Though you've never really moved to a new place before."

"That's true," Josie said softly, her eyes narrowing as if it were the first time she'd realized it. She'd never really moved before. Apartment to apartment, sure. To a different borough, once. But never outside the city limits. It was suddenly so obvious she'd never taken the time to consider its implications. "But I think I'm getting the hang of it."

"You said you have a son?"

A weight was lifted inside Josie. Small talk with a stranger was so hard before she had kids because she could never decide what about her someone else would find interesting. Her job? No. No one ever really understands anyone else's job. Her hobbies? Swimming was too personal, too existential to be a topic of conversation, and no one else ever shared her taste in movies, not even Travis. But once she was pregnant, she could talk for hours with just about anyone. Parents had nothing but tips and anecdotes to share, and people without children always listened with a level of intrigue and curiosity that felt almost academic, as though motherhood or the very act of being a parent was some hypothetical thing that couldn't possibly exist outside of a classroom. When Henry was born, she fell in love again, and what's more fun to talk about than a true love?

"Yes," Josie said. "Henry. He's four."

"A great age," Ellie said. "How's he liking Billington so far?"

Typically, Josie bristled at the question, since she learned the person asking was really using it as a sly backdoor into any number of other inquires. Was Henry happy? Was he depressed? Are you worried you made the wrong decision? Have you created a safe space for him? Do you regret the move? Will you move back? Or worse, are you miserable in this new place and do you fear you'll never leave? That you'll stay here until you're dead? But with Ellie, Josie didn't put up any defenses. Maybe she was happy to have been saved from Maria's ramblings, maybe being put on potato salad duty had made her feel vulnerable, or maybe she just liked Ellie—the way she gently touched her shoulder as an introduction and asked with such kind and curious eyes—and felt she seemed genuinely trustworthy.

"You know, he seems to be just fine," Josie said, and it was the truth. "I was worried that he wouldn't. That there would be, I don't know, a learning curve to such a small town after leaving Brooklyn behind, but he's the same Henry that he ever was."

"What more could you ask for," Ellie said, smiling more brightly than before, as if this strange child's happiness brought her a much-needed contentment.

"If I have any worries, it's just about finding him some friends. But that's hard enough without school. We moved a year early, though I can't complain about the free childcare."

"Travis's mom, I take it?"

That Ellie was right didn't surprise Josie; it was more about being right so casually. Here was a woman she had never met—didn't even know existed until a few minutes ago—and somehow, she knew more about her life than so many of her acquaintances back home. "Yes," she said. "We're so grateful. And he loves it over there. Really."

"At the Compound?"

"You know about it?" Their conversation was slowly gliding into the candid, gentle complaining of old friends, and she was happy to give in to Ellie's familiarity with her in-laws. "Oh, what am I saying, who doesn't know about it. It's practically got its own zip code. You know they wanted us to build a new house there, Travis and me, but"—she shook her head—"I couldn't do it. Not right away, at least. I *want* to live in town. Get to know it, you know? How else am I supposed to feel like I— Well, anyway. I won that battle."

Ellie nodded. "It is beautiful country up there, though. I'd love to move a little farther out of town."

"What's Houston like? I've only been to the airport."

"It's big and hot and sticky. No need to visit."

"And how old are your kids?"

"I had a son. He passed about twelve years ago. He was eighteen."

"Oh, I'm sorry."

Ellie wanted to give her a hug right then and there. Her whole life, even before Kenneth passed, she never understood why so few people realized those two words were good enough; that "I'm sorry" isn't merely a prologue to some more grand declaration of their sympathy, that it usually said everything you needed to say about someone else's grief. But here was Josie, and she was simply sorry. In that moment, Ellie decided she had just made a friend.

"His name was Kenneth. Kenny. When we moved here, he was twelve, so it was probably a little more difficult for him than your Henry. But you find your way in, somehow. It's just like anyplace."

"I hope."

"You keep doing that. Just don't worry."

"It's in my nature," Josie said, her eyes gliding over Ellie's shoulder and noticing the wine bottles behind her. "Do you mind if I grab a drink?"

Ellie laughed. "Allow me. Red or white?"

Josie eyed the gargantuan bottles and imagined them all as identical drinks colored with two different dyes. "I'll take red, I guess."

There wasn't much left in any of the bottles, so she grabbed a cup and poured what remained of each inside. "Let's call it a blend."

Josie laughed. She decided she'd made a friend tonight, too.

"So, potato salad duty. Is it as bad as Mary Alice made it seem?"

"Hate to break it to you, but it's considerably worse."

"How many times have you done it?"

"Never. I'm her best friend, so I get a pass."

Josie laughed. "Didn't you just tell me to stop worrying?"

"I didn't tell you to worry, I just said it's going to be hard. But you'll be fine. Before you know it, it'll be Saturday afternoon and you won't have to think about boiling potatoes for at least a year. Unless, of course, Mary Alice runs you out of town before then."

"I think we're here to stay," Josie said. "Especially once this pool is done. Travis and I are putting one in. I think the whole process has aged me a year in the past month."

"Oh, I heard," Ellie said, instantly regretting it.

"I figured," Josie said, utterly unfazed by the confirmation that her domestic drama had become, at least on some level, the talk of the town. "The pool men told us it would be a pain in the butt to dig through the rock, but I told them to go ahead. Cost a small fortune. Travis could have stopped me, but he didn't." She paused and breathed quietly but heavily. Her heart rate increased. Ellie stayed quiet, cocking her head as though willing her to keep going. "And if he had, I would have fumed. I would have absolutely fumed. So, it's all my fault, this big, expensive mess in the backyard, but at least the story ends with me getting to swim laps. Sorry."

"No, no. Sounds like you needed to, uh"—she waved the air in front of them in circles as she searched for the words—"air that out."

"Well, thank you for letting me. Is it silly I was dreading this?"

"Oh, I know."

Josie squinted at her, and Ellie smiled, leaning forward conspiratorially. "I told you," she said, pointing at Mary Alice in the corner, now the recipient of Maria's ravings. "That one's my best friend."

The warmth Josie felt from hearing Ellie gush about her best friend made her take stock of the roomful of women, all of whom were old enough to be her mother. Mary Alice's scorn aside, she was happy to have been invited, but this wasn't exactly the social situation she expected. Where were all the Billington women her age? Oh right, she realized. They were probably home with their children.

ELLIE STAYED TO help Mary Alice clean up after the others went home. With two sets of hands, the whole process didn't take more than twenty minutes, which the two of them spent talking about everything but Josie. But once the empty bottles were all in bags and the leftover snacks were sorted among Mary Alice's immense and admirable collection of Tupperware, neither of them could hold it in any longer.

"I saw you hit it off with Mrs. Kerr," Mary Alice said in a tone that wasn't quite scornful, but nowhere near playful.

"Figured as much," Ellie said, tightening the pull-string on the last of the garbage bags. "I like her. And to tell you the God's honest truth, I think you would, too."

"Shows how well you know me," Mary Alice said.

"I thought that was the point of all this," Ellie said. Without explanation or even a gesture, Mary Alice knew exactly what she was talking about. "We're getting to know each other all over again, and I think that's fantastic. Just about the most fantastic thing that's happened to me in a while. But if you're going to bring me back into your life, and if I'm going to bring you back into mine, you're going to have to stop being so damn stubborn all the time. Can't you give it a rest? At least now, when it's just us? I'm trying to tell you that there's more to Josie Kerr from Brooklyn, New York, than you seem to believe is possible."

Mary Alice inhaled sharply and stood up straight. "What I know is that I want nothing to do with a woman like *that*."

Ellie laughed, and Mary Alice asked her what was so funny.

"You're the most ridiculous person I've ever met. 'A woman like that,' you say? What does that mean, exactly? Someone who's apologetic when they show up late? Someone who responds to your punishing assignment without complaint? Someone who I happened to get along with?"

Mary Alice gave the counter one final wipe-down and set the bottle of cleaner on its surface with a *thud*. "Yes." Her voice may as well have been a gavel.

"Well then, you're in for a miserable stage of your life," Ellie said, her eyes narrowed, the edges of her mouth turned down. Mary Alice remained silent and waited for the good-natured chuckle or joke that inevitably softened the edges of their occasional spats. But none came, and Ellie walked the garbage out her back door to the cans in the yard.

With Ellie outside, there were no traces of any type of gathering left in the house. No sign that anyone else had recently been inside at all, let alone a group of boisterous drinkers. She could have sent the assignments over email, sure, but then when would she have had her friends over? What sort of break in tradition would that have required? And what did Ellie mean by "miserable stage"?

The rough whirr of the sliding door knocked Mary Alice out of her spiral. "Now it's like no one was ever here at all," Ellie said. "See you tomorrow?"

"See you tomorrow," Mary Alice said. "Thanks for your help."

Ellie waved goodbye with an upward flop of her hand and disappeared into the backyard. Mary Alice watched as the motion-activated floodlight caught Ellie hiking through the side yard. Once she was inside, a line of windows illuminated as she traipsed through the house, diffused by long beige curtains. The kitchen, the living room—on, then off. The hall, on as she climbed to the second floor. By the time the floodlight switched off, the only light that remained came from the bedroom, and Mary Alice wondered how long Ellie might read before shutting it off.

6

A KNOCK AT THE FRONT DOOR STARTLED MARY ALICE OUT OF her trance at the kitchen window. It was too late for company—dark-thirty, her grandfather used to say—but she was relieved to have a distraction from her thoughts. She turned back and marched through the living room, assuming someone had forgotten their phone or keys, or maybe lost them between her couch cushions. Without asking who it was or flipping the drapes aside to check for a familiar face under the harsh orange light, she opened the door.

"Don't take this the wrong way, but I was half expecting to find you dead on the floor," the woman on her doormat said. Her hair was in a tight ponytail that pulled her face taut. She had Mary Alice's narrow, severe eyes and thin lips, but with an extra feature that was hers alone: a birthmark on her cheek that gave her an imposing elegance. It was Mary Alice's little sister, a twin born three years late, and she was eager to come inside. "You won't answer a phone call at noon, but you'll open the door in the middle of the night without asking who's knocking?"

"Katherine," Mary Alice said nervously, uncertain whether or not she had fallen asleep and this was all a terrible dream.

"Can I come in? I don't really want to do this through a doorway, and I need to use your bathroom. The drive was longer than I remembered." Mary Alice stepped aside; no words felt appropriate or even possible. After charging through the threshold, Katherine dropped her two bags under the coat tree—a Louis Vuitton weekender and a large, bulging floral tote—and beelined to the half bath by the stairs. "Sorry to go straight to the facilities but it's urgent," Katherine said.

Mary Alice stood with her hand on the knob, dumbstruck, and turned her head from the bags to the bathroom door, then back again. She checked her watch and, suddenly jarred by the late hour, crossed her arms. If someone were dead, she thought, Katherine would have gotten out with it immediately. News of death was impossible to hide, and even someone as brusque as Katherine couldn't help but wear it on their face. This wasn't death, Mary Alice decided, dreading the sound of a flush and the faucet. This was something else. This was life.

The last time Mary Alice saw Katherine was at Samuel's funeral. She flew in from Atlanta, then rented a fire-engine-red Mercedes in San Antonio for the ninety-minute drive to Billington. Mary Alice remembered standing not too far from where she stood right now, holding her husband's ashes in her hand, berating her sister for showing up in a red convertible. "Did you know they're really just crushed bone?" a young man in the waiting room of the crematorium had asked her just hours before. "They throw the ash away and just give you the pulverized bits of bone that don't burn."

"You've always had a nasty habit of flaunting your money in front of me," she told Katherine that night in a gruff whisper, hoping Michael had already fallen asleep upstairs. "But I didn't think you'd stoop so low as to do it at my husband's funeral."

"It's not my fault they gave me a free upgrade," Katherine said, almost laughing. Her voice had a way of skirting into something vaguely mid-Atlantic ever since she was a teenager. Strangers found it alluring, but Mary Alice heard French tips on a chalkboard. Another performance. Another desperate attempt to leave her old home behind.

"Oh, isn't it? You think they would have just handed that to any old person? You think they would have handed one out to me?"

"Are you the 'any old person' in question?"

Mary Alice used to wonder if she would have thrown the tin of ashes against the wall if Katherine hadn't needled her in that moment, and whether Katherine would have found a way to make another joke had this one not been so gracefully set up for her. But for the sake of Mary Alice's own sanity, she decided that it would have happened eventually. This fight had been in the stars since Katherine was five and she was eight, when a friend of her father's at church called Katherine "even prettier than her sister," an observation others repeated in various ways throughout their adolescence. She just never expected it to culminate in a cloud of human dust.

All these years later, the cloud was still hovering between them. Mary Alice narrowed her eyes at the front door, as if it were daring her to escape. A sound of flushing startled her, and she slammed the door shut and walked to the kitchen, where she pulled out a box of tea. When Katherine walked in, she headed wordlessly toward the bar and sat, watching her sister fill the kettle.

Mary Alice pulled down two mugs, dropped a sachet of something fragrant and flowery in each, and rested her hands on the counter while the coils in the kettle hissed behind her.

"How have you been?" she asked, struggling to maintain eye contact.

"How have I been? That's the first question you ask?" Katherine's voice had a piercing, high-pitched frequency she wasn't used to, but one that still felt familiar. As the sound of heating water grew louder, Mary Alice began tapping her foot to camouflage the shiver that she felt taking hold of her body. "Mary Alice, are you hearing yourself? I haven't seen you since . . . last century."

"And yet you still look exactly the same. That sort of self-preservation must have set Jonathan back a pretty penny."

Katherine took a deep breath, held it, and shut her eyes. When she began speaking again, the edges of her voice had smoothed. "I've been calling you for days. I've left messages on your cell phone. I've left messages on your house phone. I've sent you emails."

"Well, I try not to look at my cell phone and haven't checked my email in months. In case you didn't know, I'm retired now." She turned to take the kettle off its base, widening the gulf between her and her sister.

"Mary Alice, it may be the first one I've seen in a decade, but I know an answering machine when I see one. And I also know what that little red light means." Her guilt wasn't working. Mary Alice remained silent. "Tell me something because I can't do all the work. Why do you think I'm here right now?"

"Not because you missed me, I'd reckon."

Katherine grabbed the air beside her ears with her fists and took a few breaths. Her tension was quickly and visibly dissipated by about half, even though she knew full steam ahead would have been more than reasonable. "When I told John I was going to fly down here and fix your mess, he said I was being sanctimonious. Sanctimonious! As if I had a choice to do something else! He said he didn't believe a person could be this stubborn, that I wasn't trying hard enough to reach you, but I guess he never got the chance to know you, did he? So I buy a plane ticket. I drive to the airport. I get delayed five hours. Eventually I fly to Texas. I rent a car. I drive down here in the middle of traffic and knock on your door after dark, exhausted, miserable, part of me worries you're dead, because who would have told me, and you say nothing. You just make me, what is this?" She sniffs the mug Mary Alice set in front of her. "Chamomile?"

"Lemon ginger."

"*Lemon ginger tea,*" she said, contempt oozing from each syllable. "That's the question you answer. You haven't changed a bit."

"You've been here ninety seconds. Don't pretend to know a single thing about what's changed and what hasn't."

"Then ask me. Ask me what I'm doing here. Because I swear to you, Mary Alice, I've done enough work. Over the past few days, over our whole damn lives. You've got to put in some effort here. Please."

Mary Alice blew on her tea and looked for a shred of confidence in the mug but saw nothing but darkening water. She raised her eyes to meet her sister's and saw her face at twenty-three, before her own life had been blurred by tragedy. It's not that she didn't want to remember her sister, it's that she didn't want to remember why she had come.

"Fine," she said. "What are you doing here?"

"Please quit treating me like I'm an idiot."

Certainty is a leading cause of nervousness, and Mary Alice was both at the same time. "You heard from him," she said at last.

Katherine nodded. "Two days ago, I heard a knock at the door. Middle of the afternoon, I was doing some work in the study. Thought it was a FedEx man delivering the new end tables I'd ordered, so I opened the door with a big grin. But it wasn't my end tables, Mary Alice. It was a goddamned ghost."

Mary Alice's deflated in her chair. "So he's OK?"

Katherine slammed the mug on the credenza beside her. "Are you listening to me? I nearly had a heart attack. I thought Michael was *dead*. We all did."

"Is he OK?" she repeated, speaking louder and more slowly.

"He's in one piece, if that's what you mean, but he's a drunk, Mary Alice. Just like Dad, just like Grandpa. I don't know how he made it to our house without killing someone. Hell, maybe he did."

"What did he want?"

Katherine shook her head. "That never came up."

"How does he look?"

"Awful. Nice clothes, I did notice that, but awful. Dirty. Unshaven. Stunk like a bar bathroom. I'm surprised I recognized him."

"So why'd he come to you?" she asked, shaken but not unstable. "He needs money?"

"I told you, I don't know. He's acting all locked up and I don't know the password."

"And what, you think I do?"

Katherine scoffed. "Who else would?"

"Well, why didn't he come here himself?"

"Why do you think I've been calling? I'd hoped his mother would come right up, but she doesn't like being disturbed, now does she. And I sure as hell wasn't going to make him travel. Not like that. That boy needed rest. Looked like he hadn't slept or eaten in weeks. Would've broken your heart. Sure as hell broke mine."

"Where is he now?"

"Holed up in the guest bedroom. John's checking in every hour in case," she said, her voice finally breaking. "Just to see if he's OK."

"I never told you he was dead."

"Right," she said as the vein in her forehead made an appearance. "You just let me believe it. You let everyone believe it."

Mary Alice bolted up and pointed in the empty space beside her, as though she were surrounded by invisible foes. "I had nothing to do with that obituary. Once it was in the paper, everything was out of my hands. What was I supposed to do? Ask them to print a retraction? You have no idea how much that hurt me."

"There you go again, focusing on the wrong damn thing. Your son is *alive*, Mary Alice. And he needs help. From you."

"Well then, why did he go to you?"

Katherine responded as though she was running out of energy. "How are *you* going to interrogate *me* when you're the one who owes us all an answer?"

"We had a fight, that's all. I told him he was dead to me, he didn't argue."

"And so he just left and never came back?"

"Exactly. Wrote his own damn obituary and sent it to the *Trevino Herald*."

"Jesus Christ. And you never thought to look for him . . ."

Mary Alice's eyes returned to the cooling water. "What did you expect me to say?"

"You want the God's honest truth? Nothing," Katherine said. "After all this time, I nearly expected you to be dead. And you know what, Mary Alice? If you had been, it would have made this trip so much easier. Because by now I'd already be on my way home." She had started crying before she even finished her sentence.

Each of them expected the other to fill the canyon between them with something, anything, but instead they let out what was left of their tears in silence. Mary Alice grabbed Katherine's empty mug, pulled the bag out of the bottom, and tossed it in the trash can. She loaded the dishwasher, turned it on, and rubbed her hands on her pants. "If that's it for tonight, I'm headed to bed. I'm sure you've had a long day and are tired. You can have the guest room, it's on the left upstairs."

"I know."

"Towels in the bathroom. Everything's clean."

Katherine scoffed with resignation at her sister's predictable roadblock. "Sure. Fine. We'll talk in the morning."

Mary Alice lingered as though wanting to offer one final word, then left her alone. Katherine listened closely to her sister's steps, which creaked on the wood, and the sounds of her bedtime routine, waiting patiently until they stopped some ten minutes later, when she was sure Mary Alice was under the covers, staring sleeplessly at the window. What she couldn't have predicted was Mary Alice taking out her phone and texting Ellie from bed. No coffee tomorrow, sorry. Will call you later.

The next morning, Mary Alice woke to the smell of bacon. She sprung up, the blanket and sheets catching the morning light while falling to her lower half. This was the first time she'd woken up in her own bed with someone else in the house since Michael left, knowing someone was making themselves at home in her kitchen, even if that someone was family. She felt prodded by the sounds and smells seeping under her bedroom door but refused to let it show. So she showered and dressed herself—jeans and an oxford shirt, tucked in without a belt. She put her hair up with a clip and checked her reflection, which was older than it was the night before, and summoned as much confidence as she could before opening the door and descending her stairs.

Near the bottom, she heard Katherine speaking in a hushed voice. "And he hasn't said anything? But he's eating? Are you sure? I think she'll come around, though. She has to. She's his mother."

My God, she thought, the palms of her hands pressed firmly against the wall. *This woman sounds exactly like me.*

1

"GOOD MORNING," KATHERINE SAID.

"Morning," Mary Alice said, trying to hide the mortification she felt over knowing someone else had spent the better part of the morning rummaging through her things. "I don't normally sleep in this late, in case you were wondering."

"I wasn't," Katherine said, her gaze staying on the sizzling eggs.

"Where'd you get the eggs? I thought I finished off a carton yesterday."

"Where do you think?" Enough scrambled eggs to feed a small army were cooking in the cast-iron pan. Katherine gently swirled them around, a low and slow method Mary Alice had never had the patience for. This was just like her, Mary Alice thought. Coming into her home and finding ways to flaunt the time and money and tricks she had. She wasn't cooking breakfast, she was showcasing the leisurely pace of her life. And Mary Alice was so, so hungry.

"You went to Carlye's?" Mary Alice leaned on the barstool but didn't take a seat, making the difficult choice not to succumb to such an inviting scene. They were still fighting the same fight from last night. Hell, she thought, they were still fighting their fight from 1982.

Katherine grinned, her gaze still on the pan. "You want the truth? I mainly went because I wanted to be recognized." Mary Alice raised her eyebrows to feign a bit of shock and drummed her fingers on the bar. "But the only people working were a young man at the butcher counter and a teenager up at the register. Had no clue who either of them were, not even who they could be the children of. So, no luck. Oh well."

"C.J. and Emily. Good kids. Taught them both." Mary Alice eyed the pan, watching the eggs solidify ever so slowly over the faint blue flame, and realized she was salivating. She swallowed as subtly as possible as Katherine continued her stirring.

"Is Carlye still alive?" she asked.

"Amos is long dead, but Eric's alive as ever," Mary Alice said. "His birthday's this week actually. Seventy. Having a party at the center."

"Seventy! How funny," she said, closing the oven door and putting her hands on her hips. "I always thought of him as an old man, but I guess he was never more than a few years older than us."

"That's how it always goes when you're a kid. I started teaching seventeen-year-olds when I was twenty-two. They thought I was ancient then, so I must've been practically dead by the end." She lifted herself up with a grunt and took a mug from the cabinet.

"Forty years of teaching," Katherine said with a sigh of either admiration or pity. "Now what?"

"Until last night, I would have said nothing." She didn't want to bring up the night before, but she didn't want Katherine making a hotel out of her house, either. With nothing to do, she leaned into both aggravations.

"So do you want to tell me what happened?"

"There's nothing to tell, Katherine. He left. And now he's come back."

"Twelve years after everyone thought he died," Katherine said, pointing at her with the dirty spoon. "Don't forget that part." As if Mary Alice could possibly. "You know he was in New York City all this time?"

Mary Alice poured a cup of coffee, impressed that her sister was able to operate the machine without paid help. "I did. I knew more than you think."

"Like about his friendship with Kenny?"

"What's that supposed to mean?" Mary Alice snapped.

"You're the one with answers here, not me."

"I can assure you that if something had happened to him, I would've been told."

"Hell of a leap of faith for someone who only goes to church because she's afraid of what people like her would say if she didn't," she said, twisting back around to the stove and turning off the burner. She dropped two pats of butter in the pan and gave the dish one final punctuation mark of a stir and began dividing the dish between two plates already on the counter.

"Oh, don't get sanctimonious with me. What I believed about Michael had nothing to do with faith or church or God. And might I remind you he was an adult when he left. I couldn't do anything to bring him back even if I tried." Katherine knew that wasn't true, and so did Mary Alice.

"He was your son. Didn't you care?"

"Of course I cared. I think your bacon's burning." Bacon in the oven, too, Mary Alice thought. Yes, it was better that way, more evenly cooked and without the messy, snapping grease of pan-fried, but it took so much longer. Again, she was jealous of Katherine's abundance of time. Sure, retirement had suddenly left her with plenty, but she lacked the experience one must have to use it properly. Idle time was new to her, daunting and unwieldy. There was so much of it, so suddenly, that she may as well have had none at all.

"Shit," Katherine said, hopping around to pull the charred, smoky strips from the oven. "Well, damn. Ruined a whole damn package."

"I'm sure they're still edible. You like 'em crunchy anyway."

"So do you," Katherine said, a glimmer of relief in her eyes.

Katherine added a few strips of blackened bacon to each plate, cracked a heaping dusting of black pepper on both, and placed them on the bar, which Mary Alice only now noticed had been prepped with place mats, napkins, and silverware.

"Oh," Mary Alice said, incapable of offering anything more.

"Take your coffee and sit. Time to eat."

"And talk, I assume," Mary Alice said, her defensiveness obviously wearing Katherine thin.

"You think I came here to *talk*? You think *talking* will make any of this better? I came here to take you back to Atlanta." They were both seated, unfolding their napkins in a few gentle shakes and spreading them across their laps like mirror images. If you walked in and saw them just now, just like this, you would think they were not only sisters, but twins. You'd think they were each ten years younger. But the first thing you'd think is that they were friends. So familiar and comfortable in their actions—until they started talking and you'd realize you were wrong about everything you'd thought. And then you'd think something else: you'd think you should leave before someone got hurt.

"You want me to come back with you?"

Katherine threw her fork onto her plate with a sharp crash that caused Mary Alice to flinch and spill egg from her fork. "Why are you making this so goddamned hard? Do you know how difficult this is for me, coming home and trying to figure you out for the first time in our lives? Tiptoeing through this house and pretending I don't see all the ghosts?" Mary Alice stared at her eggs. Her mouth was dry now, her appetite gone. "I didn't want to come here, I came here because your son can't get out of bed and you can't be bothered to pick up your damn phone. Oh sure, I'd love to just talk. To find out why any of this happened in the first place. But I feel like I have a pretty good idea. What was it? He told you he was in love with that dead boy and you kicked him out of the house?"

Mary Alice scoffed. "You think everything must be so simple, because you've never lived a day in your life where that wasn't the case."

Katherine clenched her jaw and pushed her stool back, causing a rough squeak to echo through the house. "I knew you'd be difficult, but I didn't expect you to act like such a child. I guess now's as good a time as any to tell you I'm flying back tonight. And you're coming with me. My treat, if you want to call it that."

"I can't," Mary Alice said in a defiant tone that surprised even her.

"You can't?"

"The picnic is on Saturday. If I leave now none of it will get done."

"Oh, come on now, Mary Alice. The picnic will go on. It did before you and it will when you're gone," Katherine said, uncertain whether she meant dead or just away.

"If I leave now, everyone will ask questions. You know that."

"There it is. You don't want to be embarrassed. Well, I'm sorry, but it's too late for that."

"Give me this, Katherine," Mary Alice said with a tremble in her voice that her sister didn't recognize. "Give me this weekend. One last picnic. Then I will pack a bag and I will go with you for as long as it takes. Or for as long as I'm welcome." Mary Alice's eyes welled up but her tears remained steadfast, communicating everything they needed to without falling.

Katherine covered her face with her hands and inhaled like a machine, as if she wanted no air between them. In the course of her breath, time seemed to stop, and the two of them stood opposite one another, motionless in the harsh kitchen light. Only when she exhaled calmly did the room come back to life. "Fine. I'll call John and tell him to expect us *immediately* after the picnic."

"Do you think he'll mind?"

"Do you care?"

Mary Alice's nod looked more like a tremor. "Thank you," she said in a near whisper. It was the quietest she'd spoken in years, and the timidness embarrassed her, even with an audience of one. She looked back up at her sister and cleared her throat. "Thank you," she said once more. "I mean it."

"I know."

Mary Alice returned to the kitchen. Breakfast was a total loss, she thought while shoving the eggs and bacon into the garbage disposal with a wooden spoon. But at least this gave her something to do. In under twenty minutes the pans would be stripped of their grime and the counters would be spotless. The plates and forks and knives would be hidden in the dishwasher. Her home would be clean again, and she would have done it herself.

8

ELLIE'S HOUSE WAS COZIER THAN MARY ALICE'S. WARMER.
Her curtains were heavier and more intolerant of light, the cabinets
were bigger and darker, her couch was more inviting and easier to
nap on. Ellie hated overhead lighting and enjoyed the act of turning
on the lamps when she entered a room. It was second only to the act
of turning them off as she left, which made her feel as though she was
taking a tactile approach to her life. That was the thing you'd be
struck by if you scanned Ellie's living room. It was filled with things
that didn't only look nice, but invited you to find out why. It was a
home meant for enjoying, which is to say it was a home meant for
living. As much as she enjoyed and often truly loved spending time
at Mary Alice's home, crossing her own threshold, where everything
seemed a little warmer and more inviting, always gave her a sense of
relief. Every house is tainted by a dusting of the owner's memories,
and sometimes they're too sad to bear if not your own. Ellie's

memories may not have been any happier than Mary Alice's, but at least they were hers. And on this Wednesday morning she was alone with them.

Though she'd only been spending mornings with Mary Alice for the past three months, the ritual had become such a reliable part of her daily routine that drinking coffee by herself filled Ellie with anxiety. Coffee from the same pot she would have poured from anyway tasted bitter in her own kitchen, alone with her own thoughts, without Mary Alice there to make everything seem sweeter by comparison. After one mug, she dumped the rest of the pot down her sink. What a waste, she thought, watching it swirl around the drain and then rinsing it with water from the tap, removing any proof it had ever been brewed at all.

She was dressed and adequately caffeinated forty-five minutes before she normally left, but she couldn't decide how to fill this strange new morning void. Before Mary Alice invited her over, she watched the local news and did the *New York Times* crossword on her iPad. But returning to that former version of herself wasn't as easy as turning on a TV or unlocking her iPad. There had been a murder, the reporter said. A photo of a smiling old man appeared above his left shoulder, and the reporter read the introductory details with an affected sympathy that made Ellie turn off the set before she could find out whether or not the police had any leads on the previously happy man's killer. She took her iPad, covered in a bright pink faux leather case, from its basket on the credenza and tapped on the crossword puzzle app. It loaded quickly and reminded her that she'd lost her previous streak, but solving the first clue, "Koppel or Williams," provided no pleasure. T-E-D, she tapped, filling the boxes as the editor intended, but the grid no longer felt like a challenge. So she locked the iPad and set it aside, feeling a little free. The words were someone else's responsibility now.

So, she thought, she would leave for work early. She held the arm button on her alarm, walked through the kitchen door into the garage, locked the dead bolt behind her, and got inside her car, a green compact SUV, tight and comfortable and just high enough off the ground for her to feel like she was a little safer on the road. When the front half of the car was through the garage, she tapped the brakes and looked to her left to see any signs of Mary Alice, but the morning sun's reflection obscured all the windows. Then, after pulling out fully, she saw a white SUV in the driveway. A model so new she imagined how it smelled. This must be why Mary Alice canceled, Ellie thought, instantly putting the explanation away and trying not to speculate about who it could be. She turned on the radio to 101.9 and let the second verse of what sounded like an old Jewel song carry her through town and onto the highway.

If Trevino were a body, the hospital would be the liver—sort of in the middle though not quite in the center, and ugly as hell. She could have gotten there in twelve minutes that morning, but she stopped at the Coffee Wagon instead. Even as she pulled in, she wondered what she was thinking. Paying for coffee at a café when she could make it at home or have a cup from the hospital's bottomless supply always felt like the most unforgivable waste of money, and all her coworkers knew it. "Ellie's happy with the sludge," Xavier, the oldest nurse, would say if one of their coworkers left for a coffee run during a break. Once he had poured a drink from the Coffee Wagon in her hospital mug to see if she'd notice.

"What happened here?" she'd said after the first sip. "Since when did we start getting good coffee?"

"So you *can* taste the difference," Xavier said. "I'm not sure if I'm relieved or just more annoyed that you keep drinking the office stuff." Ellie thought that trick was just awful, though she pretended to be amused by the whole thing. She wasn't a stubborn coworker. She was easy to talk to. Everyone liked working with her. So why did they pick on her for this one little thing? Why was it so embarrassing to think saving money on coffee was some kind of small virtue?

When Ellie told this to Mary Alice over the summer, long after it happened, Mary Alice scoffed and told her young people don't appreciate the value of a dollar. When she told Mary Alice that Xavier was her age, Mary Alice told her that you didn't go to work to make friends.

It wasn't until Ellie had waited for the orders of two customers ahead of her that she realized she should probably scan the tables for her coworkers. How would she explain this ethical swerve to them all? she wondered in a flash of panic before seeing the coast was clear. "Ma'am," said a voice in a tone that forced the panic right back. "Can I take your order?" Ellie turned to see a young woman with no hair on the left side of her head and many different colors of hair on the right waving her forward.

"Oh, yes, sorry," Ellie said, embarrassed by how frazzled she must have appeared. "Good morning. I'll have, hmmm . . ." She scanned the menu with her eyes squinted, grimaced, and heard someone clearing their throat to her left. Without looking but quickly getting the point, she pulled her head back and returned to the cashier. "One medium cappuccino," she said, playfully over-enunciating every syllable as if this were the most fun she'd had in days.

"What kind of milk?" the cashier said.

Ellie almost said, "Cow." Then she looked carefully at the cashier and realized it wasn't the kind of thing someone with that kind of hair would ever laugh at. "Just regular old whole milk," she said. "I haven't had breakfast."

"That'll be $4.25," the cashier said, as if that was simply how much coffee should always cost. As though no one had ever taught her how to make it at home.

Ellie gave her a painted-on smile, unzipped her wallet, and pulled out a five-dollar bill. When the change was returned in a quick dance of their hands, she let the coins drop into the tip jar, which surprised the barista enough that she said, "Wow, thanks," instead of saying nothing, which Ellie expected. "Can I have your name?" she added, pulling a cup from the middle stack and readying the Sharpie in her hand.

"Ellie," she said.

"Next in line?"

Ellie felt so hurried and out of place. Beyond the sheer financial loss, which she didn't even try to understand, she wondered how people could do this every morning, and why they would add to their workdays—which were already cacophonous jumbles of people and lines and bad moods and decisions—the possibility for even more distress. She pretended to read on her phone while waiting for her coffee to be ready, thoughtlessly thumbing through the headlines while listening to what everyone in line ordered. A young man got an iced coffee, black. The man behind him, a cold brew with half-and-half. Then came a woman with an iced latte with an extra shot, which made Ellie raise an eyebrow and let out the smallest of gasps. Not until her order was called a few seconds later did she realize, of course, the woman wanted espresso, not whiskey.

To everyone else in line, this was a normal Wednesday. To her, it was the smoking embers of a house Mary Alice had built and then destroyed. For a moment Ellie was angry at her, creating a routine only to thoughtlessly abandon it with hours' notice. But no, that's unfair, she thought. Mary Alice didn't owe her anything but respect, and the text, though late, was a sign of that. Once back in the driver's seat, five-dollar coffee in hand, she remembered the car in the driveway and Ellie's anger morphed into sheer curiosity. Mary Alice hadn't been behaving weirdly during the planning meeting. Apart from that ridiculous behavior toward Josie, she seemed more contented than she'd seen her all summer.

Ellie understood all too well why Mary Alice behaved so strangely around other people in town. She had suffered through not only the loss of her husband and son, but the endless whispers that accompanied them. She commanded respect as the town's most accomplished teacher, the person whom all their children feared and, in most cases, learned from. And though she was never exactly beloved, her classroom became icier after Michael. Being feared was preferable to being pitied, so she leaned into it.

Ellie noticed the change firsthand. It began with a slow, steady reduction in phone calls. When they did happen, they were quick check-ins that reeked of obligation. Four months after Michael was gone, what were once twice-weekly conversations—long, meandering dialogues during which they would chat while cooking or drinking a glass of wine or staring up at the sunset—had stopped entirely. Around the same time, she began hearing more open complaining about Mary Alice's harsh grades and piles of homework while browsing the four small aisles at Carlye's. Once she even heard Betty Flores tell Lucy Lutz to hush when she was spotted through the stack of cans. *Don't let Ellie hear*, they meant. *She and Mary Alice are thick as thieves.*

She could have corrected them. She could have said, "Don't worry, Linda. Your complaints are safe with me. Mary Alice and I don't speak anymore since our children died." She could have distanced herself from Mary Alice and tried to find a replacement of sorts, a new best friend, but that doesn't just happen. It's always unnerving to discuss friendship in transactional terms, as a product that didn't simply manifest organically between two people without much work, but rather a relationship one went into willingly and maintained with countless more choices over time. Every new moment between yourself and a friend is fundamentally the result of an effort to keep the friendship active. An active decision that, no, you will not let this falter. You will put in the work. You will see this through to the end, by which you mean death, though you'd never be so blunt as to admit it.

That's what "friends forever" means, isn't it? Friends until one of us dies. But the acronym for that doesn't look good on a sticker or a necklace or a mug or a card or a hashtag. And though forging new ones requires a combination of dedication and luck, it's so much easier to focus on the former. To think of friendship as a kind of magic, when it's really closer to alchemy. Still, Ellie felt she didn't need a new friend after Mary Alice. Though maybe it was because she knew, deep down, she just needed to wait for Mary Alice to come back to her. If only she'd known back then that she'd be waiting twelve years.

Ellie pulled into the staff parking lot of the hospital at 8:35, twenty-five minutes earlier than usual, and sighed after putting the car in park. The radio was playing "Underneath It All," and she tried to remember the singer instead of heading in early. Avril Lavigne? Britney Spears? Nelly Furtado? She waited for the song to finish so she could have her answer, but in place of a song ID came yet another one. Five songs and two recognizable artists later, it was 8:55, time to walk inside. She grabbed her cup of coffee, which she had all but forgotten to drink from, and headed for the door.

In movies and TV shows, you're bound to hear someone say, "I hate hospitals." Ellie always hated that. In her experience, no one ever says it, because it is far too obvious. Grieving parents and spouses and friends and family members don't look down a bright teal corridor and say, "I hate hospitals," with a shiver. Being in a hospital as a healthy person, when it's not your job, is never going to be fun, but it's not the place to talk about things you hate. It's not the place to complain. It's a place to worry and to hope, and Ellie noticed, if anything, a place with an unreasonable amount of positivity, not disdain.

People often asked Ellie what it's like to be surrounded by death all day, and over time she constructed an answer that combined shades of the truth with enough comforting whimsy to keep them from asking more. "I'm not surrounded by death all day," she'd say, as though searching for the words and coming up with her answer on the fly. "I'm surrounded by life." This put people at ease, which was a major part of her job. Yes, she administered drugs. Yes, she communicated patient problems to the doctors. Yes, she bathed and clothed and took care of some of the patients' most obvious and fundamental needs. Yes, she wore cute scrubs to soften the edges of the attending staff's harsh, overly crisp white coats. But people never wanted to talk about that. Instead, they just wanted to praise her for making them feel safe and secure and comfortable around all the more callous people doing the life-saving.

She was good at all of those things, too, which everyone at Trevino General knew. Even the patients who had never met her would sometimes say things like, "Oh, I've heard you're the best." She never asked who they heard this from, and pretended not to care, but it made her feel important. Today's rounds: a broken arm, an esophageal spasm, a busted lip that needed stitches, and a recommendation for a dentist who took walk-ins. Trevino General was rarely full, rarely empty, and rarely filled with tears. On their first date, which they didn't realize was a date until it had become a weeks-old memory, Gerald had asked her how she could spend day after day in a place as sad as a hospital. How do you keep going when a core aspect of your job is being reminded of death? And she told him what she must have told a dozen people before. Whose job isn't?

Gerald texted Ellie at 12:32, right as she was heating up lunch in the break room. The ding came from her locker, where she kept her phone all day to avoid, yes, distractions, but also in an attempt to prevent herself from becoming as addicted to the device as her friends and peers. If she never got a taste for social media, she would never need to worry about breaking the habit. But still, the sound of her text tone gave her a jolt of serotonin. The only people who texted her these days were Mary Alice and Gerald, and Mary Alice knew better than to interrupt her during work.

DINNER TOMORROW? it read. His use of all caps was cute, even if something about it seemed, she thought, strangely elderly.

Yes.

BUCKHORN?

She pulled her head back from the phone, worried by the question. They'd never been to the Buckhorn together, as a couple. Dinners had been at his house or her house or one of the three Mexican places in Trevino. It was too early, she thought, knowing better than to relay that message to him. Instead, she simply countered.

> My place? I can stop for steak on
> the way home. The only
> problem is the wine.

IF YOU INSIST. SMILEY FACE.

She didn't know what embarrassed her more: how much she enjoyed their rapport, or how quickly it had developed. The all caps, the text-based descriptions of emojis, and her coy acknowledgment of his burgeoning wine snobbery. They were a couple, she thought, even if neither of them had used the words.

> I insist. How's 7:00?

HOW'S 6:30?

> What's the rush?

WHAT ISN'T?

Her girlish giggle caught Fran, a pediatric nurse, by surprise. "Who're you texting over there, your boyfriend?"

Ellie gasped. "No! Just a friend."

"Sure."

She didn't like revealing too much about her personal life, though she was certain all her coworkers knew the bullet points by now. Got married to a rotten man. Had a son with him. Divorced him because she didn't want the rot to spread. And then the son, the opposite of rotten, died before he had the chance to grow up. She never got over it. It wasn't quite right, more of a soapified abstraction of her history than a proper biography, but it filled in the blanks in a way that left her pride intact without inspiring much additional questioning.

She slipped the phone back in her purse and slammed the locker shut. Her lunch was getting cold. As she slurped down a spoonful of the lentil soup she'd made in bulk on Sunday night, she stared up at the mounted TV and pretended to watch a celebrity tell a more famous celebrity about her marriage, hoping no one in the break room would notice she was thinking about something else entirely. Even if they did, they would never guess she was thinking about the best side to serve with steak that didn't involve potatoes. She ought to surprise him with something less obvious, she thought, embarrassed to be excited about a side dish.

9

SOMETIMES THE GREATEST FRIENDS IN LIFE EMERGE OUT OF thin air the moment you need them. They may not be the longest-lasting, like a childhood friend who knows you from diapers to retirement, or even the ones you see most, like roommates or co-workers, but they fill a hole in your life that you never knew was human-shaped until they walked right in, uninvited, and fit there, perfectly. Or, at least, this is how it was with Mary Alice and Ellie.

When Samuel died, Mary Alice was inundated with visits from people she'd known most of her life. These people—out of a noxious combination of guilt, pity, discomfort, and aimlessness—reached out to their newly widowed friend with invitations for friendly dinners and game nights and girls' nights and playdates. And for months, she accepted nearly all of them. There were visits to the Landry place, where Michael and the other kids swam in their aboveground pool as the adults drank beer in the shade of an umbrella on the rickety deck. There was the book club run by Wilma Hueber, where Mary Alice was the youngest member by at least a decade and, at least on her one and only visit, the only participant who had actually read the book (*The Bridges of Madison County*). And at least a dozen other failed attempts at friendship that never lasted more than three visits before the momentum ran out.

So when the Wilsons next door shocked the town by announcing their plan to move to Dallas to be closer to their grandchildren, Mary Alice didn't have high hopes that the buyer, who only viewed the property once before making an offer, was someone she'd ultimately befriend.

"You know she doesn't have a husband," said Linda Kerrigan at that first and last book club meeting, after Mary Alice went through the differences between the film and the novel in gruesome detail.

"I did," Mary Alice said, though she hadn't. "Is that a problem to you?" One thing she had learned since Samuel's death, something she occasionally thought of as the only good thing to have come from it, was that it allowed her to be more honest with people. She could say what she felt instead of opting for what was polite, because, as everyone knew, she was a single parent in mourning. No one had ever thought of her as mean until she was suddenly allowed to be. And then they realized it must have been who she was all along.

"Of course not," Linda said, feigning shock and putting her fingertips on her chest. "I just think it says a lot about someone— denying a boy a father. I just feel bad for him, that's all." The others moaned along with Linda. Yes, they all went on to say, that poor boy and his poor mother, escaping God knows what, probably an abusive man, and moving out to the country. Their country.

"Where do you think she works?"

"I heard she's a doctor," said Maria.

"I heard she's just a nurse," said Lucy, with a heavy air of judgment despite the fact that she herself hadn't had a job since she bagged groceries at Carlye's in the fifties.

"How old's the boy?"

"Twelve."

"Will he be in Michael's grade?"

"I'm not sure. I suppose I haven't received the dossier everyone else has."

The remark went over their heads, but Lucy continued, "Maybe he'll be good at football or basketball. That should make it easy on him."

"I just hope he's not too good."

"What I don't understand is why she'd choose Billington of all places."

Then, as she decided she would soon have to leave, Mary Alice scanned Wilma's living room, taking in the tables and credenzas covered in doilies and angel statuettes. Above the couch, a wall of crosses. Paperback copies of *The Bridges of Madison County* being used as coasters for glasses of wine. These were no longer her people, she realized. Would this Ellie person be like the rest of them?

The next week she watched from the living room window as the moving truck was emptied. A large U-Haul driven by a tall young man with a mop of floppy hair whom Ellie laughed with and touched politely. Siblings, Mary Alice thought. Or at least family. She'd bought a bottle of wine from H-E-B and baked a tray of lemon bars, deciding to put both in the fridge and wait until the next day to do her introduction. Moving day was always stressful enough.

From a hundred yards away Ellie seemed to be about Mary Alice's age, give or take a few years. And the boy, whose name no one cared to find out, could have been Michael's shadow. The kind of tall that looks stretched, and a pound or two over worryingly skinny. He hid in the house after taking a few small boxes in from the truck. It all became clear on that day as she watched them settle into their new home. This was her chance. These weren't just the neighbors she'd needed for six years; they were going to become the neighbors she'd cherish for the following six, and if everything went well, the six after that. But when Ellie turned and noticed her new neighbor staring blankly through her front window, Mary Alice threw the curtain closed and ran back into the living room, her heart racing. Tomorrow she would go and welcome them. She would explain that she had been watching, not eavesdropping and sighing with relief. Most crucially she would bring Michael. His presence would, she believed, solidify the connection, or at least make it harder to deny outright. They would become friends, Mary Alice kept repeating to herself. They had to become friends.

She rang their bell the following day, a Sunday, just after 1:00 p.m. to give them time to sleep in. Ellie swung the door open without a hint of trepidation and greeted Mary Alice with a generous smile. "Hello."

"Hi," Mary Alice said, holding a bottle of wine in one arm while extending the other. "I'm Mary Alice Roth and this is my son, Michael. We're your neighbors, just there." She pointed at the house, and Ellie followed her finger. Mary Alice had always been proud of her house, but it looked more beautiful than she expected from this angle, even in the harsh light of midday. She hoped it seemed that way to Ellie: friendly, inviting, the platonic ideal of neighborly.

"Ellie Hall," she said, shaking her hand with a firmer-than-expected grip. "My Kenneth's inside. He's watching at the top of the stairs, isn't he," she said loudly in a motherly tone. "He's just nervous."

"Being new in town's nerve-racking for sure. Anyway, we just wanted to bring you this to say welcome to town." She nudged Michael, who had been awkwardly holding the plate of lemon bars at his eye-level as though it were a bomb.

"That's very kind of you, let me take those. Want to come inside? I just made tea."

Mary Alice looked down at her son. "Want to go inside and meet the neighbors?" He shrugged and twisted his mouth to bite the inside of his cheeks. "He's a young man of few words."

"Oh, I recognize that look completely," Ellie said with a sly smile. "Come on in, and *please* pardon the boxes. I can't imagine we'll have this place looking like a home in less than a couple of months. But as long as it's good by Christmas . . ."

Michael followed his mother inside and shut the door behind him, taking a moment to peer through the etched oval of glass and consider his street from a new perspective. Still boring, he thought before returning to what the two adults had just said right in front of him. What was it about parents, he thought, that made them treat their own children like jokes just because they wanted to bond, or whatever, with other adults? Were they even jokes? Like the time, he remembered just then, she was on the phone while he was in the room, and said, "Oh, they can be so filthy, can't they? Michael refuses to start wearing the deodorant I bought him." He shot her a look from the couch, where she *knew* he was sitting, but she didn't see him. Was that one of the perks in the guidebook for parents? You get to use your kid as a punch line? He didn't remember much about his father anymore, but he couldn't remember his father using him as a punch line. He'd seen fathers scold their sons for this and that, crying over a scraped knee or striking out after three pitiful swings, but no such memory of his own dad existed. Maybe he was too young, but maybe—and this was the option he preferred—his dad was better than all the others. Maybe he lost the best thing that ever happened to him before he could really happen to him.

As Michael and Mary Alice walked into Ellie and Kenneth's house for the first time, he wondered whether or not they would have done this if it had been the three of them. He knew his mom was lonely, and he used to feel sorry for her, but lately it seemed more important to feel sorry for himself. Why did they have to invade this family's space? Because his mom wanted a friend? His dad would have waited a few more days, or maybe he would have invited them over for a barbecue. Michael had no idea that his father was the lousiest cook in the county, but that didn't matter. The father he'd created in the six years since his death was more powerful than the one he barely remembered ever had been.

As he followed his mother and Ellie through the living room, Michael realized he had never been in this house before, despite living next door all his life. Who even were the neighbors before these two? he wondered. They were old, and they were always in their yard picking weeds or planting flowers or sitting out in their lawn chairs. He and his mom waved at them as they drove past, but did he even know their names? No, he realized. He didn't. Was that normal for someone his age? Was it something to worry about? Past the piles of boxes in the living room and awkwardly placed furniture came the kitchen, a large, light-filled space in the back of the house that opened up onto the giant porch. They'd be sitting in there, it seemed, which relieved Michael, as it was the only room downstairs that seemed to be even remotely finished. This room felt like a room. The others felt like construction zones.

"Oh, I always loved this kitchen," Mary Alice said. "Not that we came over much when Willy and Frances lived here, but I did envy it when we did. So much space! And the porch. I always did want a wraparound. We've just got the patio."

"How long have you and Michael lived next door?"

"Thirteen years. We moved in just before Michael was born."

"Oh, he and Kenny are the same age then!"

"Really? I saw him from the house and thought he and Mikey might be in the same grade," Mary Alice said, holding the mason jar of tea up like she was about to make a toast. "I was watching from the house, by the way, I think you may have seen that. I didn't mean to pry, though. It's just a bit of a big deal to have a new neighbor in Billington. People don't tend to leave or show up. They just stay."

"What about me?" Michael asked, staring into his tea.

"What do you mean, sweetie?"

"How did I get here?"

"You were born here. That's what I mean. Most people here were born here because their parents were born here, and they were born here because their parents were born here—you know how small towns go. Where are you and Kenneth from, if you don't mind me asking?"

"Houston, but I'm from Beaumont originally. Not a small town, but smaller than Houston. So I know what you mean."

A wave of silence rippled through the room as they all took more sips of iced tea.

"So it's just you two? No other siblings or . . ." Ellie said, correctly detecting a single-parent vibe from her guest.

"Nope, just the two of us. We make do, though. We're a powerful duo, aren't we?" She tapped on Michael's knee and watched with embarrassment as he rolled his eyes.

Ellie laughed. "He and Kenny are like twins." She turned to the doorway and cupped the side of her mouth with one hand. "Hey, Kenny, get in here! Don't be rude to our neighbors."

The floor above them creaked, as though he had been listening to every word and was preparing to be summoned. "He's a little shy, forgive me."

There it was again, Michael thought. Another parent talking about their kid like they didn't have brains. It made him so mad he wanted to say something, but what could he say? Complaining in his head was so much more effective than complaining out loud. But his brain stopped looking for things to be disgusted by when Kenneth walked through the doorway.

Kenneth didn't look like the other boys in his class. He didn't stand up straight the way his mom was always asking him to. And he didn't have on a shirt with some stupid phrase on it, like the ones everyone else had about how such and such sport is "life" and every-thing else is "just details." Kenneth was wearing a shirt he could have sworn his own mother tried to buy him a few weeks ago, a bright red polo shirt that felt instantly familiar: too wide and still not short enough, because sizes don't work for anyone whose body exists out-side the norms. There was a palpable awkwardness to Kenneth, a discomfort he made almost no effort to hide from anyone in the room—not his mom, not two complete strangers on whom he was about to make a first impression. And Michael understood it all. From the moment he saw Kenneth, Michael felt like screaming, "You understand me!" But he would never do that out loud. Like complaints, he'd keep it inside.

Kenneth went straight for the empty chair beside Michael and, suddenly, the table was full. Ellie wondered how long it had been since all four seats were taken. Mary Alice wondered what Kenneth's father could possibly look like, given how much he was a twin of Ellie. Michael and Kenneth wondered the exact same thing: *When can we leave?*

But they stayed, and after five more minutes of listening to their mothers babble on about their jobs, Michael and Kenneth realized their afternoon wouldn't change for the better unless they took the initiative. It was Michael who spoke first. "Mom, can I show Kenneth our house?"

"What do you think?" Ellie asked Kenny, whose lowered head meant his eyes were doing all the work. "Want to go next door with your new neighbor?

"We can play Super Nintendo. I have two controllers."

"I don't play with him enough," Mary Alice said, a gentle nudge in Kenneth's direction. "I'm sure he'd love to have a second player."

Kenneth raised his head and looked up at his mother, pausing just long enough to cause a simmer of discomfort among the other three. "Can I, Mom?"

"Be my guest," she said. "Or, I guess, be theirs!"

Kenneth rolled his eyes and stood, Michael did the same, and they went.

Each of them remembered this first meeting a little dif

but they all agreed that Michael and Kenny's near-instant bond made the whole slightly awkward affair go down as a success. Overall, Mary Alice thought the afternoon thrilling, and had no suspicions that Ellie, with all her chatter and hospitality, was masking feelings of dread and discomfort. As nice as Mary Alice seemed, she couldn't shake the fact that you just never know with some people. Still, they finished a pitcher of tea while chatting long after Michael and Kenny shuffled out the back door. Michael remembers his mother embarrassing him and acting like, well, someone else. As he grew older, he realized it was the moment she changed for the better. But more than anything, he remembered Kenny, who didn't look up or listen enough to their mothers to form any kind of memory other than Michael's. It was the day they met, and for that, it was the best day of his life.

As soon as the door slammed shut, the two women turned to each other with matching eyebrows. "That was easy," Ellie said.

Mary Alice laughed. "I'd say kids are better at making friends than adults, but to be perfectly honest, it's not Mikey's strongest suit."

"Kenny's, either," Ellie said, noticing just how much this nervous, hunched-over boy and her son had in common. She'd always noticed Kenneth's disinterest in sports and fondness for solitude, as well as his lack of male friends, but it wasn't until the previous summer, when her mother asked Kenneth if he had any girlfriends at school, that she saw a new kind of fear and shame wash over his face. She remembered how he looked at her in that moment, quietly pleading with her to change the subject, which she promptly did. But she hadn't yet worked up the courage to ask him what his discomfort actually meant. She didn't think asking "Are you gay?" was an appropriate question to ask anyone, let alone a twelve-year-old. He'd always been sensitive, and *sensitive* was a word she felt comfortable with. So sensitive is where she would stay. Anything beyond that was a question for a later time. And with any luck, she thought, he'd tell her before she had to ask. She took another sip of tea to distance herself from her thoughts. "We didn't know who'd live next door. To be honest, I should have done a little more research, but this was sort of a sudden move."

"Oh?"

"Long story; nothing too interesting, just a divorce."

Thinking only of her own hatred of probing questions, Mary Alice avoided asking one of Ellie. "I'm sorry."

"Don't be," Ellie said. "I mean it. What about you? Was there ever someone else?"

Mary Alice parted her lips but felt her voice get stuck somewhere just behind them. It was the first time she'd ever been given the opportunity to tell her story on her terms, without gossip tainting the waters of the narrative. Ellie was the first person she'd met in years who knew nothing about her, and Mary Alice hadn't prepared to tell her anything, let alone everything. Talking about Samuel never got any easier, even to people who knew all the sad little details. Even now, it was the same exact amount of hard. Though, she thought, at least Ellie didn't know. At least Ellie wasn't knowingly putting her through something again.

"It's just me and Michael. Samuel, that was my husband, died six years ago."

"Oh, I'm very sorry."

"You don't have to be sorry, either. That can be the first rule of our"—she paused to choose her words carefully—"neighborly friendship. No feeling sorry for each other. How's that?"

"I like it. I think we're off to a great start."

"Looks like it was as easy for us as it was for them."

"Looks like it."

A football field away, Michael was leading Kenneth up the stairs to the landing of their second floor, where a television sat in a wall of shelves filled with books and VHS tapes. Nothing was alphabetized or categorized, which, Mary Alice thought, led to a pleasurable kind of chaos. It didn't look messy, it just looked full. Underneath the television was a small shelf where sat Michael's prized possession, a Super Nintendo he'd convinced his mother to buy him for Christmas the year before. He didn't own many games—they were yet another expense and part of the compromise was that he'd have to buy them with his own allowance—but one of them was for two players. So he popped *The Legend of Zelda* out of the dock, pursed his lips and gave the cartridge for *Super Mario Kart* a quick blow—more out of habit than because it had any effect on game play, like how his mom tapped the can of her beers before opening them—and shoved it into the console. "You play *Mario Kart?*" Michael asked, flipping the switch to ON.

"I have before, but we don't have a Super NES. Just the regular one."

"My mom gave ours to my cousins when we got this one," Michael said. "Sucks because we had a lot of games for it. But I guess it's fine."

Kenny did not reveal that he played *Mario Kart* at his own cousin's house all summer, and that he had been undefeated for the entirety of his final two weeks in Houston, but Michael realized he was dealing with a ringer after two cups.

"Jeez, you're good at this," Michael said.

"Sorry."

"No. I mean, it's cool. I just thought I was pretty good."

"It's only because I played my cousins, who were great. I feel like the computer players aren't as hard."

Michael bristled at the casual way Kenneth mentioned his playing video games alone. Did he have FRIENDLESS LOSER tattooed on his forehead? Was there something about him everyone noticed that didn't reveal itself when he looked in the mirror?

They played another cup, and Kenneth won again. "You did a little better that time," he said.

"I hope you're not letting me win."

Kenneth turned to Michael and held his gaze until it was met. "Well, you didn't win, did you?"

Michael laughed and wondered if maybe Kenneth was the opposite of what he had thought earlier. Maybe it wasn't that Kenny was seeing what everyone else in town saw, it was that he was seeing what everyone else couldn't. At this point, anything he saw was an unformed, unknowable thing. But the idea of it was there. The glow of a difference that only the most perceptive people could pick up on. Come to think of it, Michael realized, it could have been precisely what he noticed about Kenneth.

"Excited about seventh grade?" Michael asked.

"I don't know," Kenneth said. "I'm not excited about a new school. What's everyone like?"

Michael, convinced of his and Kenneth's kinship, could have run down the class in alphabetical order, articulating his precise grievances with each of his classmates, but he lost the nerve. It was too much for right now. They were neighbors, after all. He would explain his problems next time they played *Mario Kart*. "They're fine. I don't know. They've been my class since kindergarten. Apart from Derek and Ernest. Both of them flunked second grade, so they held them back. You play any sports?"

"No," Kenneth said without the slightest pause. "You?"

"I do, but I hate it."

"Which sports?"

"Baseball. Basketball. Football. I'll probably run track in high school. That's all of 'em."

"Y'all don't have soccer here?"

"Nah. I mean, some people play it, but they have to go to Trevino. You play soccer?"

"Not really. I just like it more than everything else. Maybe. I don't like . . ." Kenneth said before rubbing his eyes. "I don't like teams, I guess."

"Yeah," Michael said. That must be it, he realized. "I don't like teams, either."

After their tenth cup and Kenneth's tenth straight win, the phone rang. Michael bolted up from his spot on the floor and grabbed the old, corded phone on the small table behind them next to the couch.

"Hello," he said, annoyed.

"Hello, Mikey. This is your mother. Would you mind bringing your new friend, Kenneth, back to his house? He's been summoned."

"Yeah, be there in a sec." He hung up. "That was my mom. She says your mom wants you to come home."

"OK."

They walked the short trip in silence until approaching the Halls' back door. Michael hesitated, thinking it best for Kenneth to open the door to his own house. Instead, Kenny just stood there, squeezing the muscles in his face either out of frustration or because of the midday light. "You think you'd want to come over once we finish unpacking? I've got a lot of games. Board games, I mean."

"Yeah, sure, just let me know. Bet your mom has our number by now."

"Cool." He opened the door and found their mothers in front of an empty pitcher at the table.

"Look who's back," Ellie said.

Mary Alice smiled at her son, whom she could tell was a little lighter than before, even though she knew he would never smile back in front of people. "We should probably let the Halls keep unpacking," she said. "Thanks for letting us barge on in like that."

"It was our pleasure, believe me. We'll have you over for a proper dinner once we're all unpacked."

"Likewise," Mary Alice said. She put her arm around Michael, who bristled at first, then found a comfort in her nook. "Enjoy the rest of your day. Bye, Kenneth." Kenneth stood silently in the doorway to the living room like a windup toy ready to be released.

"Later, Kenneth," Michael said.

"Later, Michael. And it's Kenny."

"Good, and I'm Mikey."

Their eyes met, and so did Mary Alice's and Ellie's. *Our sons are friends*, their silence said. This move could be the best thing that ever happened to either of them. And when Ellie turned back to her son, Mary Alice's eyes remained on Ellie's, lingering on the slope of her nose and the way she blinked—slowly, calmly—and then, how she grazed the edge of her empty glass with the tips of her fingers.

The near-instant friendship between the Halls and the Roths proved to be a relief to the Billington residents who might otherwise have felt pressure to welcome their new neighbors a little more warmly.

Outsiders didn't often move in, but when they did, they were given an elaborate orientation—the husbands were invited to the Lions Club, the wives were invited to the Altar Society, and the children were invited to every classmate's birthday party. Connections didn't always form, but they were always tested. Though not for the Halls. Thanks to Mary Alice and Michael, those who would have attempted to fold Ellie and Kenneth into their own lives under normal circumstances felt relieved of that particular burden. What a blessing it was that these mysterious strangers had found Mary Alice and Michael, they thought, forever refusing to unpack such a thought.

10

MARY ALICE STARED AT THE BOOK IN HER LAP BUT WASN'T reading a word. Her mind was on Katherine and Ellie and Michael, how much each of them knew and the blanks she would inevitably need to fill in once they stopped letting her get away with silence. Ellie had probably noticed the rental car in the driveway but was too polite to call her with questions. Michael had probably told Katherine more than what she let on, and he could easily be telling John everything else while they sat there. She suddenly regretted canceling today's coffee with Ellie last night, realizing that Katherine's presence would be public knowledge soon enough. The quicker everything blew up in her face, she thought, the quicker she could emerge from the rubble—that is, of course, if she made it out alive. But she was never good at working up the nerve to have a difficult conversation. The things she never wanted to say somehow always burst from her without any warning at the worst possible time, making her seem thoughtless and cruel. She sighed, knowing this time would be no different, perhaps even the worst of them all, so she began preparing an apology. None of this would go well, but with a week of work, maybe her apology could help repair everything she'd broken, even if only a little bit.

The sound of the sliding glass door behind her made Mary Alice's eyes dart back to the page of her novel, pretending to look busy. It was one of those crime thrillers everyone seemed to not only love but respect. She'd bought the author's first book expecting to be disappointed, as most books about murder felt like they pandered to a reader's most primal fears and emotions, but she found herself captivated by the sustained dreadfulness of the landscapes juxtaposed with tenderly written, broken people doing the investigation. Despite the abundance of dead people, it really was her favorite kind of novel, a meandering story about sad people who get a little less sad by the end. She was used to those sad people living humble lives in the suburbs of small American cities; these sad people just happened to be solving a murder. This was the author's latest. Not her best, and thus far, arguably her worst, but Mary Alice kept reading because she found the author's voice comforting. And because the chair beside her was empty.

"What're you reading?" Katherine asked as she sat down, twisting her head to read the spine. "Looks scary."

"A murder mystery," Mary Alice said.

"Yuck," Katherine said, setting a box of crackers on the table between them. "I grabbed these from the pantry, hope you don't mind."

"Of course not. You're welcome to anything inside, not that there's much."

"I'm glad to hear you say that," Katherine said, pulling a handful from the box. "I assume the same sentiment applies to the old place?"

"The old place? What do you want with the old place?"

"I always liked it down there. And how often am I here to visit? I just need a ride because I sure as hell won't find it on my own."

"Well, I don't want to go there. Sorry, but I think you can understand that."

"Well, it's mine as much as it's yours, and I want to go."

Mary Alice looked up from her book for the first time since Katherine sat down. "Go ahead. Key's on the hook next to the garage. Still got the rabbit's foot on it."

"You know I'll never find it on my own, all those turns. You're the one who always drove."

"So you want me to take time out of my day to drive you to my least favorite place on planet Earth?"

Katherine laughed. "Yes. I expect you to agree to this teeny-tiny little favor, because it's just about the least you can do considering the circumstances."

Mary Alice grew stiff. "Let me get my pages in."

"Fine," Katherine said, rolling her eyes as slowly as possible. "Get your precious pages in. But I'm staying right here while you do."

Katherine picked up the paper and unfolded it with a whip in front of her. By the time Mary Alice set the bookmark in her novel, Katherine had read every word of the main section. "Five minutes," Mary Alice said. She stood up and left her sister behind, knowing there would be no argument, knowing that, once again, Katherine was getting exactly what she wanted.

It's not uncommon for people in large cities to spend their entire childhoods with the same group of people, but it's an entirely differ-ent experience in a town as small as Billington, where there's more space to play, but fewer options about who to play with. One of Mary Alice's earliest memories was her first day of kindergarten. It was an atypically hot day in what was already a typically hot month, the sort of cruel swelter that laughs in the sweaty faces of people who drone on and on about the benefits of "dry" heat. Her teacher, Mrs. Schlortt, only wore prairie dresses and smelled like menthol cigarettes. When her mother, Loretta, a tall and gentle woman who slept in long gloves and had a different dessert recipe for every possible ailment or trag-edy, dropped her off at the classroom door, Mary Alice refused to let go of her hand. She squeezed so hard that Loretta gasped. Mary Alice could remember it so clearly, that sudden, awful feeling that she was making her mother feel pain. So she let go and began to cry, unaware at the time that her tears only made Loretta hurt more.

Inside the room were twelve children she'd already known all her short life, quietly playing with blocks and crayons, not thinking any-thing was strange about the scene unfolding in the doorway. Even then, as a small child, Mary Alice noticed the uncomfortable discon-nect at play, how her agony was being seen and heard, yet wholly ignored. Her mom bent down and said, "I promise it's going to be all right!" There was pity in her voice, but also amusement. *My silly little girl*, she must have been thinking. *Always making a mountain out of a molehill.* She gave Mary Alice a kiss and said, "Look! There's Ma-ria!" And she looked up and saw Maria holding a picture book against the far wall. "Go say hi to Maria."

And that's what Mary Alice did. She ran across the room and grabbed Maria, who recoiled at the gesture and asked, "What's wrong? It's just school." The other children in Mrs. Schlortt's class were the same ones she grew up with for the rest of grade school, plus or minus two or three whose families came and went. There would never be cliques. There would never be feuding cafeteria tables. There was simply the class of 1975, and a year was something no living soul could escape.

"Remember how scared you were?" Loretta would sometimes say to Mary Alice, as though she could ever forget. "I never understood it! The day before, you were riding bikes with at least four of them, but in that room they were strangers." It wasn't a nasty recollection, but Mary Alice wondered how her mother was never able to see that moment as a defining piece of her life. The event that focused all her traits and solidified her into the person she would never stop being: someone afraid of being left behind. Some irritating presence that no one really cared enough to remove.

By second grade, teachers knew she would be the senior year valedictorian, not because she was exceedingly brilliant, but rather there weren't many other options. By middle school, a growth spurt made her the tallest person in her class. She was taller than all the boys in her class, while Katherine fit snugly, just below their arms, a place Mary Alice had never once desired to be. And though bullying never got physical—only the boys in her class fought with each other—nicknames were persistent. For years she was Stretch, which led to a brief period of walking with a hunch. (A habit her parents quickly rid her of by having a doctor scare her about scoliosis.) She began shaving her legs after being called Hairy Alice, and the nickname remained long after she bought her first razor. But no nickname hurt worse than the one that was never designed to. There was a simple elegance to "Katherine's sister" that cut so deep it could have drawn blood.

She never understood why everyone seemed so surprised by their differences. No two people were exactly alike, not even actual twins, so why did the disparity between her and Katherine bring the town to its knees? Mary Alice did more work, so of course she did better in school. Katherine talked to more boys, so of course she went on dates. And people complimented Katherine's appearance because, after being disappointed by Mary Alice's tomboyishness, Katherine was raised as her mother's doll from birth. She became the plaything Mary Alice was never asked to be. She dressed better than Mary Alice, meaning she wore dresses; and she wore more makeup than Mary Alice, meaning she wore makeup at all. But at night, when they put on their matching sleep shirts and crawled in bed beside each other, their twin mattresses separated by a single long nightstand, they looked like one young girl who'd been split in half. If only the rest of town could see them like this.

The summer before Mary Alice became a senior and Katherine became a freshman is when it all came to a head. Now, suddenly, Katherine was able to date. It was the rule in their house—though until then it had been entirely theoretical, as Mary Alice never took advantage of the privilege after entering high school. Katherine, on the other hand, awaited the moment with a kind of glee she'd never seen before. In that final summer of their joint childhood, the two of them spent more actual quality time together than they had since Katherine was a baby, as if they knew it was the last hurrah before Katherine would leave Mary Alice forever in favor of athletes and binge drinkers.

They drove into Trevino to buy records and ignored the boys when they approached, instead shuffling away in a fit of giggles. They bought Cokes and rode their bikes down to the brick yard. But the happiest memories were spent at the old place. Not quite a ranch, which would technically have required livestock, and not quite a second home, which would have required more creature comforts; the old place was just somewhere to be when you didn't want to be anywhere else.

It was about twenty minutes outside of town. Not east, toward Trevino, or north, toward the Hill Country, or west, toward Mexico, but south, toward nothing. Getting there required directions, not a map, and a series of turns you had to memorize on roads without signs. You felt the trip there as much as you saw it. There were the harsh sounds of cattle guards, and the way the car began to handle differently when the road changed from gravel to dirt. There were turns you made out of confidence, not because you saw anything that looked like an actual road. And if you did everything right and made sure not to forget the keychain with the old white rabbit's foot on it, you could unlock a dull silver gate with a POSTED sign on it and drive toward a dusty brown two-bedroom house with a tin roof and an inviting porch that sat fifty yards from a small lake surrounded by tan grass and a mess of brush and mesquite trees. "The old place" is what Mary Alice and Katherine's parents always called it, because they couldn't for the life of them imagine a time when it was new.

The land had been in the family since the Parkers arrived from the old country, Germany, back in the early nineteenth century, when families chose central Texas as their new home because they were promised three hundred acres of land as part of their journey, despite its then occupation by the Lipan people. Over time, those hundreds of acres of land an original family began with would split and fuse, contract and expand, due to any number of contentious inheritances, disagreements, and business propositions that may or may not have been wise. The old place was all that remained of Mary Alice and Katherine Parker's great-great-great-great-grandfather's initial claim, a scraggly sliver of a shard measuring some thirty-five acres on which nothing could be grown or raised without total dedication, something which no one in the Parker family had wanted to do in decades. Once Mary Alice and Katherine's parents were the rightful owners, the old place was little more than a watering hole, somewhere for the family to escape to for a swim or a barbecue. Mary Alice remembered the occasional Christmas in that house, a birthday party or two, the weekend when Katherine swears they were both nearly killed by a cougar, but mostly she remembered the swimming.

The two of them would spend entire days in the water as their parents stayed inside doing whatever their parents did when they were alone. They would swim laps or float in the center on a tube, Mary Alice reading *Once Is Not Enough* or *Jaws* or whatever she'd grabbed from the library as her sister lay out on the grassy edge. Miles away from everyone else, she and Katherine were free to be best friends. It was like magic. But their remote sanctuary would soon become found, as even the most unpolished of silver linings always has a little luster to lose.

It started with a funeral. A cousin, second or third, who died in a car accident in Uvalde. They were likely three sheets to the wind behind the wheel, but because no one else was involved, the family decided not to dwell. A man was dead and hurt no one but himself. Mary Alice would have gone to the funeral, but Katherine asked if the two of them might stay home while their parents took the trip alone. Mary Alice never even considered this an option. Going was just what had to be done. But it was Katherine whose naïveté sometimes manifested as something almost radical, maybe even feminist. Why should they go along? For tradition's sake? Is there a value to public mourning or is that in and of itself a selfish act? She didn't say any of that, of course, just asked if the two of them could be left behind, but Mary Alice always projected a kind of righteousness on her sister, as though she was always trying to meet her powerful potential. And in a way, she did, because their parents agreed to let them spend the weekend alone.

"I've already invited everyone," Katherine said with a conniving glee as soon as the view faded on their parents' departing Rambler.

The announcement hit Mary Alice like a hammer, her mind reeling. "Where? And who's everyone?"

"Jack knows the way, so everyone's just going to follow him. It's a perfect weekend to have a party at the old place."

Mary Alice had never thrown a party in her life, and neither had Katherine. Until then, their parties had been thrown for them, and consisted of little more than cake, a few choice presents, and music played softly enough to speak over. But Mary Alice knew this wouldn't be a time for cake and their parents' collection of 45s. This would be like the party she went to at the Kerrigans' place the summer before, where she had two Shiner Bocks and spent the rest of the night asleep on the couch. This would be like the parties she knew Katherine went to when she said she was sleeping over at Linda Attaway's, and that's why she said, without missing a beat, "No."

"No?" Katherine said, her face contorting into shock and despair.

"No," Mary Alice said. "Mom and Dad will absolutely kill us."

"Not if no one tells them, and I know I won't."

"What if the other parents find out?" Mary Alice said. "It could get back to Mom and Dad in any number of ways."

"We'll be miles away from the nearest parent. Believe me, no one coming is going to tell their folks. If you actually went to parties, you'd know this."

That was probably true, but it didn't calm Mary Alice's newly frayed nerves. Nor did the sudden realization that her sister, no matter what she said, had no intention of agreeing to Mary Alice's arbitrary rules. This was happening, she realized, whether she liked it or not. And, come to think of it, maybe it wasn't *that* bad of an idea. There was a small pleasure in succumbing to Katherine's wishes, and Mary Alice quietly began anticipating the party not long after her sister made the decree. What would she wear? What would she talk about? What would she drink? Katherine saw the growing excitement behind Mary Alice's disapproving frown and grabbed her arm to drag her to their bedroom.

"I'm going to do your hair," she said, pausing to take in her sister's tall frame. She looked so unsteady Katherine wanted to tap her forehead to see if she might tip right over. Instead, she just squinted, and kept speaking with a confidence no one else in their household was capable of mustering. "And I'm going to do your makeup. And I'm going to tell you exactly what to wear."

"But are you going to let me think for myself?"

Katherine crumpled up the right side of her face for a moment's thought and said, "Yes, but run all your thoughts by me for approval." She pulled a pair of black slacks from the left side of their shared closet, jammed a hand into the dividing line between their possessions, and smashed all of Mary Alice's clothes to the left in one dramatic, squeaky push. "That's it from your side. You'd never fit in my pants." She flipped through blouse after blouse before landing on a paisley print she'd sewn herself earlier in the year. "This. Tuck it in. Wear a belt."

"Like, with a buckle?"

"No!" Katherine shouted. "Oh my God, you're impossible. Just a normal belt. Don't you have one?"

"I think so. I thought you'd want me in a dress," Mary Alice said.

"This isn't that kind of party," Katherine said, a devious smile appearing on her face.

"What kind of party is it?"

Katherine turned and bit her lower lip, holding in a giggle. She thought hard about how to answer the question truthfully but didn't want to send her sister bolting from the room forever. "The fun kind. Trust me." It worked.

It was still morning. They wouldn't need to leave for the old place until around five o'clock, and while Katherine was happy to spend the day lying on the floor watching television, Mary Alice couldn't ease the tension she felt about the evening. She sat in a compact ball on the armchair behind Katherine, her knees under her chin, looking years younger than her seventeen. She'd drank before and knew she could easily avoid the pressure of overdoing it, but she'd never been around boys in such an open, unchaperoned context. At the Attaways' party, her home was visible—a series of flickering lights on the horizon. Escape was easy. But out there, at the old place, there was no escape. Only darkness and brush, and maybe even a cougar.

The phone began ringing at 3:00 p.m. One of Katherine's friends after another, asking what they should wear, if they should pack a swimsuit, what they should tell their parents, and which boys were confirmed to be attending. "Something casual but cute—pants would do the trick, but please, no jeans. Yes, unless you want to skinny-dip. That you're spending the night at Maria's house in Trevino while her parents are out of town, but that it's a girls-only slumber party, because it's just specific enough to prevent any alarm bells. All of them." She delivered the same response to girl after girl with a sustained enthusiasm, not once appearing annoyed by the questions, instead seeming increasingly delighted by the answers.

By the tenth or eleventh ring, Katherine was as practiced as a career receptionist. "Hello!" she said in a singsong and smile that quickly drained when an unexpected voice on the other end spoke up.

"The phone barely rang, were you hovering over it?" said Loretta.

"Oh, yeah," Katherine said, adjusting her voice to the gentle tone that kept her parents happily ignorant of her more vibrant personality outside the house. "I just got off with Linda Attaway. How's the funeral?"

"Well, awful," Loretta said. "It's a funeral. But I'm with Uncle Joe and Aunt Delores and they want to say hello to you girls. Get your sister to pick up the other phone."

Katherine put the receiver to her chest and told Mary Alice to grab the kitchen phone. She obliged immediately.

"Hi, Mom," Mary Alice said, slipping back into her default tone of someone's reliable daughter. "How's the funeral?"

"Why do you girls think that's an appropriate question to ask someone? 'How's the funeral'? Think about that when you hang up. And say hi to Aunt Delores and Uncle Joe."

Mary Alice kept the phone to her ear and listened as they droned on and on about how badly they were missed, and how they could not believe Mary Alice would soon enough be out of the house. She responded in polite laughs and yeses and nos while walking toward the kitchen door, phone in hand, so that she could silently commiserate with her sister and roll her eyes at the situation. Katherine covered her mouth to hold in a laugh, and in a few short minutes the conversation had run its course. They hung up and burst into laughter, recalling the time Delores had had so much wine with Christmas Eve dinner that she started snoring during Midnight Mass.

Secretly, Mary Alice hoped Katherine would cancel the party, or that her parents would have announced they were coming home early. The two of them alone together was too nice, too special. She had a nagging feeling that this would be the last time they would ever have so much fun together, laughing at shared memories in their childhood home while their parents were away to pay respects to a dead man. But they had places to go.

That Mary Alice would drive them was assumed by both of them, as she was the only one with a license, but she nonetheless resented Katherine's presumption. She rolled her eyes as Katherine entered the passenger side before Mary Alice had even grabbed the car keys, a princess awaiting her chauffeur. By the time the doors were locked, and a select few lights were turned on so as to keep the neighbors assured of the house's occupation, Katherine was sitting calmly in the passenger seat, waiting for her driver to arrive.

"We need to stop for beer," Katherine said.

Mary Alice would have slammed on the breaks. "What? Why? You said the boys were bringing plenty," she said, her head shaking violently back and forth before pulling out onto the road.

Katherine was twisting a few fine strands of her blond hair between her fingers, staring languidly out the passenger window. "Well, they hit a snag, so it's up to us now."

"How do you know they hit a snag? You didn't mention that earlier."

"Linda told me on the phone just before we left, didn't you hear her call?" She kept talking, seeing as how Mary Alice's answer couldn't have mattered less. "Jack couldn't get his cousin to buy us any, and Martin wimped out once he got to the beer barn because he saw his uncle in the parking lot."

"Well then, we just won't have beer."

"Mary Alice! Grow a brain! No one's coming to this if there's no beer."

"Then they can just be disappointed. It's not like they'll leave if we don't have any."

Katherine guffawed. "That's *exactly* what they'll do."

"Why! We can swim. And the stereo Dad keeps there is better than the one in our house!"

"Which of us has been to more parties, huh? Trust me on this."

Mary Alice scoffed and tightened her grip on the wheel. "Well, I don't know what you expect me to do," she said, already fearing her sister's response.

"What about that new boy in your class? Doesn't he work at the H-E-B in Trevino?"

"Samuel Roth? I can't ask him to buy us beer. I don't even know him! And he could get fired!"

"He wouldn't be buying it. We would. We'll just go through his checkout line."

"What if he's not working today!"

"He is. Linda told me."

"I'm sorry, but how does Linda know everything?"

"Linda doesn't know everything, her cousin knows everything, and they talk all the time."

A silence passed between them as they waited at the main intersection off Front Street. Mary Alice's turn signal was blinking right, ready to take them straight to the old place.

"I have plenty of cash from babysitting and I brought everything from your desk drawer."

"You stole from me?"

"I didn't steal, I borrowed because the boys promised to pay me—I mean, you—back!"

This is how it always went with Katherine; a genuinely lovely moment free from conflict was always tainted with the realization that she had been a few steps ahead of you all along, filling in the cracks and potholes of whatever path she was dragging you down. Like most beautiful people, she was used to getting what she wanted. What made her so talented was that she rarely had to ask.

Katherine slowly moved her hand onto Mary Alice's shoulder, breaking her trance. "Please? Can we just try? What's the worst that could happen?"

Mary Alice knew the question was hypothetical but couldn't help but ponder the possibilities. The worst that could happen was that they would be arrested. Though, sure, that was unlikely. The second-worst that could happen was that they would fail and someone in the store—be it the manager or a nosy shopper behind them in line—would somehow get news back to her parents, getting them both in months upon months of trouble. Then there was the possibility that Samuel would be offended by the request and immediately lower his opinion of Mary Alice, a mortifying proposition given the fact that they knew nothing about each other, which meant it couldn't have been all that high to begin with. A purely personal embarrassment, sure, but in some ways the worst of them all. First impressions are a precious commodity in a small town, and Mary Alice couldn't remember the last time she was able to make one. She wanted to make this one count. Sure, it would be sending the wrong messages— that she was someone with a lot of friends, someone who partied, someone who was trusted enough to be responsible for acquiring alcohol, not to mention someone who was confident enough to take the job—but at least that sounded more interesting than the truth.

Mary Alice let out one more performative sigh and flipped the signal from right to left, turning toward Trevino. The two of them didn't speak for the remainder of the drive, which Katherine must have realized would happen after just two miles, when she turned on the radio. "The Night the Lights Went Out in Georgia" was playing, one of Katherine's favorites, though she didn't sing along as she normally would have in less tense situations. As frustrated as she was, the silence from the passenger seat disappointed Mary Alice, who always enjoyed listening to her sister sing along to the radio. There was a tinny quality to Katherine's singing voice: just off-key enough to exist in the extremely narrow range between insufferable and charming. Mary Alice's enjoyment of Katherine's blissfully unaware wailing wasn't schadenfreude, per se, but something gentler. She liked to be reminded that not all of Katherine's flaws were hidden psychological quirks only noticeable to her. But even more, she liked to know Katherine enjoyed things that had nothing to do with anyone else. That she derived at least a tiny bit of pleasure from her own mind, her own abilities.

In the parking lot, Katherine gave her sister the rundown, which was less complicated than Mary Alice had expected. "As much beer as you can buy with this," she said, handing her a wad of bills that, once flattened and counted, amounted to around fifty-two bucks.

"So I'm just supposed to walk in there, put fifty dollars of beer in my cart, walk up to Samuel's line, and hope that he plays along?"

"No," Katherine said with a hint of frustration. "Look, the only way this works is if he gets something out of the transaction, too."

"So you want me to give him some of the beer? What if he doesn't drink!"

"You're not paying attention. What I'm saying is . . ." Katherine said before hesitating again. This was going to be the toughest part, she thought: doing her best to sound confident while delivering the most crucial aspect of her pitch. "You have to flirt with him."

"But," Mary Alice said, suddenly looking for something to do with her hands, "what if he doesn't like me? What if I don't like him!" She was rubbing her wrists, as if she were desperate to be in hand-cuffs. She couldn't do this if she were in handcuffs.

"This has nothing to do with either of those things, this has to do with flattery. This guy is smart. He can read between the lines. He'll interpret the fact that you're going to *his* line as a compliment. It means you trust him!"

"Or it means I think he's an easy mark."

"To guys there's no difference. They don't care as long as they're getting attention."

Once again, Katherine was, unfortunately, making sense.

A few steps from the door, she turned her head back toward the car and saw her sister waving her on through the windshield. At least fifty yards between them, but the force from Katherine's invisible push nearly knocked her over. She grabbed a cart from the chrome caterpillar underneath the awning and pushed it inside. The store was brightly lit and sparsely crowded for a Saturday, which made Mary Alice feel even more self-conscious. She began by weaving through the produce area, then through dairy and past the butcher. For a moment she thought she recognized the man behind the meat counter, tall and old and mustached and wiping bloody hands on his white smock, but it was just any old man.

Past the slabs of cow and pig came the frozen food, then finally, the beverages. There was a small rack of wine, a mere acknowledgment of the drink's existence, but what filled the bulk of the space was the beer. Few options, but plenty of everything. Budweiser and Shiner Bock and Lone Star and Miller and ZiegenBock, plenty of each. She fingered the prices. ZiegenBock was cheapest, so Ziegen-Bock would do. After calculating the math in her head, she decided that they could get five twelve-packs of the putrid stuff. She looked behind her to check for witnesses. No one. She put the first twelve-pack in the cart and checked again. Again, no one. After the second was loaded, she crept backward, dragging the cart along, to check for approaching customers. Satisfied by her privacy, she loaded the fifth and final twelve-pack. It was all going so well, she thought. This must be how bank robbers feel. A few short, wonderful seconds alone in the clouds with your prize before falling back to Earth, forced to contend with the bigger problem: escape.

Mary Alice pushed the cart toward the entrance, fingering a few items and examining their boxes and bottles to put on the show of a normal, trustworthy customer. No one was watching her, but she wanted to commit to the act, because even crimes deserve 100 percent of one's effort. Samuel hadn't made the biggest impression on her when the school year began a week earlier, and she worried she might not remember what he actually looked like, trying to recall the most basic details. He was taller than the other boys, though not as tall as she, with a fumbling, unsteady control over the gaunt frame of someone who just had their final growth spurt the night before. He had tightly cropped brown hair and flushed cheeks, and wasn't yet handsome, but he would be. Mary Alice knew it, and wondered if he soon would as well. She took a deep breath, shook out her nerves, and marched to his line.

Their eyes met, and she smiled first. A wave of confidence brushed over her, and she began unloading the beer from her cart as though there could never be a problem. As if she had never been questioned in her life. The trick, she quickly realized, wasn't pretending to be older, it was pretending you were the kind of person who never believed they could be told no.

Samuel eyed the drinks, then Mary Alice as she placed them on the conveyor belt. He, too, was now playing a role. Their individual tensions seemed to melt away, as if they had been pretending all their lives and only now were being themselves.

"Having a party?" Samuel asked as he entered the price of the first twelve-pack of ZiegenBock.

"Sure am," Mary Alice said without even the most microscopic of twitches.

"That sounds fun," he said, adding another twelve-pack to her order.

"I hope it is," Mary Alice said, rolling her shoulders and asserting her height.

When he finished scanning, his finger lingered over the button that completed the order. He took a breath and held it, looking down at the cash register as though it might contain a script to follow. Finally, after another moment of hesitation, he gave up and pressed down. Hard. The bell of the machine rang, a rewarding sound for them both, and he gave her the total: $43.68, just under her budget.

Mary Alice fiddled with her pocketbook and removed the freshly smoothed-out bills as Samuel placed the beer in two large paper bags. She handed him the money once he returned to the register, and he responded with the sort of beaming, dumbstruck smile you might offer a magician, or the satisfying finale of an elaborate heist movie. "Your change is seventy-nine cents," he said, placing the coins in her hand and making sure their skin touched.

"Thank you." She grabbed the bags, one in each arm, and glided toward the door as the guilt finally crashed down on her. This boy had done her a favor. Not only had he done her a favor, but he also played along without missing a single beat. The whole charade was so charming and, she couldn't believe she was thinking it, fun. Had she ever had that much fun in her life? Maybe. But maybe not. And definitely not with a boy.

So she stopped, did a smooth 180 on her left heel, and returned to Samuel. His arms were already crossed, his head cocked to one side. "Did you forget something?" he said, surprising both of them with his suaveness.

"We're in the same class, aren't we?"

"Yes, I believe we are," he said, tilting his head to the other side.

"Well, we should get to know each other, then. Free tonight? In case you forgot, I'm having a party."

"So you've said. I think I am, actually. When and where?"

Mary Alice set the bags down on the counter and told him to pull out a pen and paper because this would take some time.

Katherine popped up from her seat when she saw Mary Alice emerge triumphantly from H-E-B, and nearly jumped out of the car to congratulate her before remembering it was no time to make a scene. Mary Alice opened the rear passenger door, loaded all the beer, then slammed it shut. When she was back in the driver's seat, an electric silence passed between them. Katherine stared at her sister, dumbstruck, like she was some new version who had left a wrinkled cocoon of the girl from earlier somewhere in the canned foods aisle.

"Well," Mary Alice finally said as she turned the key in the ignition. "Don't you have anything to say to your big sister?"

"Yes," Katherine said. "Holy shit."

They both laughed and Mary Alice told her all about the game she played with Samuel as they drove. She talked to Katherine about Samuel longer than she talked to Samuel, delighting more in the details as she remembered them than she did as they happened. She was still talking about him as they pulled into the old place, the gravel crackling beneath the tires as they came to a stop.

The party began slowly, like all parties do, with the first guests, Ignacio and Maria, arriving a little too early and acting as though there was nothing at all uncomfortable about the situation. Mary Alice and Katherine held their ZiegenBocks, Katherine more gracefully than Mary Alice, and made small talk with their classmates, wondering how it could be possible to know someone for the better part of one's life and truly know almost nothing about them. The feeling struck them both, but was more overwhelming to Mary Alice, who was less used to seeing people outside the context of Billington ISD. Ignacio and Maria were suddenly human, and, Mary Alice realized, so was she.

For the first two hours, Mary Alice had trouble maintaining eye contact with the guests who deigned to talk to her. Being the center of attention, or at least sharing the role with her sister, didn't come with the discomfort she'd expected. People were speaking to her as though she wasn't practically invisible to them back at school. In that moment, she belonged there. But despite the temporary popularity, her focus kept drifting toward the door, with its square window and tiny little curtain pushed to one side so that the blurry head of a visitor could be seen from inside. Every time the door opened—as well as every time a noise came from the front of the house—her eyes darted to the frame, searching for Samuel's modest but imposing silhouette.

When she went to the refrigerator for her second beer of the night, a hand grabbed her own before it could pull open the door. "Where's your boyfriend?" Katherine said, slurring her words due to either actual drunkenness or learned performance.

"He's not my boyfriend, and I don't know."

"You're nervous, aren't you?"

"Of course I am! Why wouldn't I be!"

"He's just a boy. No boy should make you nervous. And I can tell you right now, he's going to show up."

"How do you know that?"

"Like I said. He's just a boy. And boys show up."

Mary Alice pulled two beers from the fridge and offered one to Katherine, who responded with a headshake and a bitten lip. Her eyes widened and she subtly pointed to her right. Mary Alice's eyes followed the pulsing of Katherine's index finger and landed on Samuel, towering over the other guests, his eyes surveying the tops of everyone's heads before finding Mary Alice. They smiled the same smile at precisely the same time.

"I don't need another beer," Katherine said. "Give it to your boyfriend."

When Mary Alice looked back on this moment—as she did at least once a day—she considered it as the end to the prologue of her life. This moment was the start of everything else. And all of it, absolutely all of it, was Katherine's fault.

11

"DO YOU WANT TO TAKE THE RENTAL?" KATHERINE SAID earnestly.

Mary Alice scoffed. "Take whatever car you please. I'm not coming along."

"You're not coming along or you're not driving?"

"This is your business, not mine."

"But you're the only one who knows how to get there. I've never driven there myself. I'll miss every turn. There's no way those roads are on my GPS. Plus, I doubt my phone will get service out there."

"You're right about that, but I can write you some directions. Pour yourself a cup of coffee and I'll take care of that."

Katherine opened her mouth as though she was ready to keep up the protests, but she shut it after remembering the particulars of her sister's stubbornness. She'd once been stern and knowing but malleable, convincible. But tragedy had solidified everything about Mary Alice that once had some give. She was overfired.

Mary Alice opened the drawer of the secretary desk behind the breakfast table and retrieved a yellow legal pad. As she spread her palm against the paper and clicked the ballpoint pen in her left hand, Katherine thought it looked like her sister had just been electrified. There was a newfound sharpness to her movements that she quickly realized was a sense of purpose. When she had shown up bringing news of Michael's return, Mary Alice seemed to collapse from the news, as though it had been so long since she'd been a parent that she didn't know how to do it any longer. But writing out directions, preparing a sort of lesson plan for a student, this is what she knew how to do. This was a muscle that hadn't yet atrophied.

Mary Alice worked quickly and without even the smallest mistake. She didn't have to drive to the old place to remember how to get there; she went there every day. She was going there now, in fact, her daily journey to the most inescapable memories of her life. And though she always longed for them, in her mind there were never any roadblocks, any gates she couldn't open, or any waters she couldn't cross. It was right there, always.

"Done," Mary Alice said as she ripped the page from the tablet and smiled at her work. Her handwriting was crisp and pleasurable to read, as precise as a font but with a delicate flow that had to be human.

"Does Bubba still go check up on it like he used to?"

"Once a month."

"You pay him?"

"He'd never accept it."

"You ever try?"

Mary Alice scoffed with a wry smile and handed her sister the directions. "Good luck. Call me if you run into a gate I didn't mention. Wouldn't be surprised if someone threw up another, even if it ain't theirs to meddle with."

"You sure you don't want to come, even if I'm behind the wheel?"

Mary Alice nodded. Even though she'd hated the question, it was sweet of Katherine to ask. "It's not being there that I can't do, it's getting there. I don't like—" she said, taking a sharp breath before continuing. "I don't like remembering the last time. The waiting. The wondering."

"That's sad," Katherine said almost imperceptibly. She regretted saying it out loud, but it was the truth. Not that Mary Alice would agree, but sometimes the truth needs to be spoken. "I thought you always wanted to fix it up. Retire out there."

"Sammy did, or at least he said he did, but it's not just a fix-up. It's a reconstruction. It's tearing down and rebuilding and spending money I'd rather use on something else."

"Such as?"

"If this is your way of saying you want to go all HGTV out there, be my guest."

"Ha! John would rather die. I just, I don't know, I always saw you ending up out there. Someone ought to."

"Out there? Sad and alone? Far from everyone else?"

"Happy, Mary Alice. Happy."

Katherine's eyes bulged as she scanned the directions. "How the hell did we ever do this at night?"

"*We* didn't. I did." She added a laugh to soften the critique.

"Well, thank you. This is perfect." She grabbed her keys and walked outside to her car.

It was the first time Katherine had seen her old home in the full light of midday since arriving, and she nearly gasped at the sameness of it all. These were not memories she returned to often, and on the plane ride there she wondered if she would be unable to even recall them. Would the sights of Billington and its residents be all but brand-new to her? Had she willed them out of her past? Would anyone even recognize her?

Names darted into her mind as she passed each house. The blue gravel on the Langfelds' drive. The steep slope of the Attaway roof. The small corner porch at the Richardsons', where she had her first beer. The Miller place, twice as far from the street as any other house, not an ounce of character to the empty, closely cropped front yards. The Schlortts' and its eerie arches. And then the Meyerses', the last house on the road, and one she'd never once entered, which felt strange to her, even then.

After crossing the railroad track, she pulled to a stop and waited for the light to turn red. The dangling, faded yellow thing was new to her, though not spanking. She remembered how fast she and her friends used to drive down this stretch of 90—flat and straight, all the way to the horizon. Oh, the way people used to drive when she was in school. It's a miracle she made it out alive. As her blinker continued its low click, she remembered Kenny. Of course they put up a light. When the light turned green, she turned right and passed the sign that told visitors not to drive through their heavenly town "like hell," and laughed. Who on earth ever thought that would work?

She drove west for a few miles before taking a left on an unmarked dirt road that stretched halfway to the sky, where it was obscured by a line of mesquite. The low, gritty hum of dirt roads pleased her. That is, until it became more dirt than road. *Once you're in the trees, start looking right*, one of Mary Alice's steps read. Katherine gripped the steering wheel more tightly as she wobbled between the gnarly branches and squinted back and forth from the directions to her right side, hoping the brush opened up enough for her at each turn to make an accurate count.

"One . . . two . . . THREE!" she shouted before making a sharp right as a plume of dirt filled the air around her. The next few minutes were just like this: counting and turning, counting and turning. And then: hoping she'd counted right. Her breaths became louder and shorter, slowing to a crawl unwarranted by a car as powerful as the one she'd rented.

But the simmer of anxiety she felt throughout the drive dissipated the moment the old place appeared in the distance, just when she thought it was about to boil over. The house, the Porta Potty–sized toolshed, and then the pond, which stretched from the windshield into the passenger window.

After fiddling with the lock on the front door, she jiggled the knob and shook the whole thing violently before finally getting it to turn. The door opened with a *pop*, like a cap freed from its bottle, and Katherine walked inside, shutting it behind her. She closed her eyes and tried to return to the good memories from this place, but they wouldn't come. She sat on the couch, coughing as it exhaled a puff of dust, and scanned the room from a lower angle, but still felt nothing but a tickle in her throat. She was surrounded by junk, not memories. That's all junk is, she thought. Objects with no stories to tell. But then again, she just wasn't exactly in the mood to listen.

She emerged from the house, wiped her hands on her pants, returned to the driver's seat of her rental, and pulled out her phone.

"Hi," John said calmly on the other end.

"Hi. How is he?"

"Fine. Watching TV upstairs. I made him breakfast, but he didn't eat much of it. Drank coffee, though. Where are you? What's up?"

"I'm at the old place."

"Just you?"

"Mm-hmm. Mary Alice gave me directions."

John sighed louder than he would have in person, like he wanted to make sure the phone got the message, too.

"How's it look these days?"

"Depressing."

"So you won't be going for a dip?"

An extended silence passed between them, one that neither knew how to interpret. With the phone still on her ear, Katherine inhaled and looked at the crumbling sprawl of memories surrounding her. The house needed new paint, new siding, a new roof, new every-thing. And the water, well, it needed more water. She wondered if it was still deep enough to drown in. "I just want to come home."

THE LAST TIME Mary Alice had been to the old place was twelve years before, the day after Michael ran off. She'd only stayed for a minute or two—just long enough to make sure he wasn't hiding out there, that he was actually gone for good. She found empty beer bottles and rustled sheets; small, happy scenes that broke her heart. But that visit didn't really count, she thought. It was little more than a drive-by. Nothing like the last time she went to check in on Samuel.

Kenny and Ellie were still years away from moving in, and up until recently she and Samuel were happy, at least she thought they were. Or maybe it was just that she thought Michael was happy enough for the two of them. That was the summer they went to Sea-World. The summer her and Samuel's marriage grew tense and quiet, without acknowledgment from either of them. It was the sort of change that hurt them both, the sort of change they should have talked about, but isn't that what always happens? You hope for the best for long enough, and by the time you're done hoping, you've settled into an understanding that "the best" is out of reach. Unhappy becomes normal, easy. The issue with being happy is that it takes work.

When Samuel said he was going to the old place to swim, the darkest of thoughts crossed her mind like a fly buzzing through one ear and out the other, off and away, never to be seen again. She was in the kitchen, giving Michael a snack—he loved hard-boiled eggs back then—and heard Samuel come down the stairs. The final step had always creaked, and still does, but after she heard the noise, he didn't appear around the corner. There was a pause. Must have been fifteen, twenty seconds, she remembered now. Fifteen seconds watching Michael smile as he grabbed wiggly slices of egg and shoved them in his mouth, wondering why her husband was just standing at the foot of the stairs, staring at a wall.

When he turned the corner, she noticed the smile pasted on his face. "How's someone enjoying their snack?" he said before tickling Michael's arms.

"It's good," Michael said. "I was hungry."

There was relief in that exchange, Mary Alice thought, but it went as quickly as it came. Samuel's smile changed after he'd interacted with Michael; it didn't disappear, or even stop being a smile, it just took a cue from his drooping eyes and turned into something melancholy.

"Going somewhere?" Mary Alice asked when she noticed his hands were clutching a set of keys.

"Yep," he said. "The old place. Gonna go for a swim."

She looked down and noticed he was holding his overnight bag behind his leg, as if he were trying to obscure it, as well as his swim trunks. It seemed off, even if it were the most normal thing in the world: he was leaving to swim and was bringing a change of clothes. At that moment, she wasn't sure what her worry was made of, or where it had come from. It was a nebulous thing, existential worry, and one that had been manifesting more and more frequently since the summer began. More like a vision or a force; her worry had become something biblical. A burning bush appearing from time to time in the corner of a room as she watched her son play with his toys, or under her bedroom window the moment she woke up, or to the left of her husband, underneath an old painting of an oak tree. But she ignored the flames and waved goodbye, reminding him to be safe. Those were the last things she said to him, in fact. "Be safe." A ridiculous thing to say to anyone, really. It takes a special kind of self-delusion to presume anyone could have that much control over the world around them. But still, she said it. She remembered her cadence precisely. Samuel looked at Michael, then turned his head to his wife, but what he didn't do was move his eyes. His face was pointed at her, the gesture was there, but his attention was not. He maintained focus on Michael, and walked into the garage. The door shut softly behind him. And then he was gone.

"When did he say he'd be back?" was the first thing Maria asked when Mary Alice called to see if Samuel was at the Buckhorn hours later. She could count on one hand the number of times he'd gone there without her, but still, it was the first place she'd thought of.

"He didn't," Mary Alice said. "He just left and said he was going for a swim. I thought maybe he dropped by on his way home, saw Frank's truck in the parking lot. But I guess not. Maybe he fell asleep after his swim."

"I certainly get tired after being in the water. An afternoon dip in the summer? I'm out like a light the moment I lie down."

Mary Alice threw Maria a kind laugh and thanked her. "Well, anyway, I'll see you later." She hung up.

It was dark. Nearly ten o'clock. Michael had been asleep for hours, and while she knew he wouldn't wake up in the hour it would take her to run there and back, that would be awful, leaving him alone like that. She wasn't that kind of mother. She wasn't the kind of neighbor who called her friends after dark for a babysitting favor, either. So she made the difficult decision to wake up Michael. He would be miserable, she was certain he'd throw a brief fit, but there was no other option.

She entered his room without flipping the switch beside the door. Too harsh. No one likes waking up to that. A sliver of light from the hall and a spinning dinosaur contraption on his nightstand were all that illuminated his face. She watched him for a second, worrying that worry, and then shook his right shoulder until he stirred. "Sweetie," she said. "You have to come with me in the car, OK? We have to take a drive." He was conscious, but unbothered. He didn't ask questions, he didn't raise his voice, he just let her lift him up and walk him downstairs, and into his car seat. She snapped the belt shut and noticed he had already fallen back to sleep.

The highway was dark. No one else on the road, just Mary Alice and Michael and the moonlight. She turned the radio on at a whisper, just loud enough to drown out her own thoughts. It was a different kind of dark when she parked, thanks to a whisper of clouds covering the moon and diffusing the light into something gray and eerie. Her headlights sliced through the darkness and landed on Samuel's little red truck, then as she turned to park, the front of the house. There were no lights on inside. There were no signs of life at all.

Mary Alice looked back to find Michael sleeping, his arms squirmed up around his head like a cat avoiding an overhead light during an afternoon nap. She pulled out the keys and exited the driver's side softly, so as not to stir her cargo as she stepped onto the gravel. The night was loud, the white nighttime noise of crickets surrounded her. The first thing she noticed that alarmed her was the front door; it was slightly ajar. She pushed the ancient thing open as quietly as she could, but the hinges seemed to scoff at her attempt to be silent. They released a wail of squeaks as Mary Alice noticed a note propped up on the kitchen counter—the one with her name written out in perfect cursive. She didn't even read it. She didn't have to.

Briefly forgetting her sleeping child, she ran back to the car, swung the door open, and reached inside for the headlights. Once they were on, she ran the twenty yards to the lake, but it didn't take more than five for her to see it: the outline of Samuel's back, floating in the far end of the water. His head was fully submerged, limp at the neck, as were his legs. It was an awful, unnatural pose, the kind of thing a body would never allow if given the choice.

As she screamed, she felt a moment of shame. She wasn't the type for hysterics. But it just erupted from her core, like something that had been waiting impatiently to escape her entire life. She screamed and screamed as she ran to the lake's edge, where her cries were drowned out by the chaotic splashing. As she pulled Samuel onto the bank, it was easy, not because of adrenaline, but because he was light. Because he was floating. This wasn't a rescue, or even a dive, she was just pulling a dead man out of the water. There were no revolting muscles of a drowning person. There was hardly any friction. All she had to do was pull, and there he was, Samuel in his swim trunks.

Michael was crying now; she heard him once the splashing stopped. How long had he been wailing? she wondered, running back to the car and leaving her husband behind. Inside, he was trying to wriggle out of his seat, but the belts did their work. He couldn't move and was much too small to see over the dashboard and into the water. All he knew at this moment was that Mommy was upset. She didn't have to tell him why.

"It's all right," she said, fully aware of how scarring this bit of improvisation might be. She was going to lie to him, and the lie was what he would remember forever. "I just got scared in the dark, but now I'm fine! Now I'm fine. Settle down, sweetie. OK? Settle down. I'll settle down, too, I promise. We'll both settle down."

She unbuckled the straps and lifted him out and into her arms, making sure to keep him facing toward the dark. She walked him inside the house and put him in the bed, still made, and told him to wait. "Mommy will be right back, OK?"

"OK."

Mary Alice took the phone from the receiver, an old rotary that had been hanging in the kitchen since the fifties. This was before 911 had come to this part of Texas, so she dialed Maria, hoping she would be able to get the sheriff. Time slowed as she watched the rotary recoil after the first digit. As she dialed, it was like she was being punished, laughed at, and ignored all at once. She didn't know which of the seven numbers was worse. Ninety minutes and countless wrong turns later, flashing lights shot through the old place's window.

She wasn't surprised to find him dead, though she'd never admit that to a single person, including herself. The pause at the bottom of the stairs is what did it, and for the rest of her life she would wonder what he was thinking for those few seconds. Was he taking in the entryway for the final time? Extracting as many memories as he could from the walls and photographs and windows? Was he staring out the cut glass of the front door at the distorted view of their front yard, deciding which words would be the last he'd ever speak to his family? Or maybe he was thinking, *I hope they can't tell. I hope they can't tell.* Of all of them, that's the explanation she liked most. A final gesture, the thought. The kindest thing he could do was leave Michael with a happy memory.

When the police arrived, they noticed the things she hadn't: the books on the coffee table, the change of clothes in his overnight bag, and a receipt for a full tank of gas on the passenger seat of his truck. These were not the signs of someone planning to take his own life, they said, but if there was anything else they should know, she should tell them. She said there wasn't. She never told them about the note. She never told anyone about the note.

The death was ruled an accidental drowning with the swipe of a pen in a small room thirty miles away, after which she closed his bank accounts and submitted a claim for his life insurance. When the check came in the mail weeks later, the number was so big she nearly wrote them back to tell them the truth. Instead, she deposited it into Michael's college fund. She wouldn't have to think about it for at least a decade.

Katherine came down for the funeral, ready to repair their estranged relationship in the face of this new tragedy. She had more than enough luggage in that little red car to prove her intentions, and for a few hours, absolution seemed to be exactly where the two of them were headed. After Katherine swept up the ashes, she went out onto the porch and held Mary Alice in her arms until her cheeks were dry. For a moment, their heartbeats were in sync. Their wounds, sutured. At the funeral, they sat on either side of Michael, a seemingly unbreakable chain of held hands. People looked at them and saw two sisters holding each other together, not two sisters stuck in the middle of a decade-old confrontation. One that hung between them, festering but fully unacknowledged. For a week they went through the motions of normalcy, running errands, cooking, eating together, playing with Michael in the backyard, but every night, once Michael went to sleep, they shared little more than silence before heading to bed themselves. All of Katherine's attempts to talk about what had happened went ignored at first, until they were angrily rebuffed.

"I just want you to feel comfortable talking about it," Katherine said, sipping from her bottle of beer on the couch. Mary Alice was cross-legged in the love seat, looking almost childish and staring out the front window.

"I don't *want* to talk about it. I don't ever want to talk about it. How does talking about it make it any better? It happened. He's dead. I'm alone. What else is there to say?"

"It's not healthy, Mary Alice."

"Is that what your therapist told you?"

"As a matter of fact, it is," Katherine said before finishing her drink. "And you're not alone. You have Michael. And you have me."

"Pretty soon you're going to leave and be a thousand miles away again. And in no time Michael's going to leave me, too."

"But I'm here now."

"Why is that, by the way? To make yourself feel better? Or are you just trying to dig up a little dirt on your poor big sister?"

Katherine scoffed. "What are you talking about? Dig up dirt? Mary Alice, I'm here because you need me."

"I don't need anybody. Samuel knew that all too well."

"What the hell does that mean?"

"It means I'm tired. I'm so damn tired, Katherine." The many clocks in the living room filled the air with ticks and tocks, and when they all chimed at the hour, Mary Alice stood up and put her hand on Katherine's shoulder, giving it a gentle squeeze. "You can go home." The next day, she did.

Mary Alice put Samuel's note in the old trunk in their bedroom the night of his death, but didn't read it until months later, a Friday night in November, when she was still getting used to dark's early arrival. Her students had been restless and combative at every level, and when she picked up Michael from Mrs. Wools's house, where he spent his days along with three other kids in town, she was informed he was sick. The early stages of a cold. Dinner was leftovers, not that either of them were in the mood to eat, and when she finally got him to bed after a dose and a half of cough syrup, the night seemed like it would never end. Saturday felt impossible, as did everything beyond it.

So she pulled out the note and lifted the flap, which, to her disappointment, had never been sealed. She wanted to smell it, the glue he would have licked. She wanted a piece of him. She didn't want ink, she wanted actual DNA. But what she was given was a single sentence: *I love you both eternally, and I'm sorry I could not love myself.* And then his name, *Samuel.* Just *Samuel.*

Tears did not come, nor rage. Only sadness. At a certain point, she decided then without argument, life becomes a straight line with no branches, a road with no exit ramps. Grief would define the rest of her years, and it was time for her to get used to that.

12

THE THING IS, JOSIE ACTUALLY LIKED HER IN-LAWS. WHEN she explained the dynamics of her husband's family to friends back home, they would laugh at her descriptions of the Kerr Compound, and at what was, to them, an antiquated notion of family as a unit formed by God that shalt never be broken up.

"You know it sounds just like a cult," her coworker Francesca told her over lunch, just a week before the move. "A bunch of houses filled with people who believe the same things, separated from the rest of society and unwilling to open themselves up to outsiders?" Francesca had always been the kind of person who would make cynical declarations as an attempt to project confidence and intelligence and a sophisticated sense of humor, and so, in fact, had Josie. But from the moment they decided to leave New York behind, she grew woefully tired of what she believed to be an affect unique to her hometown. Even when you're sitting across from a friend who may be leaving you for good, someone who doesn't want commentary, just a friendly ear and quiet companionship, you're playing for the cheap seats. For what felt like the first time in her adult life, she actually listened to what she said to people. And not only that, she also listened to how she said it. Had she always been a pessimist who treated every conversation like open-mic night and ate twenty-dollar salads for lunch without the slightest hint of enjoyment? All it took was one foot stepping beyond the five boroughs for her to realize how excited she was to escape them entirely.

Josie laughed before explaining, "Well, that's not really the case, is it? I mean, they let me in."

Francesca dipped a forkful of kale into a small tub of blue cheese dressing and took a bite. "Yeah, but you had to marry him for that to happen," she said, showing off the pulverized greens as she made her case. "You literally had to sign a legally binding agreement to be taken seriously."

"I shouldn't have described it that way then, because it's not really as strange as it sounds. I just don't want to, you know, begin my time there so far outside of town. If I lived at the Compound, I'd be even more of an outsider. But I don't think I'd have any real problem living *close* to them. It's a twelve-minute drive, and there's never traffic. And the best part? Free childcare! Faye is so lonely now that Leonard passed."

"I get that," Francesca said. "But when you live on a literal compound, are you ever alone?"

Josie didn't know why she bothered telling any of her New York friends about her soon-to-be life in Texas. Her excitement for it required a nuance they were all too stubborn to understand. And Josie sympathized; she'd been on the other side of the conversation countless times before, playing the role of a friend who was expected to provide the perfect balance of genuine support and playful contrarianism. It was the sort of well-practiced attitude required of young coastal professionals when one of their own jumps ship for a place with no direct flights out of LaGuardia.

Josie knew her husband came from good stock, but the Kerrs exceeded every expectation she had for how welcoming and kind a family could be. Knowing how much the stresses of teaching would make her treasure her weekends, Faye had suggested moving their traditional big Sunday-night dinners to Wednesday night, hoping they would provide Josie a midweek reprieve, one that would be more emotionally helpful than a time-consuming Sunday-afternoon affair.

They'd kindly begun the Wednesday dinners the week of Josie and Travis's arrival, saying there was no use getting them hooked on one routine only to throw a wrench into the whole thing two months later once the school year began. And those early weeks had been lovely, but this Wednesday was the first dinner of the school year, and Josie was surprised to find herself so looking forward to it as the clock ticked toward four-thirty in her classroom.

Fortunately, Mary Alice's stunt earlier that week hadn't made too much of an impact. No student was behaving more or less disrespectfully than she expected them to, and the lesson plan she'd created over the summer was proving to be well-paced for all of them. There would always be outliers who needed more or less of her help—that was part of the job and always would be. But, she thought, while putting her folders into her locking desk drawer at the end of the day, her worry had been all for naught. Mary Alice's interruption was sure enough old news by Tuesday when Greg McAllan called Josie "Mom."

Every aspect of the job was quieter than it had been in New York, and the small classes afforded her the opportunity to give every student the amount of attention she believed they deserved. Three days in, and she knew she'd made the right decision. Three days in, and she could picture herself five, ten, even twenty years from now, and that picture didn't make her recoil in shame. She didn't want to admit it to herself, but part of her was even looking forward to it.

As she twisted the key on her drawer, she heard a knock on the doorframe. "Mrs. Kerr," said a voice, whom Josie soon saw belonged to Amy Huntz. "I have a question."

"Come on in," she said with a pronounced, shoveling wave.

Amy sat down and clutched the front of the desk. She was small for her age, not more than four and a half feet tall, but had the sullen face of someone twice as old. Her eyes were big and brown and alert, and typically focused on some invisible thing on the ground to her right.

"What's up?" Josie sat back down so that she didn't appear rushed.

"Um," Amy said, keeping her gaze on the bottom corner of Josie's desk, a sturdy metal thing that was at least forty years old. "I let Jason borrow a pencil earlier and then I lost mine and I was wondering if I could borrow one to take home tonight. I think I'm . . . I think I'm out." A pause. "I'd bring it back, duh."

Josie nodded. "Yeah, you know what, I think I've got one right here." She picked up the cup on her desk, which was overflowing with a firework of pens and pencils and markers of all colors and sizes, and held it out toward Amy. "Take your pick."

Amy's eyes widened as they turned to the cup. "I only need one, just because I'm out, and I need to do the homework."

"Well, why don't you take a pencil and a pen just in case. Never know when you'll need an eraser."

"Sure. Good idea."

Amy chose a slim yellow pencil and a plain black Bic, the humblest instruments in the cup. Josie saw her thinking, and tried not to react to the pulsing ache deep inside her chest. "All good?"

"Yeah. Thanks, Mrs. Kerr."

"You're very welcome. You good on the homework tonight? Everything making sense so far?"

"Yeah, Mrs. Kerr. I get math."

"You do?"

"Yeah, English is tough this year, though."

"Really? What've you been reading so far?"

"I gotta go, actually." She stood up and unzipped the front pocket of her backpack, an old maroon Jansport that had seen its share of brief youthful obsessions, drawn on, then removed or drawn over. Patches covering patches. A safety pin holding the cup holder to the side. "I'm going to bring them back, though. The pen and the pencil."

"I trust you. But if you need them longer, just let me know."

"I won't." She flung the backpack on her shoulders and clutched the straps with her thumbs.

"OK then! See you tomorrow."

"Bye, Mrs. Kerr."

Once she was out the door, Josie took a deep breath and forced a smile for the empty seats—a trick she learned at her first job teaching fifth graders in Manhattan. She hated seeing a kid with the odds so clearly stacked against them. She hated knowing there was only so much she could do. But she also knew to avoid waterworks in front of the kids; she'd been told by her first vice principal. "The moment they see you cry, they'll either join in or lose all respect for you," she said. "And neither of those options will help your cause."

One more breath and she locked up the room and strolled to the parking lot, where she learned that it took just eight hours for her car to be blanketed in bird shit. *Ah,* she thought, *this is why no one has taken this spot all week.* It was shaded, it was close to the entrance, and it was home to no fewer than seventy grackles for whom life consisted of little more than digestive target practice. But now she knew.

THE NICEST THING about Wednesday dinner at the Compound was that Josie and Travis didn't have to plan a single aspect of the meal. All that was required of them was to show up by six-thirty. There was no pressure to bring wine or beer or a dessert, and Josie never felt a shred of guilt for showing up empty-handed. Surprisingly enough, this wasn't one of those scenarios that would lead to years of building resentment, and some enormous meltdown a decade from now in which Josie would be branded as lazy or, worse, thoughtless. Faye just wanted to spend time with them, and thanks to young Henry, Wednesday dinner was as pure and expectation-free as an invitation could get. The love of a grandparent can be suffocating and irrational, formed without the torments of daily caretaking, but indisputable in its authenticity. And though Faye was currently acting as a sort of day care, taking care of him from 7:30 a.m. to 4:45 p.m., Henry was due to start school next fall and she saw the next nine months as the gift of a lifetime. To have Travis and Josie over for dinner once a week was the icing on the cake. But Faye's happiness, though centered around Henry, was, in her eyes, thanks entirely to Josie's sacrifice. That she agreed to leave her own family and bring that child to Billington made her immune from any criticism they could ever dole out, not that any had been festering in their pockets. To them, Josie was a hero. And that was something Josie was more than happy to let them believe.

The second nicest thing about Wednesday dinner at the Compound was that it gave Josie and Travis a rare hour or so of private time. There was no need to pick Henry up before dinner since he was already at his grandmother's, which hadn't crossed Josie's mind until arriving home that day and feeling an instant calm once stepping inside the kitchen. No afternoon snack, no running around the coffee table, just Travis cracking open two Shiner Bocks in the kitchen.

"Home before me!"

"Been here for ten minutes," he said. "But I waited for you." He placed both beers in koozies and held one back for ransom: a chaste, closed-mouth kiss. Once satisfied, he handed a beer to Josie.

"Do you hear that?" Josie said, putting her free hand to her ear and stretching her neck toward the rest of the house.

"No . . ." Travis said.

"Exactly."

"Good one. Real original."

Josie smiled coyly and took a sip of her beer, then pulled it back to examine the koozie Travis had chosen. A brewery in Red Hook, Brooklyn, where they'd gone on one of their first dates.

"When do we have to leave?" she said.

Travis looked down at his wristwatch, a vintage silver piece owned by her paternal grandfather that she'd gotten restored for their first anniversary. Thinking it ostentatious, no man in his family—or even his life—had ever worn a Rolex; he didn't wear it for weeks. Then, one day, she demanded he put it on before leaving the house. Just try it, she said. For one day. Do that for me. If you hate it, never wear it again. But the least you can do is try it. He did. And he wore it every day after that. It's funny that their fights used to be about Rolexes. It's funny that they ever had time to fight at all.

"I say, hmm, A.I.S. at six-thirteen?"

Travis proudly had several characteristics Josie referred to as his "country things." Because she was from Manhattan, any version of life lived west of the Hudson River was baffling to her, but at least cities had movie theaters and record stores and even libraries. Travis's childhood home was adjacent to a literal farm—not his family's own, but still. He said "y'all" without irony. He clapped at the television when watching a game. He ordered domestic light beer when they went out to eat. And he said, "Thank you much"—not "so much," just "much"—to anyone in the service industry. All these "country things" were genuinely charming, even cute, to anyone who encountered him. To Josie, they were also impossibly, and at times overwhelmingly, sexy.

Her therapist said it was simply due to the novelty of his personality and background, and that the charm would eventually wear off—she'd met all kinds of people from all kinds of places in New York City but had never become that close with someone who had no interest in assimilating. Travis was unlike any man she had ever been friends with, let alone dated. He thrived in the big city without pretending to be anything but a kid from the country. So many transplants tried to erase their past, whereas he wore his on his sleeve. And while she had been in public on the arms of plenty of handsome men in her time, none elicited the same response as entering a room alongside Travis Alan Kerr. He had the weathered good looks of someone who'd never been bullied in his life, the body of a baseball player who didn't wear sunscreen, and the thick, weedlike stubble of someone whose face always believed it was five o'clock. And his smile! A woman once asked Josie if Travis was single while he was in the bathroom on their third date. A caterer flirted with Travis on their wedding day, just as they finished their first dance. In the moment, these things infuriated Josie. But when seen from some distance, as a group, they delighted her. Because they meant that she had won. She was the one he chose.

"A.I.S.," though, was the first of his "country things" that had actually repulsed her. The first time he said it was just a few months prior, the night before their move. The first car either of them had ever owned in the city, bought in New Jersey a week before, was parked on their street, ready to drive them 1,900 miles to Texas. Their apartment was empty, save for a few stray kitchen essentials and their toiletries, and Travis wanted to leave as early as possible.

"So, seven o'clock?" Josie asked him as they ate what neither would admit was the last good pizza they'd have for the foreseeable future.

"A.I.S. at seven," Travis said in a tone somewhere between condescending and demanding. Josie searched her brain for what this could possibly mean. Was there an appointment she'd forgotten about? Was the A.I.S. some kind of city department? When nothing seemed to make sense, she went ahead and asked.

"'A.I.S.'?"

"Ass in Seat," he said, pleased with himself and even more pleased by the bite of white pizza still in his mouth.

"Oh God," Josie said. "I've never heard that one before."

"We've never had a car before."

She initially bristled at this new country thing, confused as to whatever could compel Travis to talk like that. But over time, as was generally the case, even the least refined elements of his character—or no, especially the least refined elements of his character—proved themselves to be inevitably sexy.

"A.I.S. at six-thirteen, you say," she asked, holding her Shiner up for a toast, which he reciprocated with a satisfying *clink*. "What should we do in the meantime?"

"You mean besides finish our drinks?"

"I think those can wait."

"You're right," Travis said, wedging both bottles between the fingers on a single hand, reminding her of his time as a part-time bartender when they first met. He set them on the bottom shelf of the fridge and lifted her up in a single, graceful semicircle of movement. And then she thought what she always thought in the seconds before they had sex: *I can't believe this is happening.* She couldn't! She really couldn't. And she couldn't tell anyone about how she couldn't believe it, either, because, well, it would just sound like she was bragging. But that was only half true, because the disbelief had a tendency to obscure her enjoyment of the sex itself. This man, the sexiest man she'd ever laid eyes on, was about to fuck her. What could be less believable than that? And why was she questioning reality just before having sex?

But right now, with both of them already breaking a sweat, the answer was, well, everything in her line of sight. As she leaned into Travis's neck, buried in the nook of her own, she examined the kitchen as though seeing it for the first time. Suddenly, it was real. They lived here, and they would for years to come, she could feel it.

The cabinets were just what she wanted, white with slate fixtures and glass fronts. The counters were quartz, so much more practical than a trendy and expensive material like marble. The appliances were all brand-new. And there, on the front of the fridge, was a drawing Henry had done of the three of them standing in front of their new house. Travis, a tall stick person with scraggly hair. Josie, a stick person of the same height with longer scraggly hair. And Henry, the only one of the three with an open-mouth smile, hands raised as a bird flew above them. To the right, a blue square with wheels. "What's this?" Josie had asked when he first showed it to her.

"The pool men," he said.

Did this make her silly? Was Henry's memory of his mother as a woman obsessed with building a frivolous and expensive therapeutic tool in her backyard something he'd return to in the future as proof of, what? Her unhappiness? Her family wealth? Her distance? She didn't even know if those things were true, but there must have been some reason he'd included it in the drawing. When she brought it up with Travis, all he'd said was, "He drew them because they was there." He was right, she thought. He drew it because it was what he had experienced. Henry had simply told the truth.

Travis took her hand and the two of them walked up to the bedroom, where she rolled off him in just a few minutes. She hadn't come, but wasn't unsatisfied. Other things were on her mind, and it was fine to let them dominate her thoughts. When she returned from the bathroom, Travis was already back downstairs finishing his drink.

"How was school today?"

"Better," Josie said. "Nothing exciting to report. It was just a day of school."

"That's good. That's what you want." She wasn't sure if he was exactly right, but he was close.

"How was the family business today?" she said cheekily.

"Oh, the same. Phone calls. Just a bunch of phone calls. I didn't leave my desk except for when I grabbed lunch from the kitchenette. I need to start taking a walk or something or I'm gonna put on some pounds before too long."

"I thought I'd miss walking, but I don't so far. The drive is nice."

"Is it even long enough to enjoy?"

"Just about. Today I zigzagged. Took a long route and added three or four minutes to the drive."

"Should I be worried?"

"Worried?"

"You avoiding anything?"

"No!" Josie laughed and took another swig. "It's the opposite, in fact. I just like being in the car."

"Sometimes I wish I hadn't learned to drive at fifteen. You New Yorkers who learn in your twenties always seem to enjoy it so much more."

"We have more respect for it. I bet if you checked all the statistics, you'd find out we're safer drivers, too."

"Maybe."

"Pool's starting to look like a pool, isn't it?"

"It is."

"Three more weeks. Think it'll still be hot enough to swim?"

"Jo, I'm sure it'll be hot enough to swim on Christmas."

It was the first time they'd had anything resembling a normal one-on-one conversation in weeks, if not months, and when they had exhausted every other topic, Josie followed a sip of room-temperature beer with a question that had been on her mind since the planning meeting the night before. Something that felt off-limits, even in her own house. "Did I tell you I met Ellie Hall last night at Mary Alice's?"

"Yeah. I always liked her."

"Did you know her son?"

"Kenny? Yeah. Nice. Smart. Shy. We weren't buds or anything. Everyone knows everyone. You've learned that already, I'm sure."

"Of course. I mean, and I know this is so morbid, but what happened there? He and Mary Alice's son died the same summer, didn't they?"

Travis's head rocked from left to right as he jogged the memory from its place. "It's just one of those sad stories, that's all."

"But can you tell it? Because I feel like it will, I don't know, help me understand these people better."

"You mean Mary Alice."

"Yes."

Travis sighed. "It was the morning after graduation, Kenny and Mikey's class. There was some big party, and on the way home, Kenny's car got hit by a drunk driver who survived without a scratch, basically."

"And Kenny wasn't drunk?"

"Nope."

"But what about Michael? That was just a coincidence?"

"Everyone was messed up after Kenny died. Everyone. It wasn't just death. It was this instant cautionary tale. It's one thing for the drunk driver to die or get hurt, but you know, this was more tragic. Sounds awful to say, but it's true." He twisted his mouth and squinted his eyes, not quite stopping a tear but perhaps preparing for it.

"Anyway, like I said, everyone's messed up. No one's taking this well. But Michael Roth is taking it worse than anyone. There was a sort of memorial bonfire for Kenny at someone's place a couple days later. More like a vigil. Pretty much everyone in school went, so did some parents. Totally dry, no booze, out of respect. But in comes Michael, absolutely shithouse drunk. Someone tried to talk to him, I remember that, but he brushed them away and drove off. I remember thinking, 'Oh Christ, he's gonna die just like Kenny,' but he must've made it home in one piece because he showed up to Kenny's funeral the next day. He brought a flask and barely tried to hide it. And that's the last I ever saw him. I think it's the last time anyone I knew saw him. Then, a few weeks after that, his obituary is in the paper. Suicide."

"Oh my God," Josie blurted out. She felt like the wind had been knocked out of her. "They actually said it was a suicide?"

"No, but what else could it have been? He clearly wasn't in his right mind and we could all see he wanted to be dead, whether by a gun to the head or driving drunk into a ditch."

"I had no idea," she said, her hand now covering her mouth. "Did you go to his funeral?"

"There wasn't one. That obituary was pretty much the last time anyone ever talked about Michael, at least that I know of. By the time I graduated the next year, it already felt like ancient history. I guess it was all too sad for anyone to think about."

"Yeah," Josie said. "I guess that sounds right. So they were best friends, Kenny and Michael?"

Travis curled his lip. "At least."

"Oh, I see. But did anyone know for sure?"

"Nah, but I mean, everyone did the math. They were pretty inseparable."

"Right," Josie said. "God, how awful. No wonder the two of them are so close."

"Who?"

"Ellie and Mary Alice."

Travis nodded, then glanced at the clock on the microwave. "Oh shit, we gotta go," he said before tossing his empty bottle in the trash and kissing Josie on the forehead. Before she could respond, he was in the garage, already far from the memory of those two dead boys.

But the image of Kenny and Michael, still basically kids when their lives were cut short, stuck with Josie for the rest of the drive. The trip to the Kerr Compound was beautiful by central Texas standards, with views of flat farmland and the hint of the Hill Country's rolling beginning in the distance. There was just enough development to avoid a feeling of eerie isolation, and to keep Josie distracted. Once outside the town limits, which they reached in just under a mile, it would be mostly farmland, with the occasional home dotting the middle distances to the left and the right every mile or so. The road was two-way and smooth gray asphalt, which had been done a decade prior. Barbed-wire fence ran the length of the crops, running parallel to the road some twenty feet from both edges of the road, and kept on going until, suddenly, there was a green-brown burst of tree line, where the crops came to a stop. It was there they turned right onto a smaller road, which they took for four more minutes, and that's when the Compound came into view.

The main dwelling—an old farmhouse with a wraparound porch and a tin roof and navy shutters—where Faye lived, was closest to the road. All the lights on the bottom floor were on, and the rooms were a blurry buzz of activity. Mae and Freddy's house looked nearly identical, apart from the fresh coat of paint, and it wasn't more than five live oaks away. Diagonal from both was the barn, which was really just a shed. Beside it, a stable for their four horses. Behind that, a chicken coop where they kept two dozen of the most contented birds in the state. And if you stood on Faye's back porch and scanned the property from north to south, you'd probably notice a shimmering patch of grass on the far end and think, *Why, that'd be the perfect spot for another house.* Or at least that's what Faye had hoped.

Josie could see it then, just as she could see it the first time they approached the Compound after their engagement. It could be scary to arrive in such an ostentatious display of wealth and comfort, in the middle of nowhere. And given more context, to know they deliberately removed themselves from the towns where they did all their business could be interpreted as dismissive or judgmental. Freddy and Mae made money surveying land for residents of Billington, and yet they chose to live fifteen miles away from them, holed up with their own, much too far to be visited for a neighborly favor. At least Travis lived in town, and Josie felt even more certain that her decision to buy Margaret Rose's house was the right one.

As they stepped in that evening, twenty-nine minutes after six, they looked at this house in a new light, still. The previous week of babysitting had sealed the deal. Even if their house was twelve miles away, this wasn't simply a visit. This was their second home, and Josie loved it. Though the structure itself had been standing for nearly a century, the interior was only twelve months old. Retirement had left Faye and Leonard with two things: a comfortable nest egg and a newfound obsession with home renovation shows. The combination proved incendiary, and led to a near-gut job of the entire house. Carpet was ripped up, rooms were combined, and walls were stripped of their paper and reduced to their most basic form, planks of wood dusted with a coating of whitewash that even Tom Sawyer would call unfinished. Josie had watched the same shows as her in-laws from the confines of her little Brooklyn apartment, and seeing the aesthetic in person was so exciting she felt embarrassed by the crazed look in her eyes the first time she saw it post-renovation. It was like walking into her TV set and into a gray, white, and brown fantasyland where space and light are infinite, time is measured exclusively on giant wall clocks, and family is always around the corner. She loved it, and that made her feel absolutely crazy.

When Henry heard the door he dropped his book and burst from the plush gray couch in front of them into their arms. "I'm hungry," he said, leaning into his flair for drama.

Josie picked him up, caressed the back of his head, and laughed. "I am starving, actually. I hope Grandma made a good dinner. Think she did?"

"Yeah. I think she made a good dinner."

"What is it?"

"I don't know."

"Chicken-fried steak," screamed Faye from the kitchen. "And mashed potatoes."

"Anything green?" Travis yelled back while kicking his shoes off, laces still tied.

"Salad!" she screamed before poking her head around the corner. "Not from a bag!"

Josie looked back down at Henry. "That sounds good, doesn't it?" Henry nodded, then wriggled his shoulders. "Oh, you want to be put down? Use your words, then."

"Can you put me down?"

"Yes, I can." She lowered him a foot and he jumped out of her arms like a cat, then he bolted down the hall and disappeared around the corner into the kitchen.

"Don't you hate 'use your words'?" Travis said. "I mean, it just sounds so ridiculous."

"Yeah, well, it works," Josie said, nipping that conversation in the bud. Their parenting styles were rarely at odds, but a stray piece of methodology would occasionally cause a rift between them. "Use your words" was one of those things.

"You two fall asleep in there? Party's in the kitchen!"

Travis rolled his eyes and led them down the hall, lined with framed collages of the Kerr family, and into the kitchen, a grand communal space that felt out of place in such an isolated location, with not one but two islands, the biggest fridge any of them had ever seen, and a farmhouse table with bench seating on the two large ends that could contain everyone on the Compound comfortably, even more if they squeezed. And no one in the Kerr family minded a squeeze.

"So," Faye said, removing a tenderized and liberally breaded slab of sizzling beef from the pan and setting it beside at least a half dozen more on a wire cooling rack. "How's your first week?" She was a sturdy, oval-shaped woman with a chic yet spartan uniform consisting of stretchy blue jeans, a tucked-in T-shirt, and a flowy plaid overshirt. A mop of wavy dark gray hair peppered with bobby pins that never seemed to serve any purpose sat atop her head, which was a vessel for two extremes: generally exuberance, but occasionally scorn. She was a woman you would describe as loud before hearing her voice; like a knob on a stereo turned all the way to the right without anything playing.

"You know what," Josie said, "it's actually fine."

"What'd I tell you? There was nothing to worry about."

"Well, there was a little something, and I guess there still might be, but maybe not."

"Spit it out, sweetheart. What you mean?"

"Mary Alice Roth came by on Monday and caused, well, it wasn't a scene, exactly, but it wasn't nothing."

"She come back since?"

"No."

"I wouldn't worry about her, then. Like I said, she's all bark and no bite."

"Then why do I feel like I've been gnawed at?" Josie reached for a chip from the bag on the island and dipped it in a tub of salsa Faye had placed beside it.

"That feeling will pass."

"Tell her about the meeting, though," Travis said, playfully shoving Josie's hand out of the way so he could grab another chip before she could.

"What meeting?" Faye asked.

"Jo decided she wanted to help out at the picnic this year."

"Why would you go and do something like that?! You're a young woman!"

"Why don't you do it, Faye?" Josie asked. "Plenty of the ladies there were your friends."

"Honey, I don't do it because I don't hate myself. We do plenty for that picnic that doesn't involve taking orders from Mary Alice Roth."

"What's that?"

"Where do you think they keep all the supplies for the booths? In our damn barn! Leonard and I always lug 'em over and set 'em up, then tear 'em down and bring 'em back every year. That's our contribution, though I guess it's just mine from now on." Faye's gaze left the room for a moment and focused on the memory of her husband, but the pop from a frying piece of steak brought her right back.

"Is it too late for me to change jobs?" Josie asked.

"If you already told Mary Alice yes, I'm afraid so. Just don't do it again! Let this year be a lesson to you."

"She yelled at me for being late. In front of everyone."

"She's just mad that you took her job."

Travis swallowed another chip and interrupted them. "She didn't take her job, Mom. She got a job that happened to be the one Mary Alice resigned from."

"What I'm trying to say is she's intimidated by you," Faye said, dropping her tongs on the spoon rest with a force just shy of confrontational. "What do they say about wild animals? They're more afraid of you than you are of them?"

"So you're saying Mary Alice is, what, a bear?"

"More like a mountain lion."

"That's not any better!"

"Fine, then. She's a, I don't know, a bee."

"Still stings."

"Then what happens? It dies."

"Well, that'd be helpful."

"Oh, there goes my mouth again. I shouldn't have said that. That poor woman's been through enough death."

"Her son died, right? Ellie Hall tried to bring me up to speed at the meeting and Travis filled me in a little earlier."

"Ellie Hall, now, there's a friend you want. You know she lost her boy, too, just a few weeks before Mary Alice. They were best friends. But did you know about Sammy?"

Travis groaned. "Mom, can we please not do this?"

"What! The more you know. Might help dull all this misery she feels about that poor woman."

"It's gossip."

"It ain't gossip if it's the truth."

"I don't think that's true but whatever."

Just then the back door swung open and in came Mae, Freddy, and their seven-year-old, Brooklyn, a name Josie always had trouble saying without a smirk. "Hello," they shouted in a singsong, directing most of their energy toward Josie in particular. After the awkwardness of the week, that sort of greeting was like a salve, she thought. Her parents and siblings had always been close, and she loved them deeply, but their love was more like a steady simmer, and rarely boiled over like the kind the Kerrs shared several times a day. They were a family of bear hugs. Hers was a family of side hugs. One no better than the other, to be sure, but there was something to be said about a big, booming hello to make her feel not only welcome, but essential.

"What're we talking about?" Freddy said as he nudged Brooklyn toward her cousin.

"Samuel Roth."

"Oh God, why?"

Until that moment, Josie wasn't quite sure she wanted to be let in on every detail of Mary Alice's life, but she couldn't help but find something titillating in the various Kerrs' reactions. All she'd known was that he'd died long ago, when Mary Alice was a young mother, and that she'd never felt like remarrying, or even seeing someone else. That was enough, she had assumed, to paint a clear enough portrait of this woman. But she was starting to suspect the version she'd created had gotten the colors and features all wrong.

"Well, first of all, he probably killed himself," Mae said.

"Mae!" Faye said, admonishing her daughter while conveniently overlooking the fact that she herself had started the conversation.

A hint of red appeared on Josie's cheeks. "Oh, I had no idea it was a suicide."

"Well, it wasn't," Faye said. "At least not officially. But her boy killed himself, too, and depression's in the genes, so it all makes sense. They found Samuel's body in the lake over at their place way out west of town. You think we're in the boonies? They've barely got electricity out there."

"So people think he . . ." Josie said, too nervous to finish her thought.

"Well, there wasn't a note, and he brought a change of clothes along, and I remember something about a tank of gas," Freddy said. "But, what can I say, you'd just have to have known him."

"Oh please, you were practically a baby when it happened, so don't pretend you know any more than what your father and I told you. Anyway, Josie'll never have the opportunity to know Sammy Roth at all."

"I didn't realize they were both suicides."

"There wasn't even a funeral for poor Michael. But I can't say I blame his mom. After going through all that death, who could bear it." Faye went silent for a few seconds, as if realizing she may have disrespected the dead. "Now, who's ready to eat?"

Henry raised his hand and ran to his normal seat at the table, reminding Josie, and every adult in the room, that they had been discussing something so terrible in front of someone so innocent. They quickly changed the subject and spent the rest of dinner talking about better things, things that had nothing to do with anyone in town. Things that were even farther away from Billington than they were. But Josie's mind stayed on Michael, and Samuel, and the tragedy of the Roth family. There was something about them, Michael in particular, which she couldn't shake. Even with the ultimate ending, his story felt strangely unfinished. Maybe it was because he was about her age. Maybe it was because she thought it would help her understand Mary Alice. Whatever the case, she knew she had to find out more. More than that, she knew she could.

13

AS MARY ALICE FELL ASLEEP WEDNESDAY NIGHT, SHE WENT
over her terrible day from sunup to sundown to figure out what exactly had gone wrong. It would have been easy to blame everything
on Katherine—she often did that anyway—but to do so in this particular instance felt unfair. Right now, Katherine was a conduit for
Michael, who was only gone because of Mary Alice. But the act of
blaming herself was a bridge too far—and crossing it certainly
wouldn't help her insomnia. So she decided to place the blame away
from herself and chalk up all the discomfort to the absence of something. Ellie. Ellie made things feel normal, and Ellie was missing from
her morning, and mornings set the tone for the day, so, yes, it was
Ellie's fault that Wednesday was terrible. This solved everything.
Bleary-eyed, Mary Alice grabbed her phone from her nightstand and
typed out a message. It wouldn't be seen until the morning, to be

sure, as Ellie always went to bed before eleven o'clock, but that would be enough. Ellie, reliable Ellie, would happily change her plans.

> Coffee tomorrow, if you don't
> mind a third. My sister came for
> a surprise visit, but she'd love
> to see you.

It wasn't technically the truth. Katherine hadn't mentioned Ellie at all, but there was no ill will between them, so what could it hurt? After tapping send, she let her head sink into the pillow, and sleep finally came.

Once again she awoke to the smell of breakfast. Katherine must have tried again. There was the undeniable fragrance of bacon, which meant there must be eggs, as well as perfectly toasted bread, the kind that's mere seconds away from burning. Then, hovering underneath was the smell of coffee. Carlye's didn't have anything but Folgers, but Katherine must have used something to make it smell better.

Then, a voice. Distance muffled its particulars, but the cadence was there. Ellie, being polite. And then Katherine, doing the same. Two wordless yet identifiable clouds of sound that Mary Alice took a brief pleasure in trying to decipher. Whatever they were saying wasn't important; there were too many pauses and not a hint of anything bright. But still, they kept talking, filled with a nebulous unease, which she would have enjoyed had it not come from both sides.

She darted into the bathroom and did the bare minimum of a morning routine, as there was no time for a shower, not with her friend suffering God knows what horror story in the kitchen.

"Good morning, sleepyhead," Katherine said, her back to her sister while pulling the perfectly cooked bacon out of the oven.

"I don't know what's come over me the past couple of days," Mary Alice said, smoothing down the sides of her shirt. "I see you've been entertaining Ellie. So sorry about that, by the way, I'm such a dingbat, sending you that last-minute text and not even being here to greet you when you came."

Looking at Katherine and Ellie, Mary Alice found the whole scene surprising and, honestly, more than a little upsetting. What she'd imagined as a tense affair from inside her bedroom was actually a rather relaxed conversation between two women who may as well be old friends. Ellie was smiling a real smile, the kind Mary Alice knew and loved so well, and Katherine was in the middle of a story about her husband, whom she had barely mentioned to her own sister in the thirty-six hours since her arrival.

"He said, 'Katherine! I swear to God, if you don't come over here quick, these burgers are going to catch fire!' And he was right. We opened the oven, and the patties looked like they'd been napalmed."

Mary Alice squinted disapprovingly in both their directions as they laughed. She had no interest in hearing how that story began, or why it was so funny to the two of them. No, no. Ellie was just being polite, she thought. And then she noticed the full carafe Ellie had brought resting on a trivet and insisted it was time for coffee.

"Oh, hell. Thank you for bringing that. Sorry we're not outside."

"I don't mind a change," Ellie said.

"You hear that?" Katherine said, filling three plates set side by side on the counter with equal servings of eggs. "Your friend here's a modern woman. Not as rigid as some of her neighbors."

"OK, OK." Mary Alice turned back to Ellie. "What've you been getting on about?"

"Oh, just catching up. She tells me there's quite a fuss happening in Atlanta right now."

Mary Alice would have dropped her mug onto the floor, making a bigger mess than she had in, oh, hours, but a heroic muscle in her arm remained tense, saving the room from chaos. "Really? What's the fuss in Atlanta?"

Katherine turned to her with a devious eye. "Homeowners association." She took the tiniest pleasure in watching Mary Alice unclench. "They've turned authoritarian. New rules about lawns that've turned everyone on the street into raving lunatics."

"Ah, of course. I don't envy that."

"I'm sure you don't."

Ellie sighed and took a large glug. Mary Alice looked at her quizzically, as though Ellie had something else to say. When it became clear she didn't, Mary Alice's face tightened and she put on a wry smile.

"Speaking of neighbors," Mary Alice said, her voice turning sly and conspiratorial. "You know what I've seen when I look out the window for the past ten years? An empty driveway. You know what I've seen recently? Gerald Harbison's brand-new truck. I didn't think accountants needed to make that many house calls."

"Gerald Harbison?" Katherine said before Ellie could respond to Mary Alice's prodding. "I remember him. When did his wife pass?"

"She died, oh, must have been ten years ago at this point," Mary Alice said.

"Eight," Ellie said quickly.

"Well, it's about time he moved on," Katherine said. "You, too. No harm in dating at our age. You know, I actually think I kissed him once."

Mary Alice wondered when it had become so easy to talk about death. She tried to remember her adult life before Death had gotten himself so involved. The thought of someone other than herself dying was something she never considered. Friends and family seemed permanent; it was her own mortality that was ever in doubt. So she tried to stay active. She wasn't prone to gluttony. She didn't sneak cigarettes like her sister. And when Michael was born, she even toyed with going vegetarian—a strange weeklong experiment that ended with a Sunday roast. But once Samuel was gone, any sense of control she thought she had over life dissipated. She didn't become any less healthy, but only because that would have involved the work of changing her lifestyle. Her routine was set in stone, and so were the ultimate deaths of herself and all those closest to her. It would happen eventually, and nothing she could do would stop it.

For years, Mary Alice felt like an anomaly. Her mother died of heart failure. A stroke took her father six years later. Once their high school homecoming king, Moe, died of a heart attack, her peers finally caught up with her acute sense of mortality. No conversation was over until talk of someone's funeral came up. You couldn't talk about the weather without transitioning into the results from a physical, or worse, a biopsy. Death was coming for all of them, so they might as well talk about it.

But still, Mary Alice found Katherine's comments a little too callous. "There's no alarm clock," Mary Alice said. "She's in no rush to find someone and neither is anyone else." Katherine raised an eyebrow and took a bite from the plate she held in her hand.

Ellie suddenly felt like an intruder, despite her open invitation. She finished the eggs and bacon so quickly that Katherine nearly commented on her speed, and stood.

"I think it's time for me to be going."

Ellie's obvious discomfort did nothing to faze Katherine, who waved with the hand holding her fork. "It was great to catch up."

"It was a pleasant surprise to see you," Ellie said. "We still on for tomorrow? No pressure if the two of you want bonding time."

"We'll get enough of that during the day. Don't worry, come on over if you have the mind to. I won't sleep in, promise."

"Will do. See y'all tomorrow."

She held up the plate as a show of good manners, but Mary Alice snapped, "Don't even think about it. Just get out of here and go save some lives."

"Yes, ma'am."

When the sliding door closed, Katherine turned to face her sister. "You know she'll kill you when she finds out."

"She's not going to find out."

"And how so? You're just going to keep lying?"

"I'll have you know I've never lied to that woman in my life."

"Then what do you call making sure she thinks her son's best friend is dead just like her own?"

"A misunderstanding that would hurt too much to correct."

"Oh, I see. This is for her benefit. Sure. You're a saint, Mary Alice! Move over, Mother Teresa."

"I have things to do today—errands to run over in Trevino—and you're more than welcome to come along. You're also more than welcome to stay here and find something else about my life to judge me for. Take your pick. I'm leaving in an hour."

Mary Alice left Katherine alone, another delicious breakfast not just uneaten but wasted. Is this what she'd become? A person who takes everything—from groceries to friendships to family—for granted? She escaped the room before coming to a decision, leaving Katherine behind like a canted statue lamenting the ills of domestic life. Once Katherine heard the bedroom door close, she returned to her meal and finished every bite on her plate before throwing everything else down the garbage disposal. After, she called John to check in on her nephew. Best to do it when Mary Alice wasn't around, she thought.

"He's barely eating," John said, a hint of exhaustion in his voice. "But he's fine."

"Is he talking much?" Katherine took a seat at the bar.

"A little. He talked a little about work last night, how he feels, what'd he say, directionless without his job. Watched a little TV with me before creeping off back to sleep."

"That's something."

Then, after a pause: "I wish you were here. This is hard, Katherine."

"It's no picnic here, either. Trust me. At least not until Saturday. And you know what? I have a feeling that won't be much of one, either."

"Why are we doing this, Kathy? Why are we fixing your sister's mess?"

Katherine wanted to tell her husband what had been weighing on her the past few days, that Michael was the closest thing she'd ever have to a child, and that not doing everything she could for that boy was something she would regret for the rest of her life. Instead, she just sighed and said, "Because she can't fix it herself."

Upstairs, Mary Alice sat on the foot of her bed and listened to the muffled voice of her sister, then the whirring of the dishwasher. She conjured up an image of the whole morning scene being ripped apart and flushed down the drain, just like the garbage. As though it had never happened. As though she could give the day another shot.

14

THE LAST TIME JOSIE CALLED IN SICK TO WORK, THE VERY
act of dialing a number on her phone made her right arm ache so
badly she thought a blood vessel was going to burst. She had the flu,
a nasty strain that put her in such all-encompassing, sweaty pain that
she realized she'd probably never actually had the flu before—just
bad colds, which, compared to this, weren't that bad at all. Travis had
compared it to those people who say they have OCD when they're
actually just more organized than the average person. Josie told him
the comparison wasn't helpful and to get her another jug of Pedialyte
from the bodega down the block while she phoned the principal.
"You sound like you're dying," her boss told her with more revulsion
than sympathy. "Do you need to go to the hospital?" She told him no,
that she would just sweat it out at home and take as much Tamiflu
as the box said was safe. Six days later, she returned to work and found
a large WELCOME BACK, MRS. KERR card on her desk. She teared

up as she thanked the class, and felt wracked with guilt despite the complete and total justification of her absence. The finest penmanship on the finest parchment can't compare to the emotional slaughter of crayon on construction paper.

But today's sick day was different; she was in perfect health. In the bathroom, after Travis went down to make breakfast for Henry, she checked her temperature, hoping for a slight fever—anything over 99 would be enough to assuage her guilt for skipping out on the morning classes—but the screen read 97.7, as it always did. She couldn't call the school from home, where Henry or Travis could hear, so she decided she would take the long way to work and call from a corner somewhere south of the highway, in front of one of those houses where the oldest of old-timers lived out their twilight years.

Downstairs she peered over Henry's shoulder and examined the remnants of the scrambled eggs he'd spread around his plate. "Looks like you've got a few more bites left," she said.

"No," he said, a hint of worry somewhere in the back of his throat. "I'm all done."

"You sure you're all done, or did you just spread the eggs around to make it look like you're all done?" Henry sighed and began collecting the dregs into the center of his plate. Josie wondered how he, at four years old, even thought of a scheme like that, whether he'd seen it in a movie or one of those awful shows he loved on YouTube. If he'd come up with it himself, should she be impressed by the creativity? Isn't part of being a person in society these days finding creative ways to avoid things? And wasn't that exactly what she was doing right now? "Actually, I think he's eaten enough," she said, pulling the plate out from under him.

Travis turned his head from the sink and raised an eyebrow with a smile. "Well then," he said. "You off?"

"I'm off." She loved watching him clean up the kitchen. And because he loved doing it, she loved watching it even more. The one who cooks isn't supposed to clean, but she let him finish the work without protest; this was always part of their routine. Nothing about their household roles had changed since moving to Texas; there was just more time and space to complete them. Texas was a place that let you stretch out, for better or worse, and she had every intention of focusing on the better. She would spend more time with family. She would spend more time watching, enjoying, appreciating. But not this morning. This morning she had plans.

"Have a good day," he said, leaning in for a kiss. She held it longer than a normal peck goodbye, long enough that she was worried he'd notice something was off. But he didn't say a thing, just went back to the dishes. Part of her hoped he was lying about something today, too, so that they'd be even.

On the corner of Culebra and Seco, idling beside a drooping chain-link fence, Josie called Principal Ortiz. "Hi, Judy," she said to his assistant, who'd been there since the first Bush administration, suddenly realizing she needed to sound less chipper. "Is Principal Ortiz in?"

Judy picked up on the worried tone and adjusted hers to match. Yes, she said, someone's in his office but she'd connect them straightaway.

"I'm so sorry to do this," Josie said when Principal Ortiz jumped on. "And I know it's tricky still being the first week of school and all, but I'm feeling really off and have to run to Trevino for a quick doctor's appointment. I'll be back by noon, but I do have to take care of this."

"Aw, well, that's going to be tricky, because we've got Laurie in for Mr. Gonzalez this morning," he said, doing his best to obscure his frustration. "But hey, you know what, we'll be fine. We'll be fine, for sure. I bet we could maybe make this work. Worst case, I'll fill in. I hope nothing's the matter."

Of course something's the matter, Josie thought. Why else would a woman call in for a sudden doctor's appointment? Probably because she was lying. But he didn't know that. "Thank you so much, Principal Ortiz. I won't let this happen again. Today's an anomaly."

"Don't give it a second thought," he said. "Enjoy. Or feel better. Just hope you're well. Be well. See you this afternoon."

After ending the call, she dropped the phone into her center console and let out a sigh. The conversation had been so surprisingly simple that she wondered why people didn't call in sick to work more often. What were their bosses going to do, check? Well, maybe, she thought. If it started happening too often. The point, she realized, was finding just the right line between not enough and too much. But isn't that what they say about everything? Moderation? What a joke. After her mind slowed down, she started the car back up and noticed an old man staring at her from his front room window. He was hunched over and looked older than her own grandfather had looked on his deathbed, but there was nothing sinister in his gaze. She had no sense that he was angry about two of her wheels being on his lawn. He was just looking, so she looked back and waved, feeling a strange sense of generosity for giving him something to see.

The morning buzzed with possibility. It was 7:45, which would put her in Trevino by a little after 8:00. If she could get into the *Herald* by 8:05, she'd have well over three hours to riffle through the records. More than enough time, she thought. Back in college, she loved spending an afternoon in the stacks or scrolling through roll after roll of microfilm. She had come of age just as analog archives were making their way out the door in order to make room for their instantly accessible replacements, and had just enough of a connection with the old ways to long for the tactility of it all. Even now, she'd prefer hours of riffling with her hands—squinting at indexes and call numbers—to a quick search in an address bar. But this was a small-town paper, and she didn't know whether to expect a complete mess that would take double the time she'd allotted, or a set of archives so small and well taken care of that she'd strike gold in an instant. Maybe her biggest problem would be having to kill time somewhere while she waited out the plausible length of a doctor's appointment. But that was a worry for later. After she found Michael Roth's obituary.

She pulled into the *Trevino Herald*'s parking lot at 8:24, later than she'd hoped, but instead of bolting inside, she was distracted by the courthouse across the street. This was her first time on this side of the Trevino train tracks, and she found herself in something resembling awe of the town's grandest building. It was limestone, perhaps, although not white, but a pale red. So, no, maybe it was granite? Was there really a big difference between them besides a whole lot of time? She wasn't sure but hopped across the street to get a better look. To her right, she saw a big black metallic plaque on a pole about her height and recognized it as the same kind of landmark sign in the center of Billington, the one describing the old train station.

This one told the story of the Trevino County courthouse, built in 1892 out of granite (she smiled at her guess). It took five years, the sign read, and at the time it was the largest town hall outside of San Antonio. Josie looked back up at the building and tried to imagine it back then, when it was more impressive. How it must have felt to watch something like that be constructed, to watch your town grow into something bigger. She'd never lived in a place that was anything but big, and over her three decades in New York witnessed only changes in aesthetics, not actual size. Manhattan, to her, had always just been a metropolis, and probably always would, as long as they figured out the seawall. She thought of Henry and wondered if he'd remember New York when he was her age, or if, for him, childhood would always begin at four. Looking up at the pink granite in the morning light, she hoped that it would. Maybe he'd have a greater respect for size if he started somewhere small.

A six-wheeled truck's thundering honk thrust her out of her morning daze. So she waved apologetically and ran back to the *Herald*'s diminutive building across the street. Inside, she expected a bustling office yanked out of another era, the sort of wide-open, smoky room filled with men in ties and women in dresses, all of them clacking away on their electric typewriters with cigarettes between their fingers. The reality was less glamorous, more dusty than smoky, and not a tie in sight. Not anyone, actually, until she knocked on the reception desk and let out a timid "Hello?"

A woman with tight white curls and bright-red cheeks rolled her chair out from behind a shelf and under the desk. "Sorry, ma'am. Don't usually have visitors this early. How can I help you?"

"My name is Josie Kerr, I'm a teacher down in Billington," she said, a wave of nerves rushing over her. "I was wondering if I could thumb through your archives for something I'm working on for a class. Do you even keep them in this building? Sorry, I'm new to town. Still getting to know the area."

"Well, we don't got more'n one building, first off." The silence that followed was impossible for Josie to decipher. Was this a good sign or a bad one? Would she be allowed in or laughed right out in a cloud of aging dust? "But, yep, you can follow me. Been a while since we had someone in here digging through the old stuff. Usually picks up once a semester, when the kids come in to do a report on something they can't just type in on Google. Hardly few adults, I gotta say." She twisted the squeaking doorknob of a room marked RECORDS, and gestured for Josie to step in first. "You say you're new in town? Well, I'm sure most people who've lived here for seventy-five years ain't never stepped foot in this building, let alone asked to see the, what'd you call 'em?" she said with something between a scoff and a guffaw. "The *archives*? This ain't the Library of Congress, I'll tell you that much."

Josie couldn't decide if she was alarmed by or enraptured with this woman.

"Should have anything you're looking for, as long as it ain't before 1952. The old building caught fire in '51. Lost everything."

"Oh, that's a shame. But what I'm looking for is more recent."

"Well, have at it. Should be easy to make sense of. Recent stuff starts here, then sorta zigs and zags through the rows until you get to that corner. Make copies if you want to. We usually charge ten cents a page, but feel free to copy as much as you want, no charge."

"Wow, thank you so much."

"To tell you the truth, I just don't feel like digging around for the key to the change box." The receptionist waved Josie goodbye and shut the door behind her. After turning to the stacks, a smile filled her face. She understood how gauche it was to feel such delight when hunting for an obituary, but the thrill of an archive was impossible for her to deny. It made her feel like she was in a detective novel, looking for the final clue that would solve everything, usually tucked away in the private files of an eccentric, wealthy academic. She fingered the stacks of boxes, seeking May 2002, the month of Kenny's death. If she remembered correctly, Michael died only a few weeks later. For a place that was not disorganized per se but not the most well maintained, it only took Josie a minute or two to find the right box: 2002, MAY–AUGUST. She pulled it off the shelf with a huff and dropped it on the table in the center of the room.

Each paper was a single section, about twenty-eight pages long. Obituaries were always on page six, but she kept flipping through each even after confirming Michael's wasn't inside. She thumbed through stories about restaurant openings and family reunions, teacher retirements and chamber of commerce meetings. She read a story about a grocery store chain and a Trevino girl who received fifty thousand dollars in college scholarships. And then, after five weeks of misses, there it was in the issue from July 8, 2002. There were seven printed that week, and his was the last one listed, and the shortest by far. While the grandparents above him had multiple paragraphs of memories and condolences, Michael's was only a short, single column, just over fifty words, creating an uncomfortable asymmetry on the page.

MICHAEL SAMUEL ROTH

Michael Samuel Roth, formerly of Billington, passed away on Friday, June 28, in New York City, NY, at the age of 18. He is survived by his mother, Mary Alice Roth, who suggests Michael be remembered with a donation to PFLAG.

Josie narrowed her eyes and set the paper down for a moment. She squinted into the distance, as though trying to see through the frosted glass on the door, then lifted the paper back up to read the obituary a second time, then a third. After making a copy on the ancient Xerox machine behind her, she closed the binder and coughed at the dust that erupted after its thud.

"Find what you needed?" the receptionist asked her.

"Yes, thank you."

"Well, good. Glad someone's getting some use out of this place. Have a good one now."

Josie smiled and waved, then walked back to her car. In the driver's seat she read the photocopied obituary one more time and shook her head. She couldn't articulate what exactly she didn't believe—the location or cause of death or maybe even both—but something was off. Maybe it was anxiety steering her brain toward conspiratorial thinking, or maybe it was the thousands of obituaries she'd read in the *New York Times* since childhood, but this didn't seem like it was written by someone in the throes of grief. No, she thought. That wasn't an obituary at all. It was a message.

15

GERALD HARBISON WAS A BIG MAN WITH A BIG VOICE AND A big truck. The kind of bigness that felt welcoming and spacious, as if he could fit the whole of the town inside him and still have room to spare. He seemed to like everyone and was someone whom everyone seemed to like. So when his wife, Peggy, died of breast cancer eight years earlier—a grueling nine-month ordeal that neither he nor Peggy would let anyone refer to as a "fight" (because fights, they said, are fair)—everyone, not just the single women, wondered who would be the first he'd let inside, and when. He simply had too much love that not sharing it with someone felt like a waste. But the years passed, and he showed no interest in Maretta Meyers or Gloria Pflüger, despite their shameless, if well-intentioned, flirting over at the Buckhorn. He showed no interest in anyone, claiming to be fine all on his own. And then something wonderful happened: he sawed his damn finger off.

It happened in his shed, a well-stocked workroom attached to his garage that he'd built when he turned forty-five in an attempt to cut off a midlife crisis at the pass. The shed *was* the midlife crisis, Peggy assured him with a smile. But she was happy to watch him develop a hobby. Big, burly Harbison, a man who looked like he was forged in fire, was the least handy man in town. By his thirties, after count-less failed home renovation projects, his lack of skill had turned into a gentle joke. But he never stopped believing in himself, and some-how thought that creating a perfect shed would manifest the desire to learn and master everything inside it. This, like his earlier attempts, proved untrue. But unlike before, both of them noticed, the summer he spent creating the perfect workspace was an achievement in and of itself. Yes, they decided. That's what it was. An achievement. Peggy didn't seem to mind the money spent. In fact, she welled up with pride every time she saw it, despite knowing it was more of an art installation than a functional workspace. She knew he'd be inspired to use it in time; she just had no idea that time would come after she was gone.

Eight years to the day after her death, Gerald caught the urge to build something. It happened one morning as he looked at his na-ked, sixty-three-year-old body in the bathroom mirror. Decades of shrugged-off commentary about the disparity between his size and shed-related know-how rushed into his mind all at once. Maybe the date was a coincidence. Maybe it wasn't. All he knew was that he couldn't look at himself without feeling as though he ought to be doing more with himself. *Look at this body*, he thought. *Look at this worthless body.* That afternoon he drove all the way to San Antonio— he didn't even stop for coffee and kolaches in Castroville—to buy himself a project. He'd been eyeing those expensive cast-iron barbecues shaped like mastodon eggs for a while now, ever since he saw a chef he liked use one on a cooking show one weekend afternoon, and though a sturdy metal stand could be purchased from the same company for a reasonable price (especially compared to the egg itself), he decided to build one with his own two soft hands. If done right, the egg would fill the far side of his back porch and look as though it had been there forever. As though the house itself had been built second, to match the barbecue's glory.

To his surprise, the young woman in the lumber department complimented his rough sketch of plans and didn't have too many suggestions when he explained his intended methodology to her in detail. "You designed this yourself?" she asked. He told her that it was a bit of a hodgepodge of other designs he'd seen in the backyards of famous chefs. And though he wasn't a famous chef, his barbecue was adored by his family and friends. "I could use some good brisket right about now," she said without a hint of flirtation. He nodded and agreed. So she cut the pieces he required, and he loaded them up on a big orange dolly. "We can't accept tips," she said when he handed her a twenty, so he waved goodbye and reiterated his thanks and loaded up his gas guzzler of a truck.

He started by flattening out his sketched-out blueprint and sticking it to the wall with a piece of electrical tape. Then he turned on the oldest object in the shed apart from himself, an AM/FM radio with a two-foot telescoping antenna. A familiar voice began discussing the news, and he shook his head at the first story. They'll be calling in about this one, Gerald thought, realizing he'd never once called in to a talk radio station. Next up, he'd cut the two-by-fours. These would be the legs. thirty-eight inches long each. The perfect height.

He laid out one of the massive pieces of wood, marveling at the fact that it had once been part of a tree, and measured out the first cut, then the second. He checked the length three times before deciding it was time to move on. Not double-checking was where people got in trouble, he thought. But he would triple-check. That's how he would become as great as Peggy thought he could be. Satisfied that all the segments would be a perfect thirty-eight inches, he moved to the next step.

The radio host said something about San Antonio's worthless city council before being suddenly drowned out by the whirr of Gerald's table saw. A spinning piece of ragged titanium that could cut through wood—not to mention muscle and bone—is almost too magical to be terrifying. Gerald watched it in awe, not just because it was capable of so much, but because so many people in so many places had come together to design the whole setup. Constructing devices for destruction is the job of so many more talented people than he. Fits of this particular kind of existential awe had been happening to Gerald a lot lately, but he was a little too old to blame his recent affinity for *feeling* on a midlife crisis. Ninety was believable, if unlikely given his family history, but 120? Maybe feeling a sense of wonder was just the first stage of getting truly old, that reverse aging that ends with you helpless as a newborn, all your memories gone. His finger was on the floor by the second cut.

He looked at the pathetic, bloody nub of a thing and gasped softly, not that he could hear it over the saw. The pain took a while to register. He covered his hand with a towel of questionable cleanliness hanging on a hook behind him, picked up the finger, and turned off the saw.

"Jesus, Mary, and Joseph," he repeated as he walked to the house.

"Jesus, Mary, and goddamned Joseph." He put the finger in a cup, covered that in ice from the door of his fridge, and somehow managed to grab the car keys and get into his driver's seat and onto the road before the pain hit.

For ten minutes, he screamed in a low groan, like a dying wild animal who's not sure whether to give up and drift away slowly or take one final heroic pounce at the hunter who shot him in the stomach. The same host was complaining about the same city council on the radio, but a listener had just called in to debate him. By the time Gerald parked, the conversation had drifted to food stamp regulations for reasons he wasn't conscious enough to follow.

As he came to ten minutes later, there was Ellie, holding his hand. "Mr. Harbison," she said, "you passed out in the lobby of the hospital. You lost a lot of blood on the drive here, but the doctors are taking good care of you, all right? Don't you worry about a thing." But of course he was worrying. Who wouldn't worry? Though at least he wasn't in pain.

"What'd you put in me?" he asked when the maze of IV tubes came into view.

"You needed blood, first of all. Antibiotics, too, and a light painkiller to take the edge off. That one was my idea. The doc wanted to make you suffer." Gerald didn't know how to interpret her smile, but he liked looking at it, so he just let her keep on talking. Seemed like she enjoyed the audience.

"What'd you do that made you walk in here without a finger, Mr. Gerald Harbison?"

"I'm an accountant," he said. When the doctor walked in, the two of them were laughing like middle schoolers.

Eight days later, Ellie answered her phone and heard a kind voice she couldn't quite place, a voice that not only expected to hear hers on the other end, but one that was clearly thrilled to. When the voice revealed itself as belonging to Gerald, she thought he'd dialed the wrong number. Why on earth would the accountant who lost his finger be calling *her*, anyway? She wasn't his doctor. She wasn't anyone's doctor! She didn't need help with her taxes, either. Did the hospital give him her number by mistake? Had that ever happened before? When he finally asked a question—"Would you like to come by the house sometime this week for dinner?"—the sheer directness just confused Ellie even more.

"Do you have extra food?" she asked him, wondering if he'd perhaps planned for a party that had been canceled last minute.

The question baffled him. "Do I have extra food?" he muttered under his breath, forgetting for a moment that phones worked in both directions. He cleared his throat. "It's not that I have so much food," he said. "What I mean is that I could. Or not that I could have so much food. I should have put it more simply, though I thought that I had, but in any case, I just wanted to cook for you. Dinner. I'd like to have you over and cook you dinner if you say yes."

"Why?"

He covered the mouthpiece with one hand and lowered it to his waist, exhausted by the entire ordeal. For a moment he considered just hanging up. Putting this whole thing to bed right away. Then he looked down at the asymmetry of his hands and felt a burst of confidence. Next time, he thought, he could lose an eye—or worse! He raised the phone back to his ear and uncapped the mouthpiece. "You just seemed like someone I'd like to get to know. And if you feel the same, then I think we should get to know each other."

"So you're asking me out on a date?"

"I suppose that's what I'm doing. Yes. That's what I'm doing."

Ellie grimaced, as though she'd smelled something rotten. The idea of someone asking her on a date, let alone someone like Gerald—a patient, by the way—filled her with trepidation, but she couldn't decide where it was aimed. Now, she knew Gerald as well as she knew most people in Billington. She knew which house was his. She sat across the aisle from him at church. She waited in line behind him at the post office. She bumped into his cart at the grocery store in Trevino. She went to Peggy's funeral, and she saw him at Kenny's, but everyone goes to everyone else's funeral in Billington out of a prodding mix of etiquette and boredom. She knew the edges of Gerald, just as he probably knew the edges of her, but filling in the blanks—learning the colors and shadows of a person—took time and energy she conserved for other things, like work. And, lately, Mary Alice.

"I'm sorry," Gerald said, deflated by her extended silence. "I shouldn't have called. This is inappropriate."

As she listened to him cower, a surge of worry came over her. Here was this man being as kind as she knew a man was able to be, being vulnerable to another person; and here she was allowing the shadow of doubt to prevail over how utterly flattered he'd made her feel. "No," she said, her register clearing into something forceful and intriguing. "Don't hang up. That sounds lovely."

She knew where he lived, and he knew she knew, so all he said was, "How's seven o'clock tomorrow?" As it turns out, seven o'clock tomorrow was just perfect.

And so it went. Dinner at his place during the week, then dinner at her place on Friday or Saturday night. Eight meals, just the two of them, with no eavesdropping neighbors or intrusive servers to get in the way of their conversation. Their conversation! They talked for hours at a time, as the meal was prepared, eaten, and lingered over. They talked about work and television, and they talked about food and the president and the town they had both lived in for so long. They talked about retirement and laughed, then they talked about dead people and cried. Then they talked about Mary Alice.

That Thursday at dusk, just as the fireflies started hovering around Gerald's back deck, he poured Ellie a glass of red wine that he described to her with the words printed on the label. "She's your best friend, you'd say?"

Ellie watched the glass fill up, then waited for the ripples on the surface to die down. "I guess I would say that. Don't know of anyone else who could possibly fit the bill."

"You go there every morning for coffee?"

"Since the beginning of the summer, yeah. I think she's been bored out of her mind since they fired her, or, well, since she retired," she said before toasting Gerald and taking a sip. "I'd wager it was a little bit of both, but the point is, she needed to leave that school."

"Have you two always been close?"

"Yes and no. When our boys were, we were. And then." She turned one side of her mouth up in a pitiful half smile. "We were less close."

"I'm sure that was hard."

"It was," she said. She didn't drink much on her own, and was always surprised by how quickly even the smallest amount of wine made her feel overly talkative and wistful, like she needed to simultaneously shut up and pour out every bit of her heart. "It was. It's hard to be there for someone when that someone is the person you need to be there for you. Does that make sense?"

"I think so. So she's your best friend, but have you told her about us?"

Just the way he said it made her wince, the casual confirmation that Mary Alice had somehow become the person she was closest to. A friendship can be so effortless, so free from hesitation and introspection, that it takes a spectator to point it out. She had wanted to tell her about him, but so much of this new stage of their relationship was centered around Mary Alice's own unhappiness. And revealing a relationship of her own would require a kind of delicacy she hadn't yet figured out. And now here was Gerald, finally putting a name to it: Mary Alice was Ellie's best friend. Best friends know about your relationships. But, she said, she hadn't told her yet. Though she would soon, she assured him. Tomorrow, in fact. She had it all planned out.

This wasn't exactly the truth, and Gerald could tell, but he didn't press her for details. He only nodded, and smiled the smile that Ellie quickly learned meant he found her adorable. She still couldn't believe he'd called her as much that first date night, when he served her a slice of cake for dessert. And she still couldn't believe that she'd said it back. Lucky for her, he believed them both.

"Sometimes you seem burdened by her," Gerald said, a line Ellie thought was a little too accusatory this late in the evening.

"What do you mean?"

"Mary Alice. I get that you two are close, and I get you share something that no one else could possibly share with you, but you still seem to walk on eggshells every time she comes up."

"I don't mean to. I just don't want to make her, you know, I don't want to make things any harder for her than they already are."

"We're all grown-ups, Ellie. She can deal with hard. So can you."

"I know she can, but what's a friend for if not to make things less hard?"

"I'm just saying that sometimes you making it less hard for her only seems to make it harder for you."

Ellie set down her glass and shook her head like she was shooing away a fly. "This is getting confusing," she said. "My friendship with Mary Alice isn't hard."

"That's not what I'm saying, I'm—"

"You don't know her the way I do . . ."

"Exactly."

"What do you mean?" Ellie said. She'd heard versions of this before, that Samuel's death shut her down, made her meaner, nastier, more challenging to talk to and be around. But she'd never heard an opinion from someone as reliable or as generally openhearted as Gerald.

"Ellie, I have known that woman just about my whole life. I knew her before she met Samuel, I knew her while they were married, I knew her in those days after he died. Did she become more, I don't know, *difficult* after they were gone? Of course. No question about it. Before then she was just, oh, quiet. But you're the only person I've known in sixty-some-odd years who I'd ever call her best friend."

Was that true? Ellie wondered. As long as she'd lived in Billington she'd thought Mary Alice was some kind of queen bee, the woman who knew everyone and everything. But as she thought about it, she realized Gerald was right. Mary Alice was more authority figure than friend. She wasn't a busybody, exactly, because busybodies are only successful if they pretend they aren't busybodies. She was just busy and in everyone's business. Everyone's except Ellie's.

"So what are you saying?"

"I'm saying you need to tell her. Not for her sake, for yours. It's wearing on you, I can sense it. You feel guilty that you're having fun while she's sitting at home stewing in her terrible memories. And I understand that. But if this is going where I think it's going, it's time."

"And where do you think it's going?"

Gerald smiled. "Somewhere good."

The last time Ellie had sex with someone, the night proved so disastrous to her psyche that she gave up hope that it would ever happen again. One of her old friends from Houston had called to check in on her not long after the move to Billington, the sort of call that came regularly for a couple of months and then tapered off into nothing. "You need to get back out there," the friend had told Ellie, so she took their advice and went on one date.

She was upfront with him that she had a son, mostly because she wanted to see if it would scare him off. And when it didn't, she'd thought the best of it. When he invited her back to his place after dinner, she assumed it meant he was the kind of man who was mature enough to date a single mother. Though after he offered her a beer from his otherwise empty refrigerator, it became clear he was just a regular man. The sex was brief, unsatisfying, and, to her biggest surprise, quiet. She lay there watching him in the dark, wondering why he refused to make any noise. Was there something shameful happening between them? Would she be his secret? Or worse, would she be his one-night stand? After he finished, he asked if she knew how to get home. She would never forget the way he said it, pulling his boxer shorts up while sitting on the side of the bed, not even looking up to make eye contact. Of course I know how to get home, Ellie told him. She cried on the drive home, ashamed to have abandoned her son for a night because she was, what, horny? She had no one to tell. No one to remind her that these feelings were OK. That single mothers can date without shame. Mary Alice wouldn't understand, she thought. Look at her. She's been single ever since Samuel died. He must have really been something else.

She didn't think about any of that in Gerald's bed that night. For the first time in what felt like a decade, her mind was entirely in the present. Gerald laughed as they had sex, he asked questions, he listened. She told him how it felt to have him inside her, and as she curled up into his sheets to fall asleep, she kissed his cheek and said, "Thank you."

To her surprise he said exactly what she hoped he would. "You're welcome."

16

ELLIE COULD FEEL THE EYES ON HER FRIDAY MORNING AS SHE parked in her driveway. She even laughed at the thought of Mary Alice peering through her front window the way she had the day they moved in, and it filled her with pride. This was a walk of shame, wasn't it? Or at least a car ride of shame. Though, she reminded herself while stopping the engine and checking her face in the rearview mirror, there was no shame in what she had done the night before. There was no shame in any part of her relationship with Gerald. Even thinking the word *relationship* made her feel a little woozy, or maybe that was the hangover.

She had showered at his place—it was more of a rinse, really, meant to telegraph a feeling of total comfort in his space—and went through as complete a morning routine as was possible in his spartan bathroom. But what he lacked in products he made up for in comfort; she'd slept without a single stir and woke up wanting to throw her own mattress into a dumpster. And though she could have used the extra hour of sleep, missing coffee with Mary Alice and Katherine would have led to more questions than merely showing up after a night spent somewhere else. It was hard to admit to herself, but she was excited about having the chance to share good news with her friend. Her reveal would break the ice, and she trusted that Mary Alice would then obliterate the rest of it with a pickax. With Mary Alice guiding the conversation with her questions, there was nothing for Ellie to do but tell the truth. She wouldn't even have to think about it.

She heard their voices before smelling the coffee. It was clear things were tense on the porch, so she slowed her step and waited until their conversation died down, which it did after about a minute, just before someone slammed a door. When she returned to her normal gait and turned the corner to the porch, the wrong sister greeted her from Mary Alice's chair.

"Morning," Katherine said.

All Elie could get out was, "Oh."

"Don't 'oh' me, sit down and grab a cup. Brought you a mug from inside. I'm sure you heard that shouting just now."

"I don't want to interrupt."

"You're not interrupting. Mary Alice just went inside to grab a plate of muffins."

And wouldn't you know it, out she came with a plate of fresh muffins. Ellie breathed a sigh of relief at the sight. Katherine noticed.

"Morning, Ellie," Mary Alice said. "My sister made these this morning because apparently she doesn't sleep."

"They look delicious. Smell it, too," Ellie said before taking her first large sip of coffee. "What's in them?"

"Everything But the Kitchen Sink," Katherine said, grabbing one off the top of the pile.

"I'm not too sure about that," Mary Alice added, pulling off another and examining it like an alien fossil.

"That's what they're called," Katherine said with a wad of fiber-filled muffin in her mouth. "Everything But the Kitchen Sink. Nuts and seeds and bran flakes and coconut oil. Coconut oil's good for you now. Oh, and dates. No sugar, just dates."

"Dates have sugar in them," Mary Alice said. Her face had finally relaxed after taking a second bite.

"You know what I mean," said Katherine.

Ellie kept her eyes on her muffin—which she was surprised to find quite tasty—as the Parker sisters continued their exhausting argument over nutrition, semantics, and the semantics of nutrition. She examined the stratified layers after every bite and tried to see if she could re-create the recipe in her head without asking for it. Flour, bran flakes, maybe half a cup of pureed dates, coconut oil, a dash of salt, looks like coconut flakes, chia seeds, walnuts, and what were those—pumpkin seeds? The two of them just kept on bickering, as though they had forgotten she was there. Didn't they know she had news to share? Didn't Mary Alice watch her come home? Ellie wondered if maybe she had been a little narcissistic to assume Mary Alice watched her every move, which only made her feel more anxious to talk. So she swallowed the last bite of muffin, folded the wrapper up in a tight square, and said, "I slept with Gerald Harbison last night."

"I knew it," Katherine said without missing a beat.

"We've been seeing each other for a few months, and I wanted to tell you yesterday, but it wasn't until last night that it felt, you know, real," Ellie said.

215

"So that was the first time?" Katherine asked.

"Is that embarrassing?"

"Not at all," Katherine said.

"Well, it's embarrassing for me," Mary Alice said in a near eruption. "It's a hell of a subject to bring up before noon."

"I happen to think it's a great thing to bring up whatever the time," Katherine said. "Talking about it keeps you young. It keeps you, I don't know, virile."

"I don't know that I agree with that," Mary Alice said, setting the uneaten half of her muffin on the table between her and her sister. "I think it's a private thing. Meant for the people it's happening to and no one else."

"So I take it you two didn't share everything growing up?"

Katherine let out a booming "Ha!" and adjusted her legs in her seat to get more comfortable. "No. We did not. I would have shared more, though."

"It would've been one-sided anyway, and to be honest, I didn't want to hear about my little sister's escapades with all the rotten boys in my class."

"Mary Alice, I don't know what you imagined I got myself into when you weren't looking, but I guarantee there wasn't half the debauchery as you seem to think there was," Katherine said. In the silence that followed, she had more of her coffee and began picking the top off another muffin. "For the record, I wanted to talk to you more about the boys I was seeing. Not to brag. I just wanted to complain about them. You were the only one who would have understood. But you always brushed me off. Even when I asked about Samuel! I set the two of you up, so you think I'd take some interest in how it all panned out! But no. I got nothing. I was a pest. Always was."

It's not that Ellie didn't want to hear the two of them rehash decades-old grudges over coffee and muffins. On the contrary, she so desperately wanted to know more about Mary Alice's youth, but the *speed* at which the conversation became just the two of them, like she had been shut out and ignored! Like she was Katherine and they were both Mary Alice. It was just proof that Gerald was right, she thought.

"I didn't think you were a pest," Mary Alice said. "I just, I didn't have anything to say to you. I couldn't relate to you. Still can't."

"That's what I mean," Katherine said. "Even when you could, when you and Samuel started seeing each other, you wouldn't. I was never allowed in."

"Don't you dare bring up Samuel," Mary Alice said, meeting Katherine's eyes for the first time.

Katherine sunk back in her chair, then popped back up again when she noticed Ellie watching them, remembering that they weren't alone. "But we're being cruel. Ellie, I want to know more about what happened with Gerald. Was he a gentleman? Did you want him to be?"

It was too little too late, but Ellie *did* need to talk about this with someone, so she gave in to Katherine's gossipy prodding. "I did, and he was. I mean it when I say I didn't expect it to happen. I don't even want to talk about how long it's been, but we had"—she inhaled deeply—"a very nice night. And immediately after I worried I'd ruined something, but this morning as I was driving home, I realized nothing had changed. Maybe it had even gotten better? But at the very least it hadn't gotten worse. That's good, isn't it?"

"That's everything," Katherine said. "I hope you still used protection."

Mary Alice nearly flew out of her chair. "Katherine!"

"What! You know rates of sexually transmitted infections are sky-rocketing among people our age? Widows and empty nesters and divorcées are horny as sin and unafraid of pregnancy. They get sloppy! Literally!"

Ellie was laughing so hard she had to spit coffee into her mug, but Mary Alice remained unamused. "Really, Katherine. I'm sorry, Ellie. My sister can be, well, you can see how she can be."

"I'm not offended," Ellie said. "I'm just happy to have someone to tell. That's the hardest thing about it sometimes, right? Not having someone to talk to."

Mary Alice and Katherine didn't need to ask what she meant by it. They knew right away.

They moved on from the sex talk and went over their normal morning bullet points: the weather (hot), Josie's pool (unfinished), the picnic (fast-approaching), the day ahead (jam-packed).

"I have quite a few errands to run, actually," Mary Alice said. "Picking up the pies for tomorrow in Castroville, grocery shopping, then I thought since I'll be out and about anyway, I should buy Eric Carlye a birthday present somewhere before I forget."

"Hell, that's tonight. What're you thinking of getting him?" Ellie asked.

Mary Alice laughed. "Not a damn clue, and if you think of something, let me know and I'd be more than happy to split it. Men like him are the hardest to buy for. They say they'll like anything and they mean it."

"Maybe I can help," Katherine said.

"Aren't you usually certain you can?" Mary Alice asked, instantly feeling guilty for beginning the day with contempt.

Katherine shook her head. "Or I'll stay here and stare at the wall while you make a terrible decision."

"Fine," Mary Alice said. "I'd love your help. I'll even buy you lunch if you pick something *real* good. How's that?"

"Ha! You've never bought me lunch in your entire life."

"Maybe that'll change this afternoon."

"Just so you know, she's never bought me lunch, either," Ellie said, expecting a laugh, but the two of them just looked at her wordlessly, with unconvincing smiles quivering on their faces. Ellie couldn't quite figure out what it was they were thinking, but whatever it was, they were clearly sharing the thought. Something was brewing between them, that much was obvious, and the tension was suddenly more than Ellie could bear. "I should go, actually," she finally said, shattering the silence so abruptly that Mary Alice and Katherine nearly lost their balance at the sound of her voice.

"So soon?" Mary Alice asked in a tone that didn't sound disappointed at all.

After Ellie said her goodbyes and disappeared behind the corner, Katherine asked Mary Alice if she was serious about the lunch deal.

"I'm no liar," Mary Alice said. "Despite what you might think."

"You mean despite all the lies you've told me?"

"Name one."

"Excuse me?"

"Name one lie I've told you. In my whole life."

"Apart from the one about your son being dead?"

"I never told you he was dead."

Katherine stood, feeling a sudden urge to go be alone and wanting to take a moment to look down at her sister. "You've made all these rules for yourself, haven't you? Rules that help you justify how you've behaved. How you've hurt people. But I don't care if you never said those words. You never corrected the record. That's lying in my book, and I don't give a damn what they call it in yours." She walked inside to clean the kitchen. And when she squinted out the window and saw Mary Alice with her face back in her book, she made more noise than necessary.

Two chapters later, Katherine came back outside and dangled a set of car keys by her sister's ears. "Time to go, Miss Daisy," she said.

Mary Alice swiped the keys from her and rose from the chair, her bones creaking so loudly she thought something had broken. "Where'd you get these?" she snapped.

"In your purse."

"So I'm a liar, and you're a thief then," she said without thinking. "And at any rate, I'm Morgan Freeman in this equation. *You're* Miss Daisy."

"What was his name in that movie, anyway?"

"No idea," Mary Alice said. "Never actually saw it."

THE PILE OF pies was visible through the window of the swinging door behind the cash register, and Mary Alice sighed softly when they came into view. Five years prior, when she came to pick them up, the manager assured her no such order had been placed. Mary Alice raised so much hell they almost had to call in an exorcist. There were no pies for dessert at that picnic, only slices of mismatched store-bought cakes from H-E-B, and every year since she'd feared it would happen again. But not today! Her pies were ready, and the manager handed them over with a knowing smirk, just to let her know he would never forget the way she'd behaved in the past. Still, when she asked for two small coffees to-go on top of the order, he threw them in free of charge. Loyalty trumps attitude, but he'd never tell her that.

So they had the pies, one part of the day's checklist finished. Mary Alice had two more items on her agenda, and yet when Katherine asked, in a somewhat pleasant tone of voice, "What next?" in the car, Mary Alice didn't know what to say. They were still getting used to each other, flip-flopping between nasty bickering and quietly enjoying the other's company, and the back-and-forth had left her tongue-tied.

"Well, I need to get Eric's gift," Mary Alice finally said.

"All right. Where?"

"That's what I haven't figured out yet."

"What does he like?"

"Katherine, he's a seventy-year-old man," she said, rolling her eyes like a teenager. "I have no idea what he likes."

"What about a nice pair of boots? No man I know in town would be upset about that."

"You think I know that man's shoe size?"

"Fine, a gift certificate."

"Gift certificates are a cheat to get out of thoughtfulness."

"Well, I think gift certificates are wonderful; they let you do whatever you want, but I don't suppose I can convince you otherwise. So what else? Nice bottle of whiskey?"

"He quit drinking about five years ago. Solidarity with his daughter."

The two of them stared at the bakery through the windshield, searching the two layers of glass for some semblance of an idea.

Katherine realized she only ever got her husband shoes and liquor, which suddenly felt thoughtless and easy. But he liked new boots. And he liked an old bottle of bourbon. Mary Alice, on the other hand, hadn't bought a gift for a man in over ten years, and, she figured, never one that old.

"How about a tie?"

"Tie it is."

They drove to the only real men's store in the area, a friendly-looking Western storefront on Trevino's main strip called Zack's. Like so many businesses in town, it had been there for decades. But like few of them, it had aged gracefully, miraculously avoiding the strange musty odors of old age and maintaining a selection that never felt dated. When they stepped through the door, propped open between two mannequins in pearl snap shirts and cowboy hats, a big bald head poked through a maroon velvet curtain and offered Mary Alice a wide, almost worrying smile. This man had made his mark, and she looked terrified.

A buzz in her purse knocked the smile off Katherine's face, and when she saw the name on the phone, she tapped her sister on the shoulder. "I need to take this real quick. Good luck with Uncle Fester," she whispered before stepping back outside.

Back in the car, Katherine's demeanor transformed. Her shoulders stiffened and her face became taut. She hated Mary Alice for putting her in this position, mostly because she knew it was because she was so damned dependable. "Is everything OK?" she asked once Mary Alice and her new friend weren't within earshot.

"He says he wants to leave."

"What?"

"Michael wants to go to Billington. He's getting antsy and says if she won't come to him, he's going to go to her."

"Just tell him it'll be three more days. That's it. Three more days and we'll all be together. I don't want him on a plane or on the road. He's in no shape to travel without an escort, and you can't, I mean . . . I didn't mean that."

"I know what you meant."

"Does he want to talk to her? We're out shopping. She's in a store but I can grab her."

"No, he says he specifically doesn't want to speak to her unless it's in person."

"Well, just tell him to wait. Maybe grab his ID when he's asleep to make sure he can't fly." Katherine looked into the shop, hoping her sister was watching, maybe even getting curious about the conversation.

"You want me to go through his things?"

"John, desperate times. It's for his own good. Just keep him in the house, please. And hide your keys."

"OK. I just wanted you to know."

"Thanks. How you feeling?"

"Just come home soon, OK? I need you."

"I need you, too. And I miss you."

"I miss you, too. Good luck."

"Thanks."

She hung up and put a smile back on her face, just as Mary Alice stepped out of the shop. Telling Mary Alice what was happening in Atlanta wouldn't make her leave any sooner, she knew that much, and a few more days of blissful ignorance felt like a gift she suddenly wanted to give. She had come down here because of Michael, but selfishly, she realized she had really come down for herself.

"Everything OK?" Katherine asked when Mary Alice stepped in the car.

"Just fine," Katherine said, her eyes focused on the small paper bag in Mary Alice's hand stuffed with a firework of pastel tissue. "What'd you get?"

"Socks," Mary Alice said, the word falling out of her with a thud. "That man convinced me socks were the answer. More practical than a tie."

"He's probably right."

"They were thirty dollars."

"Well, it's a gift," Katherine said. "Speaking of gifts, where are you bringing me for lunch? You owe me, don't forget."

Mary Alice couldn't remember the last time she ate lunch out in a restaurant—alone or with someone else—but figured Katherine was the type of woman of leisure for whom lunching with the ladies was as integral to her routine as doing the crossword was for someone else. "What are you thinking, since you're the guest?" Mary Alice said. "Barbecue? Tex-Mex? Or there's a Sonic around the corner if you want to eat in the car."

"We're having barbecue tomorrow at the picnic, so why not Tex-Mex? Jonathan and I don't eat it enough back home. All the saturated fat. Not too good for his heart."

"It's not too good for anyone's heart," Mary Alice said, realizing too late she probably should have inquired further.

"Jonathan had, well, a bit of an episode, and we'd like to keep it from getting worse. He won't be high on the list for a transplant, that's for sure."

"Oh," Mary Alice said, awkwardly holding her keys but not starting the car. "I didn't know."

"I'm well aware that you didn't know. Sometimes I wonder if you'd be able to pick him out of a lineup."

"Why? Think he's getting arrested anytime soon? I hear tax frauds are popular with rich men these days."

"Oh Jesus, Mary Alice, my husband—your brother-in-law—almost died five years ago and you had no idea. I didn't even call you. Can't you see how wrong that is?"

"You could've called."

"Would you have answered?"

Mary Alice gripped the keys in the ignition but didn't twist. She just squeezed and held, hoping to feel blood pumping through her reddening fist. A reminder that she did, in fact, still have a heart.

"He's fine, just fine," Katherine said finally. "They found a blockage and put him on something that should break it down over time."

"Well, I'm glad he's all right."

"We're all all right," Katherine said. "For now at least."

"So, El Cortez then?"

"It'd better be."

Katherine hadn't been to El Cortez in at least twenty-five years. The place had never even crossed her mind, but the simple beige facade and dusty, free-for-all parking lot were as familiar to her as her own driveway. Mary Alice's Buick joined a mud-coated behemoth of an F-350, at least fifteen years old, in the lot. She checked the clock on the dash and realized the lunch rush must be over, but places like this wouldn't close between now and dinner, not like in Atlanta. Why bother when there's nothing else to do?

Mary Alice pulled back the restaurant's door, which was plastered in stickers asking guests to review them online alongside two different signs reading No SHOES No SHIRT No SERVICE, and let Katherine in first.

"Afternoon," said a man running numbers on an ancient calculator at an empty table in the dining room without looking up from his work. "Take a seat and I'll be right with you." No sooner had they chosen a spot—one of two booths along the windows—than menus, a basket of chips, and two bowls of salsa appeared on the table. They didn't even notice the person who dropped them there.

"What're you getting?" Katherine said, holding the menu with one hand and dipping a steaming chip with the other.

"Not sure yet," Mary Alice said, her finger falling down the first page until stopping at the enchiladas. "We missed the lunch special, though."

"Don't worry, lunch specials are fine for you now," said the same man who disappeared behind a swinging door just seconds before. "Can I take your order?"

Neither of them were ready, but there weren't too many options in a well-oiled, simple place like this, even if the menu suggested otherwise. The draw was rice and beans and cheese and tortillas; the hardest decision to make was beef or chicken. While elaborate dishes could be found between quesadillas and enchiladas and *tacos al pastor*, it was hard to find the energy to eat mole or chile rellenos when you were in a hurry. "Chicken enchiladas," Mary Alice said, triumphantly closing her menu.

The server nodded, then directed his gaze at Katherine, who trembled slightly while darting her eyes around the menu. "You know what," she said, tossing the menu on Mary Alice's, "I'll have the same."

The server nodded once again, only to be interrupted as he turned back to the kitchen. "Wait! Beef instead? Is that all right?"

"Beef," he said. "Be out soon."

Katherine didn't eat much beef, which Mary Alice suspected partly because of the nervous amendment and partly because she didn't eat much, either. Their father had died of a stroke, and though it could have been attributed to any number of factors—his drinking habit, his smoking habit, his genes—it was always his unspoken rule that dinner wasn't dinner unless beef was involved. He ate far too much of it, and both sisters internalized it as something to course correct. This little thing, they both half-believed, would give them more years on this Earth than old Edward Parker, and so far it had. Katherine was a year older than he was when he died, and Mary Alice was more than four. But what would a little sliced flank steak hurt every now and then?

In the corner, Mary Alice watched an old man lift up his bowl and slurp the remaining drops of his soup. He wiped his mouth with a handkerchief he also used to wipe sweat from his brow and then placed it back in his breast pocket.

The server pulled the plate from his table almost immediately and they had a brief exchange Mary Alice and Katherine couldn't make out, but quickly enough the old-timer was dropping a wad of bills on the table, finishing off his iced tea, and shuffling toward the door. He was shorter than he looked sitting down, older, too, and covered in a fine layer of dust that made them wonder what a man his age was doing working so hard. He should be home on his recliner watching *Wheel of Fortune*, Mary Alice thought before turning the same idea inward and feeling embarrassed for feeling even an ounce of pity.

"Thank you much," he said, opening the door with a sturdy shove, its chili pepper–shaped bells offering the room a polite little ding. That's what did it; the ding.

She hadn't cried alone in months, and she hadn't cried in front of people since Linda, Linda, Maria, and Debbie showed up to her house with a dish of King Ranch Chicken and flowers after Michael left. But the view of this old man, older than her but not by a whole hell of a lot, heading off to work opened something up in her. The tears fell when she realized what she was feeling wasn't pity: it was envy. That man had somewhere to be, and people who needed him, even in old age. What did she have, the picnic? That was just one day a year, and there were so many others left to fill.

"Are you all right?" Katherine asked, noticing the distinct, perfectly symmetrical tears running down both of her cheeks. Mary Alice hadn't even tried to hide them.

"I'm fine," she said, unrolling the tightly wrapped utensils and wiping her face with the napkin that held them. "I just thought I recognized that man."

"Him? Who just left?" Katherine turned around and got a glimpse of the man in the driver's seat of his truck. "Probably because he looks like everyone in a thirty-mile radius."

"Yeah, probably." She dipped a chip in the salsa, a watery-though-chunky concoction that she'd tried and failed to replicate at home once or twice, the sort of house dip that wouldn't have tasted as good even if she'd had the recipe.

"I know it goes without saying, M, but I do hope you come home with me next week. I wouldn't be here otherwise. I wouldn't be in this—I'm just going to come out and say it—ridiculous and, frankly, insufferable limbo with you right now. We're just going about our days as though there aren't decades between us. As though every-thing's been fine forever and nothing needs to change."

"I know."

"Hasn't all of this felt strange to you? Haven't you been uncom-fortable?"

"Yes."

"Why haven't you said anything?"

Mary Alice grabbed another chip and dipped it, dumping a few drops back in the bowl before pulling it to her mouth. "I don't have to tell you I'm not so good at talking about things, do I? Never seems to work out."

"Come on, now."

"I don't want to fight."

"I don't, either," Katherine said. They were both so calm in that moment, so attuned to the other's frayed antennae, that when the server returned with their lunches even faster than anyone expected, he just thought they were a couple of sisters who enjoyed each other's company but who may have been having a not-so-great day.

"Can I get you two anything else?"

"Two iced teas. Unsweet if you have it."

"Will do."

He was gone again, and they ate their meals slowly and in total silence, finishing every bite. When the plates were taken back by the server, Mary Alice finally broke the quiet to ask for a check. "It's taken care of," he replied.

"What do you mean?"

"My manager said not to worry about it."

"Why would he go and do a thing like that?" And then Mary Alice saw him standing behind Katherine. Had he been there the whole time? "Wait a minute," she said, her voice going up into a more scholarly register. "Oh my goodness, Juan Lopez!" She stood up to give him a hug, which both of them held with a palpable joy. Juan Lopez. Shy. Wonderful parents. Loved to read aloud in class.

"It's good to see you," he said as they came apart.

"You, too!" Her eyes turned down to his breast, where a name tag with his name and title glistened in the afternoon light. She pointed at it, then tapped it twice as punctuation. "Running this place, I see?"

"I guess."

"Good for you."

"How have you been?"

Mary Alice sat back down and began to clean up the mess she left from the chips, wiping crumbs into a napkin she held at the edge of the table. "Oh, I'm just fine, apart from turning your place into a pigsty."

"Taking a long lunch or skipping school completely?"

"Ha!" She crumpled the napkin into her hand, which Juan grabbed with his own without comment. "No, no, I'm retired now. My first semester off in about three decades."

"Congratulations!"

"It's just work. Or I guess it's just not work. But thank you. I didn't do anything special. Just got old," she said before remembering they weren't alone. "Oh, Juan, this is my sister, Katherine. She's visiting from Atlanta. Both of us were craving a nice big lunch today."

"Nice to meet you," he said, extending his hand.

Mary Alice began monologuing, talking to the empty tables and chairs. "I taught Juan, oh, ten years ago at least," she said. "Great student. Always showed his work. Not everyone does. You got an A in my class, didn't you?"

"Probably," he said with a laugh that wasn't quite genuine but also not performance.

"You got an A in every class, I bet. Do you remember any of it?"

"Math? Not using derivatives much these days, but addition and subtraction? Big ones in my industry."

"Well, you remember derivatives exist at all, so I guess that's something."

"I guess," he said, bobbing slightly in the awkwardness of their silence. "Well, it was great to see you, Mrs. Roth. And to meet you." He gave a nod to Katherine, who responded with her own.

When they walked back to the car, Katherine shut the door to Mary Alice's Buick and pulled down the seat belt in an exaggerated diagonal. "However much you paid him, it wasn't enough," she said, timing the click of the belt as her punctuation mark.

Mary Alice laughed. "I slipped him a hundred while you weren't looking."

Katherine chuckled, surprised at the warmth in her voice. For the first few days of her visit, the house balanced on a knife's edge when they were both inside. But when they were in the car, they could joke around like they used to. It put them on solid ground, always had. A shared love of a cracked window at fifty miles an hour, that absolved even the biggest of fights. And as Mary Alice drove west, into the oppressive afternoon sun and back toward home, she realized that, unless she was starting to get forgetful, they'd always gotten along on the road.

17

DRIVING. THERE HAD ALWAYS BEEN SO MUCH OF IT. IT WAS always the great equalizer in their stretch of Texas, where your vehicle wasn't merely a necessity but an appendage, a product of evolution. You drove when things were far away—in the country most things are—and you drove when things were close, because the driver's seat was always closer. When Mary Alice and Katherine were growing up, the driving age was sixteen, but just like everyone else they knew, they learned to drive at fourteen. "Just in case," was always the reason, no matter who was doing the reasoning. Just in case you need to drive somewhere and get help if an adult got hurt. Just in case you need to drive home when an adult has had one too many. Just in case you need to help out on the ranch while your daddy's operating the hay baler. Just in case you need to run to the grocery store while Mom's stirring something on the stove.

Parents in Billington believed that certain skills, like shooting guns and drinking beer and driving cars, should be taught at ages below government recommendations because, in their estimation, curiosity would inevitably get the better of an adolescent. So why not treat it like an education and cut mischief off at the pass? Better to teach your child about drinking responsibly than have them show up to a party and learn how to shotgun from a third-year senior named Hank.

Mary Alice and Katherine's father taught them how to drive on the evening of their respective fourteenth birthdays, both of which came in the dead of summer, when the idea of school was impossibly far away. Though the lessons were three years apart, they happened in exactly the same way, with the same reliable Ford F-100 Ranger, the same empty Billington ISD parking lot, and the same can of Budweiser in Edward Parker's left hand shared between the driver and the father. (Best to do two life lessons at once, their father thought. He was nothing if not efficient.) They were pros in just under ninety minutes, figuring out how to shift without stalling the engine or cracking the gears just as magic hour sank in, and both Mary Alice and Katherine had identical memories of the drive home, with their daddy in the passenger seat, finishing off his second beer of the lesson while looking proudly at their smiling faces, in profile, of course, eyes on the road, staring triumphantly at the purple-orange glow of a Texas sunset.

Both of them would only buy manual cars for the rest of their lives. They would tell people it was because they found shifting gears to be more satisfying, but in reality it was that it reminded them of their dad, whom they loved so much that even mentioning his name was enough to bring them both to tears. Their lives had expanded in different directions, but when you followed the stories down to their roots, you'd find them joined in a million different ways, a knotty tangle of memories covered in years of dirt and two deep green canopies.

The thing is, their relationship had actually gotten better in those years before Samuel died. They'd begun calling each other more, slowly trying to mend the gaping wounds slashed open at Katherine's wedding some ten years prior by pretending it had never happened. But it did, and it was the inescapable fact of their lives together; a memory they could never outrun. It was 1982. Michael hadn't been born, Samuel hadn't grown distant, and Mary Alice hadn't lost her sister to the worst man she'd ever met.

The morning of the wedding, the first below-ninety-degree day of summer in weeks, was actually quite lovely, as Mary Alice remembered it anyway. She woke up beside Samuel without the assistance of a tinny beep at 7:00 a.m., curled up in a ball on his side as usual, flipped off her alarm so it wouldn't stir him half an hour later, and crept downstairs to put on a pot of coffee. As it percolated, she unzipped her dress from the bag hanging in the coat closet, just to look at it again.

"The world's first beautiful maid-of-honor dress," Samuel said when he first saw it. He was right, too. The cut was simple—two small straps, a bit of ruffling along the bustline, and an ever-so-fitted cinch down a largely straight side. The salesperson had called it an "upscale maxi" when she tried it on at the boutique in San Antonio; whatever the name, Mary Alice knew it was the only kind of dress in which she ever really felt comfortable. "I can't believe she let you pick it," he said, gently rubbing the fabric between his thumb and index finger.

"She didn't," Mary Alice said the first time she unveiled it, waiting for him to make eye contact. "Katherine chose the whole thing herself. Knew my measurements, too, somehow. I didn't even get the chance to try anything else on, just walked in and found this ready for me. It fits me like a glove without a bit of tailoring." The rest of the bridesmaids, Katherine's friends from college, were in over-tulled, ruffled disasters that appeared to have been dyed in a dehydrated elephant's urine. It was a dark, worrying color you could almost smell. But not hers. As she stared at her dress, its bright and flattering pastel lemon almost glowing in the early-morning sun, Mary Alice was actually excited to put it on. More than that, she was excited to be seen in it beside her sister.

The wedding was at 2:00 p.m. It would include a full mass, not because Katherine or her fiancé, Jonathan Yancey, were believers but because there was no way out of it. Mary Alice's had been nearly identical; so was Maria's. And Laurie's and Betty's and Wilma's. There was always the option of flying to Spain—or even Las Vegas—and eloping, that sort of break in tradition would have been frowned upon but ultimately forgiven, but Katherine wanted the big to-do. She wanted people she knew in the audience, not drunken strangers. And in Billington, Texas, if she wanted to be seen in a beautiful dress beside her beautiful husband and walk from table to table being given the same wonderfully satisfying compliments over and over for the better part of eight hours, she would have to get married in a church. An hour listening to a priest drone on and on about the sanctity of the sacrament and a woman's place as her husband's property would be easy enough to stomach; she'd heard it all before.

Mary Alice's call time was 10:00 a.m. at their parents' house in the middle of town, a two-minute drive away. She was told to come "naked," meaning messy hair, no makeup, and with the dress in the bag. They would have champagne while one of Katherine's bridesmaids, a stylist with a salon in Houston, would do the entire bridal party's hair and makeup. It was the bridesmaid's gift to Katherine, and Katherine accepted without taking much time to appreciate the sacrifice of doing everyone's hair and makeup, including her own, in less than four short hours. Mary Alice dreaded the whole, extended ordeal, but she pushed her worries aside and arrived with what would have seemed like a positive attitude to anyone who didn't know her too well.

When she walked into the room filled with beautiful, laughing strangers, she felt ancient. No more than four years was between her and any of the other members of the wedding party—one of them was nearly her own age—but Mary Alice was the only one from Billington, a small town the girls found so novel and strange. To them, she was a creature trapped in formaldehyde, someone to observe with a curious condescension but never actually know. So, yes, she entered the room with a positive attitude, but it disappeared by 10:01.

"Can you at least pretend like you're having a good time?" Katherine muttered through a gritted smile, pulling a bottle of the cheap, too-sweet sparkling wine from a beer bucket and topping her off. She'd pulled her into the kitchen so they could have a minute away from the others, who started shrieking when "Jack & Diane" began playing on the radio. "This is a good day, remember? Your little sister? Getting married? This may not happen more than, I don't know, three or four times, tops!" Mary Alice cracked a grin. No one had ever annoyed her more, and yet no one was better at making her laugh.

"I'm sorry; you know I'm not good in groups," Mary Alice said.

"Bullshit," Katherine said. "You're great in groups. You just have to be the boss. You're a fucking teacher."

"That's different."

"Just think of them as your freshman algebra students, only . . . dumber."

Mary Alice smiled and grabbed her sister's shoulder, pulling her in for a hug. "I'm thrilled to be here, just so you know. And I won't be a grump anymore."

"Thank you."

"How're you feeling?"

"What do you mean?"

"About your wedding? To the man of your dreams?" Mary Alice tapped Katherine's forehead with her finger, a playful gesture that put a short-lived smile on her face.

"You know, no one's asked me that all week. Not one person has asked me how I'm feeling. They just tell me how they think I'm feeling. 'You must be so excited,' or 'You must be so exhausted,' or 'You must feel so lucky.'" Mary Alice felt like she had just been complimented and scolded at the same time.

"I'm sorry, Kath," she said. "I was just making conversation."

"Well, I'm feeling good. I am. Weird, but good. Nervous, but everyone's nervous on their wedding day, right?"

Mary Alice nodded, and when that didn't seem to shake the daze on her sister's face, she tapped Katherine's forearm. "Hey. Everything's going to be fine. This is a wonderful day."

Katherine gave her sister an appreciative smile just as John Cougar wailed once again about life going on and a voice from the other room cried out, "Katherine, get back here! Christine's doing the robot!"

"You go ahead," Mary Alice said. "I need to call Sam anyway and make sure he's managing."

"Ugh, he's so helpless sometimes."

"He's not helpless, he's just . . ." Mary Alice said, twisting her mouth. "Helpless, yeah. I guess he's a little helpless. All men are. You'll find that out soon enough."

Katherine bolted off and Mary Alice grabbed the rotary above the sink. She dialed their number and waited, feeling a little light-headed off the two glasses of champagne as the phone rang one, two, three, four, five times before Samuel answered, out of breath. "Hello?"

"Hello, Sammy, it's me, how's everything at the house?"

"Well, the kitchen is on fire and I can't find my suit, but other than that, I'm doing just fine."

"Ha-ha, but seriously. Is everything sorted? You're all set?"

"Yes, dear."

"Don't 'yes, dear' me ever again. Your pocket square? Black socks? Black shoes, not the brown ones?"

"Yes, it's all laid out on the bed."

"What time are you getting to church?"

"Is this a quiz?"

"Yes. What time are you getting to church?"

"No later than one o'clock, so twelve-fifty."

"Great."

"How's the war room?"

"A nightmare, but fine."

"And Dr. Strangelove?"

Mary Alice laughed, then turned closer toward the phone to make sure her back was toward the noise. "She's good, actually," Mary Alice said, twisting the tight curls of the phone cord between her fingers. "Her friends are awful, or not awful, but different. And she seems, I don't know, happy."

"It is her wedding day," Samuel said in a deadpan. "That's the bare minimum."

"I know, but it's still nice to see." They both paused, and Mary Alice broke the silence with a hiccup. "Sorry; champagne."

"OK, so does that mean it's pencils down? I passed?"

"Sure, sure. See you soon. Love you."

"Love you."

Linda had a surprisingly gruff approach to hair and makeup, but given the delicate beauty of the final product, Mary Alice wondered if Katherine had told her friend to be extra vigilant about her own makeup. She imagined Katherine whispering something like, "I know this was supposed to be a gift, but let me know if you need an hourly rate for this one." Mary Alice's hair was pulled and curled and burned to a crisp; her face was shellacked and painted and sprayed with a sticky topcoat that made her feel like she was being turned to stone. But when Linda held a hand mirror in front of her face after the forty-five-minute process, she gasped at the reflection and leaned in for a hug.

"Are you crying?" Katherine asked. "Oh my God, you're crying! And now I'm crying!"

They were both crying—Mary Alice because she felt she looked better than she had at her own wedding, and Katherine because she felt proud of herself for doing a good thing for her sister. The two of them hugged each other, then Linda, then everyone else. The wedding was in ninety minutes, and they were both delighted and drunk.

At church, the photographer, a jittery, balding man named Brian Brinks, introduced himself to the bride-to-be. His handshake was cold and soft and limp, and Katherine noticed his socks were as pink as his tie and pocket square and cheeks. "I'll be doing the snapping today, but just pretend I'm not here," he said. "Unless, of course, I scream your name like a hyena. In which case, you better get your ass over to me pronto because you won't like me when I'm mad." Brian turned to Mary Alice and gave her a big hug. "How you doing, hon?"

"I'm busting, Brian. Can't wait to watch my little sister get married."

"Don't you just love love? I know I do."

Katherine nodded and offered him a large, forced smile, then turned her head to Mary Alice, who held back a laugh. They led the bridesmaids through the grounds toward the hall, where they would remain corralled as the guests showed up and the groom's party took their places at the front of the church.

"The photographer's a bit *much*, isn't he?" Katherine said, watching Brian chat with the bridesmaids as her left eyelid narrowed as if focusing on the recipient of her judgment. "I hope you two were right about him."

"We've known him since college. He's a sweetheart, and Sammy says he's the busiest wedding photographer in Dallas. Plus, I heard about the discount you got, so don't even start complaining."

"I'm not complaining! I just think it's funny, imagining the two of you being friends with someone like him. Samuel especially."

"Why? What's funny about that?"

"Oh, come on, Mary Alice. Don't be dense. He's very . . ." she said, choosing her next word carefully. *"Loud."*

"It's not like all your friends from college are pillars of normalcy and tradition. He's a sweet man. And I'm sure you'll regret making jokes once the photos are developed."

"I guess," Katherine said, sinking into the decades-old couch in a drafty room toward the front of the hall. "I haven't been in here in forever. Remember how much I hated CCD?" A chalkboard filled one wall, and a dozen old school desks were pushed into the corner alongside a chipped upright piano. Folding chairs formed a semicircle around a table in the center of the room, where someone had placed a bouquet of flowers, cups, and a pitcher of water.

"Everyone hated CCD," Mary Alice said, flopping down beside her. "Who wants to spend their entire Sunday in church?"

"You didn't complain back then," Katherine purred as the rest of the bridal party entered and turned their noses up at the dusty old room.

"You know, it is possible to not enjoy something and to also keep your mouth shut about it."

Katherine rolled her eyes playfully and called to her friends, "Sorry it's so sad in here."

"So this is where you used to go to church?"

"Well, this isn't the church. The church is the churchlike building next door. This is the hall."

"Which is, what, a school?"

"No. They had dances here, Sunday school, weddings, funerals— pretty much any town event ended up with people eating or drinking or dancing here one way or another. The town picnic, too. I had my first kiss at one of those."

"At the picnic?" Mary Alice said, extending her neck. "You never told me that."

"Gerald Harbison."

"Gerald Harbison!"

"Who's Gerald Harbison, and will *he* be at the wedding?"

"He's happily married now. I think they just celebrated two years."

"Are any of the men here going to be single or will they all have wives and toddlers?"

Her friends laughed.

"Come outside with us," Christine said.

"But I don't want Jonathan to see me!"

"He won't. We'll stay away from the church. Being in here is depressing."

"Fine," she said, turning to Mary Alice. "Tag along?"

"No, I should go find Sam and make sure he's not a mess of wrinkles."

"Suit yourself!"

Outside, the sun hit Mary Alice like a whip. She put her hand to her face to shield her eyes and scanned the gravel parking lot for Samuel's old pickup truck. Toward the front of the lot, she saw it and smiled. Samuel was checking his face in the mirror on his visor, pulling down the skin under his eyes and examining his nose for stray hairs. When Mary Alice knocked on the driver's-side window, he nearly flew out of his seat, but the buckled belt kept him in place.

"Oh, it's you," he said, opening the door a crack.

"It's me."

"And what time is it?"

Mary Alice looked at her watch. "Twelve-forty-seven."

A wry smile washed across Samuel's face. "Are you impressed?"

"More shocked, I guess."

"Come on, give me some credit."

"Fine." She pecked him on the cheek. "Brian's here, by the way. Made quite a first impression on Katherine."

"Oh no, what'd he wear? I told him to keep it toned down."

"A black suit. Pink everything else."

"Oh, that's practically priestlike for Brian. Did they get along?"

"Seemed to. I'm sure she'll forget everything about him once the photos come back."

"Hey," Samuel said, ominously. "You doing OK?"

"Of course."

"You sure?"

"Yes."

"Good. By the way, you look very pretty today," he said.

It's not that she didn't believe him, but there was something about the way he said it that implied an ulterior motive. Samuel had lied to her so often in the past that she had no problem discerning precisely when he was telling the truth. She felt prettier than she had in years, thanks to Katherine's thoughtfulness with the dress, but she could count on two hands the number of times Samuel had ever complimented her looks. He was hiding something, but now wasn't the time to think about it, so she returned his compliment with a smile as complex as love itself, a twisty, earnest expression of anxious attachment. "Go inside and keep my dad company. I know they haven't put out the booze, but I wouldn't put it past him to find some anyway. So please make sure he's not drinking yet. If he asks you to get him a beer, just say yes but never bring one. Do that enough times and he'll forget. Just make sure he doesn't run off looking himself. Katherine doesn't need him getting in anyone's way." He gave her upper arm a rub, and kissed her on the forehead.

Mary Alice and Katherine's father, Edward, a round bald man with a permanent smile that could be read one of two ways depending on the context, was red-faced even before a day of champagne and light beer, and by the time he gave his speech later that evening, he was a cherry in black tie. "Well, that went off without a hitch, apart from the hitch," he said with a smirk in the hall. The room erupted in laughter. Even those who'd heard him make the same joke in conversation earlier that day couldn't help but give in to the old man's charms. "Katherine, you're the prettiest dang bride I've seen since nineteen and fifty-two, when your momma was settin' right where you are now. I know she's looking down smiling. Mainly because she doesn't have to deal with me." More laughs; he was doing his job perfectly. "But seriously, darlin'. I'm so proud of you, I'm so happy for you, and I love you more'n I love anything on this planet. And, Jonathan? Take care of her, OK? You may not carry a gun but I got plenty." Edward fumbled with the microphone stand, and after failing to pop it back into its socket, simply gave up and set it on the floor. He stepped to the bride to give her a big hug, which was met with more applause and warm smiles, even from Samuel, oblivious to his wife's empty stare. She shook her head subtly, dabbed at the tears welling up in both eyes, and whispered, "I'm going to head to the ladies' room."

Inside the bathroom, she stared at herself in the mirror and replayed her father's drunken speech. Everything had been so lovely before that, hadn't it? The ceremony was long but ultimately incident-free, everyone looked absolutely stunning—even the girls in their terrible dresses—but Mary Alice had long believed that no wedding was meant to go off without a hitch, to quote her father. And though no one else would have agreed—oh, how they laughed and cried right along with him—she decided her father's speech was the hitch in question. Was it wedding day puffery, calling Katherine the person he loved more than anything, or was it the truth? Had he said anything similar at her own wedding? She leaned closer into the faded, scuffed mirror and searched for the memory of her wedding but couldn't remember anything aside from dry chicken breasts and her mother's ill-fitting wedding dress, neither of which had been her choice. When Maria came into the bathroom with her young daughter, she waved hello and stepped outside for a few more moments alone.

It was nearly 8:00 p.m., the sun was down, and a breeze had lowered the temperature at least ten degrees. She rubbed her arms and looked out at the baseball field on the other side of the parking lot, remembering the summer evenings she spent reading under the bleachers instead of watching the games, letting her bright blue snow cone drip over the pages of whatever paperback she had slipped out of her mother's shelf. Her whole life wasn't just in this town, it was in a radius of about one hundred yards. Everyone she knew and loved within earshot. She'd nodded in the past when her sister called Billington "suffocating" and claimed that she felt "trapped," but standing there and feeling so close to her entire life didn't feel like a punishment to Mary Alice. It simply felt small. No, she decided then, it felt close. Never enough distance to forget. Always remembering, never looking ahead.

The door behind her sprung open and slammed the wall behind it. A smash followed by a sly giggle. She turned around and found Christine, her hair flattened by the events of the day, waving, then covering her mouth as she laughed. She bolted off to her right and disappeared behind the old schoolhouse, a three-story redbrick building abandoned since before she could remember. She'd only been inside a few times, pressured by classmates as a tween to sneak in and slide down the rusty fire-escape slide, which was finally removed after Tommy Lutz broke his leg a few years prior.

Mary Alice turned her gaze back to the baseball field, believing Christine just needed a private place to vomit up the two bottles of sparkling wine she'd had since noon. Something about the evening, her father's speech, her husband's reliability, and now this stranger's drunken glee brought the tears back to her eyes. Afraid of running into anyone else, she walked quickly to her car. The doors were unlocked, as she expected, and she sat in the driver's seat, facing the visiting team's dugout. She folded down the visor and checked her face in the mirror. *Damn*, she thought. Her eyes were still bloodshot. She took a few deep breaths to calm herself before stepping back out, then noticed the hall door open in the mirror. Jonathan had stepped out, and he hadn't been as forceful as Christine. He let the door shut gently behind him and looked left and right before running toward the old schoolhouse.

Mary Alice instinctively slammed the visor shut and shook her head to calm the storm building inside her head. She waited a few moments to make sure she wouldn't be seen, then stepped out of the car and walked back to the hall.

At the table, Samuel asked what took her so long, if she was OK. "Bring me another beer," she said.

It was possible she saw nothing. Or, rather, that she just saw two people leave a building and head in the same direction toward a relatively isolated building some two minutes apart. There was no reason to speculate about Jonathan, especially now, on his wedding day, and therefore no reason for her to drink her beer as quickly as she did. But she did all of those things, and Samuel noticed.

"You all right?"

"I'm totally fine," Mary Alice said, too defensively.

"You just seem a little high-strung."

Mary Alice set the empty bottle down on the table and began

tapping the neck with her wedding ring. "It's just a big day, that's all," she said. "My little sister just got married, and she's about to leave me forever."

Samuel sank a little into his chair. "It's not forever, and she's not going far away."

Mary Alice nodded, not out of agreement but to end their conversation. While considering ways to change the subject, she overheard her sister whispering to one of her bridesmaids a few seats away.

"Johnny's been in the bathroom for, like, half an hour."

"He probably went outside to sneak a cigarette," Mandy said. "That's where Marty and Roy and Scott went."

"Ew! No! I made him quit months ago," Katherine shrieked.

"Let him enjoy himself for *one* day."

Catching her listening, Katherine turned to Mary Alice. "You wouldn't let Samuel start smoking again, would you?"

"I never smoked to begin with," he said, poking his head out toward the center of the table to meet her gaze.

"That's true," Mary Alice said, her hand now tapping the beer bottle at a faster rate. "But if you wanted to smoke outside with Marty and Roy and Scott," she said, clearing her throat, "and Jonathan, I would turn a blind eye because it's a special occasion."

"See?" Mandy exclaimed. "Let him have fun."

"I'm not fun enough for him?"

Mary Alice rolled her eyes, but immediately felt guilty for it. "Katherine, this is not the day for worry. This is a good day, remember?" Alcohol always coaxed the teenage brat out of her sister, and Mary Alice was irrationally more annoyed by this childish behavior than what she saw—or thought she saw—outside the hall.

But now wasn't the time for scolding, so she pushed back her frustrations and rubbed her sister's back. "It's going to be OK," she said. "It's going to be OK." The loving moment must have appeared sweet to Brian, who at that moment flitted by and snapped a photo of them from across the table. The shutter made Katherine's head pop up like a cat's ears.

"Stop it," she said to him, a vicious snap that made the rest of the table shut up. "I mean it."

"Oh. Apologies, dear," he said. "I thought I'd caught a nice little moment."

"Well, you didn't, so prance away to someone else."

"Katherine," Mary Alice said gravely. "He's just doing his job."

"He's supposed to capture happiness, not this."

"You're overreacting! He just went outside for a cigarette!"

Brian shot a wide-eyed look at Samuel, who waved him away as subtly as he could.

The whole thing was on the precipice of utter chaos. Katherine was a powder keg veiled in white flint, looking for any reason to explode. Everyone at the table seemed to know it, Mary Alice most acutely. So when Jonathan burst in just a few moments later, when Katherine's outburst seemed all but inevitable, the guests breathed a collective sigh of relief.

"Where have you been, you little sneak?" she said, jumping into his arms. "I've been asking for my *husband*." The way she said *hussssss-band* in a snakelike falsetto made Mary Alice wince. Jonathan gave her the confident, nothing-could-ever-go-wrong smile she'd fallen in love with. It was the practiced expression of homecoming kings and investment bankers and presidents, a disarmingly soothing curl of the mouth that feels strong and protective because we have been

conditioned to assume it must be. The alternative would mean everything we've ever been taught is a lie. Mary Alice, used to being unde-
sired by and incapable of desiring all the men in her class growing
up, learned to see right through it early in life, but poor Katherine
had never been given that lesson. She'd always been wanted, which
tends to prove dangerous for someone who does so much wanting.

Suddenly, all was well again. The party went on, the dancing continued, everyone drank more beer and ate more dry chocolate cake.
When only family and a handful of friends remained, a droopy-eyed
Katherine stumbled into the ladies' room while Mary Alice was
washing her hands. Katherine reached around her sister as her hands
were still under the tap and squeezed hard, nearly falling asleep in
the nook below her arms. She'd stopped drinking hours ago, but the
lingering buzz made the moment feel weightless and perfect. Not
since grade school had they spent a full day together without actual
incident, and Mary Alice believed for the shortest of moments that
this was a sign of their lives to come; that their relationship had finally evolved into the kind of sisterhood she'd only read about or
seen in the movies. There was tension, sure—and maybe there always would be—but the love was more palpable than ever.

"John didn't smell like smoke," Katherine said, her voice muffled
by Mary Alice's dress.

"What?"

She picked up her head and looked up at her sister. "He told me
he had been gone for so long because he was smoking, but when
he came back he didn't smell like smoke. What do you think that
means?"

"I think it means you're thinking too much."

"No," Katherine said, pushing herself out of Mary Alice's tightening grip. "I think you think it means something. And I think you don't want to tell me."

"Katherine, I don't. You're being paranoid because you just got married. Everything is fine." To Mary Alice, the lie felt as if it were manifesting into something visible, something she could barely keep concealed.

"I think you think he did something stupid."

A pain appeared in Mary Alice's chest. There's no way Katherine could have seen anything beyond Christine and Jonathan leaving a few minutes apart, but she put the pieces together anyway. Had the two of them behaved strangely earlier in the day? Had she been suspicious of his wandering eye before? Mary Alice imagined the torture her sister must have been feeling, but knew she could never explain what she had seen, at least not now, plenty drunk on her wedding day. So she offered a tender smile and stroked her hair.

"What you need is to find your husband, go back to the hotel, and sleep off this day. It's been a blur, I bet. Exhausting. OK? I've been through it. Weddings, they're hard work for the people getting married."

"Tell me."

"There isn't anything to tell you, Kat."

"Don't do that. Don't call me that," Katherine said, shaking her head and pacing around the tiny, dull bathroom. "I'm not a child anymore. I don't want my marriage to begin like yours did."

The forced smile on Mary Alice's face dropped. "What do you mean, like mine did?"

"With secrets." Katherine wiped her eyes and checked herself in the mirror. "I don't want any of those. I don't want your life. I don't want your husband."

Mary Alice was baffled. Her brow furrowed, and her head began shaking. Every part of her was soon vibrating. "There are no secrets between me and Samuel."

"Aren't there?" She was suddenly speaking with a cool lucidity, as if something about the act of confrontation had sobered her up.

"Katherine, I love you, and it was a beautiful day," Mary Alice said, walking to the door. "But I have to go before this beautiful day turns into something I don't want to remember." She grabbed the doorknob and twisted, but part of her subconscious was daring her sister to stoke the fire.

"At least I'm sure about one thing," Katherine said. Mary Alice kept her hand on the knob and her eyes on the floor.

"What's that?"

"That I didn't marry a faggot." The words hissed out of her so easily, like a violent exhalation.

"I'm leaving. Congratulations, Katherine."

"If you aren't telling me something, I'll never forgive you."

Mary Alice turned around in a sharp movement and tapped her left foot down when she faced her sister. "I saw your husband, Jonathan, leave the hall with your friend Christine and head to the old schoolhouse together. And as far as I know, there weren't any classes today." For a second Mary Alice thought she hadn't actually said anything, because Katherine gave no reaction. She stepped closer and kept talking, her voice lilting into the patronizing tone of a bad teacher embarrassing a student in front of the entire class. "That's what you *thought* happened, isn't it? You must have expected it, or you wouldn't have asked. You must have seen the way they acted. Come to think of it, I bet you even watched them leave. They weren't exactly subtle, were they? And now you have confirmation that you weren't just imagining things. Now you know the truth. So you're welcome. Congratulations. Now you get to get the hell out of this town and spend the rest of your life with a man you can't trust. I may not have struck gold, but at least I didn't marry a liar."

"You love this, don't you," Katherine said. "You think it's exactly what you always wanted. You think you're watching me suffer from the high road. Well, guess what, I'm not as miserable as you think I am. So when you lie down at night next to a husband who sleeps as far away from you as he can without falling off the bed and think, 'At least I'm not Katherine. At least I'm being honest with myself,' just know you'll be wrong. Never forget that you had a choice to let Samuel come back to Billington alone after you two graduated. You had a choice to leave, to finally move somewhere else. But you chose otherwise." Katherine smirked, the sort of drunken grin that makes a person look absolutely vicious. "And you hate that I didn't."

"That's where you're wrong, Katherine," Mary Alice said, matching Katherine's grin almost exactly. "I don't hate your choices. I just hate *you*."

Mary Alice wanted to take it back instantly. Instead, she took a deep breath and marched slowly and silently through the door, never looking back.

18

ERIC CARLYE'S BIRTHDAY PARTY HAD BEEN PLANNED FOR AL-most a full year. His wife, Dottie, rented out the Buckhorn the week after he turned sixty-nine, not that it required a deposit, just a friendly call. Ruth and Ronnie knew they'd easily make enough at an event like that to shut the place down for a night. Hell, they figured, the whole town would probably be invited anyway. What would a sign reading CLOSED FOR PRIVATE EVENT even matter? Dottie said she'd pay the bar tab. When Eric reminded her how much people in Billington liked to drink, he expected her to renege, or at least add a cap, but she didn't. "This is your seventieth," she told him with a kiss on the forehead. "And what the hell else am I going to do with my checkbook?"

Guests began arriving at seven o'clock on the dot, and the Buckhorn was loud as graduation night by seven-thirty. When most of the guests are over forty, she realized, there's no such thing as fashionably late. There were no airs, no egos, just the most important people in Eric's life, some of whom had traveled across the country to celebrate.

"Happy birthday, Daddy," Jillian said, kissing him on the cheek and handing him a heavy bag bursting with tissue paper. Dottie had missed her daughter walking in, and jumped from her seat when she saw her bending over Eric's chair.

"Jillian! You're here! What in the world took you!"

"Traffic. I think there was a wreck on the 410 somewhere; took us two hours to get from the airport to 90."

"You should have called and let me know!"

"We texted!"

"Oh, you know I never check my phone. Well, the point is, you're here."

Amid all the noise of unhampered celebration and friendship, here was this little family reunion. It was the happiest Dottie had been since her wedding, she would tell people later. And she meant it, too. To watch everyone she loved crammed together in a restaurant filled her heart; who cares if it would empty her pockets.

There was so much joy in the room that no one seemed to notice Ellie arrive with Gerald in tow. Perhaps they'd just thought he was holding the door open for her because he was a gentleman. Maybe that also explained why he kept getting her drinks. Or maybe everyone simply knew they were together because it was the most obvious thing in the world, once you thought about it. Ellie and Gerald wished Eric a happy birthday while practically joined at the hip, and when Dottie came to say hello while making her rounds, she didn't even comment on Gerald's hand resting on Ellie's thigh.

"I told you there was nothing to worry about," Gerald whispered while brazenly pushing her hair back with a finger and nearly touching her ear with his lips.

"Get a room," Mary Alice said with a laugh when she and Katherine took the empty chairs beside the couple.

"Oh, hush," Ellie said. "Where've you two been anyhow? It's nearly eight o'clock!"

"Don't look at me."

"I couldn't decide what to wear," Katherine said. "Yes, yes, I'm a cliché."

While it was true Katherine was the reason for their tardiness, Mary Alice wasn't without a little fault. She'd actually enjoyed the fashion show back at the house, and provided more commentary than Katherine expected every time she was asked, "How's this?"

"Well, you look lovely," Ellie said. "You chose wisely."

"I was so nervous to see everyone, but I don't even think anyone recognizes me. Oh well." She took a sip of her white wine, and when Dottie began shouting, nearly spit it back out.

"Katherine Parker! Is that you?" she howled, getting the attention of everyone else in the room. "I cannot believe my eyes!" She ran over and gave her an even more smothering hug than she'd given her own daughter, pushing Katherine away from her and gazing up and down at the sight. "I'll be damned! It really is you! I had no idea you'd be here! Oh, how kind of you!"

It wasn't until then that the realization hit Dottie that Katherine may not be here for the party. Perhaps tragedy had struck, she wondered. It wouldn't be a surprise for that family, so she cowered slightly and lowered her voice. "Is everything all right at home? You're just here to visit?" Katherine gave her a sly smile and nod that would have convinced anyone they were being ridiculous.

"I'm just fine, Dottie. Just came to visit Mary Alice. That my trip managed to align with Eric's birthday is just a happy coincidence."

"Happy indeed! Maybe even the happiest! Gosh, I haven't seen you in, what, twenty years?"

It was no question, they both knew that, but Katherine humored her. Wow, she said, that must be right. How odd. And far too long. For the next half hour, the party belonged to Katherine, and guests nearly lined up to give her a hug and repeat the astonishment over the last time she visited. Or all the facts but the dreariest one: the last time she'd visited, which everyone knew was when Mary Alice lost Michael. They had all spent the better part of two decades talking about him and Kenny only when their mothers weren't around, so leaving him out of the conversation wasn't just easy, it was second nature.

"You come down here for the picnic tomorrow?" Tommy Lutz asked.

Katherine inhaled sharply, paused, and exhaled into a reassuring grin. "Sure did."

"How's Atlanta?" Tommy asked. "You're still in Atlanta, right?"

"For thirty-two years," she said.

"Has it been thirty-two years since that wedding? I remember it like it was yesterday." Neither Katherine nor Mary Alice told him how badly they wished that they didn't. "Big wedding like that, then we never saw you again!"

Katherine did her best to hide her discomfort with a laugh, but it was only convincing for people who'd had more than two drinks that evening. "Well, to be fair, I came back to visit."

"Not often enough," he said, holding up his beer as if his scolding were a toast. "But I'm happy to see you back. To tell you the truth, I always figured it'd be you who stayed and Mary Alice who only came down for funerals and seventieth-birthday parties. But you came back after, what? No more'n a year?" He was looking at Mary Alice now with an earnest inquisitiveness in the cock of his head. He paused to wait for her response, but her throat had closed up. She looked at Katherine, who had nearly never looked so confused. Mary Alice gave her sister a pained glance, then inhaled a bit of pride before turning back to Tommy and finally offering him a polite nod.

"About nine months, yep," she said with a swallow. "And it was the right decision, coming back here."

"I thought you and Samuel'd be up in San Antonio for good."

"Yeah, well. It wasn't in the cards. Can I get anyone another drink?"

Before Katherine could ask any of the questions on her mind, Mary Alice was gone for the bar, and when Tommy began chattering on about something else, she didn't even pretend to be paying attention. Her eyes remained fixed on her sister, doing their best to pierce through all those stubborn layers.

By nine o'clock the crowd began emptying out. One couldn't expect a party to last long for a crowd this old, especially with a picnic the next day to rest up for. When Mary Alice and Katherine approached Eric to say goodbye, he was sitting silently in the back of the restaurant, at the table he'd chosen as his regular decades before. His eyes were nearly closed, but he recognized them immediately. "Y'all two headin' out?"

"I think it's time, unfortunately. It was a great party, though. You really know how to throw a bash."

"Dottie takes all the credit for this one. All I had to do was show up."

"Well, you're talented at that." He reached up and grabbed Mary Alice's wrist in a sudden jerk of movement. "Is everything all right?"

"Thank you."

Mary Alice's anxiety dissipated as quickly as it had arrived, and she laughed at the old man's drunken grace. "Don't thank me. Thank the pushy salesman who convinced me socks were a better gift than a tie."

"No, no, not the socks. Though they were pretty snazzy, weren't they?" He smiled and sunk back into himself.

"Then what're you thanking me for?"

"I always hoped I'd get to see you two girls together again. I never did like knowing something came between you, and I'm glad you worked it all out."

"What makes you think something came between us?"

"Not much to do around here but notice things."

They left him clutching a bottle of beer to his stomach and swaying his head up and down as his wife took care of the bill up at the bar. From far away it looked like the languid pulsing of a drunkard, but Eric had simply been looking out at his life and nodding.

"So are you going to tell me what Tommy was talking about?"

Mary Alice didn't respond; she only started the engine and put the car in reverse. She was fine to drive. No one would have questioned her, and a Breathalyzer would have shown her BAC far below the limit. Boiling, perhaps, but not tainted with alcohol. "Can't this wait until we're home?"

Katherine turned back to the windshield and let Mary Alice drive the rest of the way in silence. More silence. She was sick of driving in silence. Even the radio was off.

Back at the house they both went upstairs to change, and when

Katherine returned to the living room she found it dark—illuminated only by a lamp next to the armchair. Mary Alice was opening up a bottle of whiskey she'd pulled from the cabinet. "Nightcap?" she asked. "I don't know how long this has been in the cabinet, but I don't suppose it's gone bad."

"Sure. Couple of ice cubes, too."

Mary Alice took her time with the two heavy pours and walked them to the sofa. After they clinked their glasses together and took that first sip, Katherine smacked her lips. "When the hell did you and Samuel live in San Antonio?"

It had never occurred to Katherine that Mary Alice had any secrets she didn't already know about, at least not before she learned about Michael. It was in part a result of her own narcissistic belief that she was better at reading people than anyone else, but more so because she thought that, despite everything that had ever come between them, every fight they'd ever had, she knew her sister better than anyone in the world. But in that moment on the couch, in the dim, warm light of Mary Alice's reading lamp, with the taste of bourbon in her mouth, she began to realize that even knowing someone more than anyone else doesn't mean knowing them all the way. And as Mary Alice filled in all those blanks, or as many as she could in a single evening before bed, Katherine felt more than surprise. She felt humbled.

Katherine's wedding was what did it. Mary Alice was acting so strange that Samuel thought he'd been found out—offering Brian the photography gig had been a risky move but still, people could be so dense—so he came clean the morning after. "I've been having sex with Brian," he told Mary Alice as she held her mug up for a first sip of coffee. "For years now, since college. But it's just sex."

Mary Alice looked up, then returned to her coffee. She blew on it and took another sip, then another. The mug was half empty before she said anything, and Samuel knew better than to rush her. "Do you think I knew?"

"I'm not sure."

"No, don't do that. Are you telling me because you think I suspected or are you telling me because you think I didn't and now it's starting to make you feel guilty?"

He began speaking, but she interrupted him. "Or are you telling me because you want to end this marriage? Don't lie to me. Don't."

"I'm telling you because I figured you knew, or at least suspected."

"Well, I didn't."

"Oh."

"Katherine did, but I didn't. I guess I'm the dumb one after all."

"You're not dumb."

"Aren't I? I really did just think you were doing Brian a favor. I gave you the benefit of the doubt! Honestly. And when I saw the way you two got along, I thought, how nice that they've patched up. I didn't think it had all started over. I spent half of last night worrying about Katherine and feeling superior for marrying a better man, and now I'm waking up to this?"

"What do you mean about Katherine?"

"Don't change the subject. Not now."

"I noticed you were upset but thought it was about me."

"So that's why you never asked what was wrong. You felt guilty."

"It's only happened a handful of times, when he can get away and I can spare an afternoon."

"Where?"

"Mary Alice, it doesn't matter where, it matters that I did it. And that I've *been* doing it."

She raised her voice. "I asked you a question. Where?"

"Wherever we can find a room."

She laughed. "How romantic. Well, now I know, so thank you. I always wanted to get divorced in my twenties."

"Well, I don't."

"Excuse me?"

"I don't want to get a divorce. I want to see if we can make this work."

It was too ridiculous of a proposition for Mary Alice to take seriously. "Making it work" was something people did back when wives didn't have jobs, or by people with children, not by two adults with the rest of their lives, and all their infinite possibilities, ahead of them. Though what was it she was really chasing anyway? It was a question that had plagued her since childhood. She could look at Katherine, her little sister, and figure her out. But to look at herself was different. Katherine had always planned on marrying rich and leaving Billington for good, while all Mary Alice wanted was, she thought, not that. Despite the outward disdain for her sister's romantic goals, Mary Alice had always been disappointed by her own unspoken and unshakable traditional feelings about romance. She wanted to be the kind of new woman who could have sex with whom she wanted whenever she wanted, and always believed college would be the time when she opened the door to all those possibilities. Billington boys were not for her, she was certain, but she would find her type in the stacks of the libraries. But then Samuel moved to town and her needy sister made her go buy beer and her fantasy was all over. They both decided to attend the University of Texas, and spent their four years in Austin as the boring couple their small collection of single friends pretended to envy while being privately shocked that anyone would give up the freedom of their youth to outdated relationships ideals.

When she knocked on Sherman Miller's door the following day, he welcomed her inside suspecting this wasn't a friendly neighborly visit to ask for a cup of sugar or milk. "Have a seat," he said before anything else, and then he watched her cry from the sticky old leather armchair across from the paisley couch on which she sat.

"I need to quit," she said.

"Why?" he said.

"Because I can't live here anymore."

"You can't or you won't?"

"Both," she said, finally looking up to meet his somber gaze.

Sherman Miller had been superintendent of Billington ISD for over a decade. Before that, he was its principal, a position he was given another decade before that thanks to a stellar twenty-year record teaching math. Yes, Mary Alice had taken over the math department after the death of Maude Martin the year prior because she was the most talented applicant—whip smart and atypically intimidating for someone her age—but also because Sherman had known her since she was a one-day-old blurry reflection of her father. He watched over her throughout her time in school, though there was little to do but marvel at her grades and the way she seemed to hover over everyone else like a storm cloud. And though he would never tell her, he always assumed she'd be principal herself one day—had he survived long enough, he would have guaranteed it. So he was not only shocked to see her there, crying on his couch and quitting the job she was tremendous at, he felt like it must have been partly his fault. "Will you tell me what happened? If it's something at school, then I have a responsibility to you to—"

She interrupted him. "No. It's nothing at school. School is fine. But I'm not, and I need to go. There's nothing you can say to fix that. Believe me, I wish there were."

"Is it something to do with Samuel?"

Mary Alice bristled at the sound of her husband's name and stiffened her pose into something approaching defensiveness before decompressing back into the puddle of nerves she could no longer pretend not to be. Of course he would ask about Samuel. He was her husband, after all.

"It's not something easy to explain, so if you don't mind, I'd rather not. Samuel is not coming with me. But I've thought about this, and trust me, I am not making this decision drunk out of my mind. I'm leaving and I'm going alone, and it would be nice if you helped me do it in a way that won't screw everything up more than it already has been."

"And you're not going to give me any details, no matter how hard I try to wriggle them out of you?"

Mary Alice shook her head defiantly, and Sherman could tell he had no chance. Mary Alice was always headstrong. It's what he admired most about her. But she looked so sad at the same time that all he wanted to do was pour her a glass of tea, or maybe something stronger, and be the shoulder she needed to lean on, but he was not her father. He'd never been anyone's father—he didn't even remarry after his wife died just a few years into their marriage—so he performed the role she expected him to play: a kind of elder adviser and confidant that existed on the matrix somewhere between parent and friend. This was what it was like to be a teacher, he thought, even outside the classroom, trusted but not opened up to, admired but not loved. He was grateful to be anything at all, but never stopped being a little sad to have never been more.

It was easy for a young woman to get a teaching job in Texas in 1982 as long as she didn't mind where she'd be teaching, but a call from Sherman Miller made the job hunt even easier. When he let Mary Alice know she'd been offered a job in San Antonio, she didn't even pay attention to the position because nothing mattered except the job's existence. It would be somewhere else, and soon, so would she. The unenforceable deal she made with Sherman, in the smallest of parts because he didn't want to lose her for good, was that she wouldn't be gone for more than a year. That had been the piece of universal wisdom he doled out in response to the problem she wouldn't explain: give it a year. That would be more than enough to approach her situation with clarity. "You're only saying that because I'm young," she told him.

"I'd be saying it if you were my age," he said, wanting so badly to wipe the tears from her cheeks. "You're never too old to give yourself time."

A two-hour drive, San Antonio was as far as she could manage to go. With the help of her new boss, an old friend of Sherman's, she found an apartment to rent down the street from William Travis Elementary, where they were in desperate need of a replacement for their fourth-grade teacher, Mrs. Wallach, who'd taken a tumble down the stairs and into early retirement.

Mary Alice had a week to get settled in the charming one-bedroom, which was simple seeing as how it came furnished with more than enough for one body to live on. A decent bed, a couch big enough for three people, not that she had plans for company, a small television set, some watercolors painted by someone who signed their name "Ethel" framed on the wall, a modestly stocked linen closet, and a kitchen filled with more pots and pans than she knew what to do with. Among her additions were a coffeepot, a box of paperbacks, and two photo albums she had no intention of opening but which she couldn't bear to be separated from. Once she moved the lot of it inside, which she did alone despite Samuel's tepid offer to come up and help, Mary Alice flipped on every light in the apartment and stared at the space, taking stock of her newly compacted life. There it all was, neatly boxed (and unboxed) up and spread thin across four rooms when it could have fit in the smallest one. A month before, such an image sent her into one of her increasingly unwieldy panics, but now, just far enough removed from Katherine's wedding, she felt a pang of pride. As she stood there, a smile slowly forming on her face, she felt something even better: she felt possibility.

Teaching fourth grade had worried her when the job fell—or was placed gently by a pair of understanding and unquestioning souls— into her lap, but all her fears dissipated mere hours into the first day. What an astonishing age nine years old was, she thought. A person remains malleable and unformed for so much longer than we give them credit for, which can be hard for those who teach anyone over fifteen to admit. But at this age it's easy to feel powerful as a person capable of molding and shaping and inspiring. She had lucked into a class that was mostly eager, with just two—Sandra and Nolan—who needed a little more help from her. And that's how it went for the first few weeks. To be a teacher is to break yourself into pieces and dis- tribute them to your students day after day, until the final grade is cast. To be a *good* teacher is to distribute them in such a way that makes every student feel as though they've been given equal shares. No student can ever *know* they're a teacher's favorite or their greatest struggle. If you had asked Nolan who it was Mrs. Roth loved most, he would have said Harriet. If you asked Harriet, she would have said Derek. If any of her students asked Mrs. Roth, she would have said nothing. But when Mary Alice scanned the class as they read silently for thirty minutes in the middle of the day, she fought the generous urge to choose everyone and settled on Nolan.

But even the most wonderful jobs were a strain on your body and emotions, and after three long months of focusing only on her classroom, only leaving the apartment to buy groceries or to visit the laundromat half a mile away, Mary Alice decided she'd like to eat a nice meal. "With whom?" was the question the others asked in the teachers' lounge, exclaiming genuine surprise when their quietest colleague told them she intended to eat out—At a restaurant! On a Friday night!—all alone. So the two closest to her age, Claudia and Carol, canceled a double date with their husbands and offered to take her to their favorite spot, a charming old Mexican place in the heart of the city where restaurants and bars dotted the edges of the narrow, gentle river that snaked through downtown. She hadn't been to the River Walk since college, when she drove down to attend the rodeo with a group of classmates who were more excited about the weekend than she could bring herself to be. But strolling through its bustling banks with two new friends—God, she hoped they were friends—as an adult, it may as well have been her first time. There was a different kind of music billowing out of every window, an interminable thunderclap of Tejano, disco, and country, and people danced so close to the river's edge as they waited for their tables that Mary Alice worried they would fall in. Part of her even hoped one of them might, just to see what would happen. Suddenly, she realized what it meant to live in a city. It wasn't the sprawl or the height of its buildings, but the potential for closeness and the unapologetic volume of all its different kind of sounds. She felt electrified by the bodies, flickering under a rainbow of multicolored lights and decorative umbrellas, and when she trailed behind her friends to close her eyes without them noticing, she delighted at the sound of all the laughter. Sure, there was yelling and plenty of unintelligible conversation, but most of all there was laughter. Just listen, she wanted to tell her new friends. Have you ever heard so many people having a good time?

Claudia and Carol didn't stay out late—they had husbands and children to go home to—but Mary Alice wasn't ready to leave just yet. After they said their goodbyes and made tentative plans to do it all again soon, she sat in her car and watched them drive out of the parking lot toward the interstate, returning to their quieter outer orbits. When their taillights faded, she took the keys out of the ignition and stepped back outside. The night was young, she thought. Isn't that what you're supposed to say when it's only eight-thirty on a Friday night?

Back on the River Walk, there were even more people her age than before. Happy hour, it seemed, was only replaced by something even happier. Not everyone in the crowd looked friendly, but most did, which was all it took to make her comfortable and curious to keep exploring. She walked back and forth, looking for the right place to step inside. Not too empty, because she'd be the center of attention. Not too crowded, because how would she meet anyone without the benefit of empty space? What she needed was a place like San Antonio Country, and San Antonio Country was exactly where she ended up.

The Country, as regulars called it, was just off the main drag, a block away from the heart of downtown but still close enough to feel its pulse, and old in the way bars used to be before old was just a look you applied to something new. The facade was covered in jagged pieces of brownish stone, and had it not been for a colorful awning over the entrance walk, Mary Alice probably would have mistaken it for an old mission, like the Alamo or San Miguel or any of the other remnants from the time Texas was part of Mexico. The building didn't have many windows; the only sign of life was the faint sound of music sprinting through the cracks in the unmarked front door. When it shot open as two patrons left together, she stopped and turned at the sudden burst of music and chatter. One of the men walking out nodded at her when he passed, as though he'd be seeing her later. It was as good as an invitation.

The cracking wooden walls inside were dark and dusty, covered with photos of patrons and concert tickets and album covers, a collage of memories that were all the more fascinating to Mary Alice because they weren't hers. A small group of young people smoking cigarettes and doing enough dancing for the whole place filled the couches in the center of the main room, and two older people—a man and a woman, both in boots more country than even the ones her father owned—sat at the red vinyl seats at the bar. There were about a half dozen open spots next to them. She ordered a Lone Star because she heard someone else do the same before shuffling back to his friends, and sipped it slowly while paying close attention to a Tammy Wynette song that had just come on. She knew the chorus, everyone did, but as she listened closely, she realized she'd never considered that Tammy wasn't being entirely honest with her audience. In that smoke-filled room full of people more interesting than she could even imagine, she decided the song was actually more melancholy than she'd ever given it credit for. Tammy was singing about compromise, not submission, and didn't that make it wonderful? "Stand by your man," she sang softly, under her breath, even after the next song began.

What happened next she'd run over in her head after getting home that night, and again and again for the rest of her life. A woman about her age set a glass of bourbon down beside her with the subtle intention of someone who wanted to be seen but only by someone who saw them back. When Mary Alice's eyes met hers, but not a moment before, she asked if the seat was taken, knowing well that it wasn't, because she'd been watching Mary Alice ever since her last drink.

Mary Alice gestured for her to have a seat, so she did. The woman's name was Vicky, she said. Short for Victoria. Mary Alice had never met a Vicky, or a Victoria for that matter, and said it back slowly when introducing herself.

"Nice to meet you, Mary Alice. Everyone call you Mary Alice?"

"I don't know everyone."

"What about the ones you do?"

"Just Mary Alice."

"I feel like I'd have a little more fun with it," Vicky said, pulling her stool closer to the bar. "Having two first names, I mean. Most people don't get that chance; they have to work with the one they've got."

"You mean you'd choose one or the other? I don't know that I like either one on its own."

"But do you like 'em both together?"

Mary Alice laughed. How was it in her twenty-four years on this Earth that she'd never considered her own name? "I guess so! Or I have no problem with it. And even if I did, it's not like a person can go around changing their name." She took a sip of her beer to hide her smile, it would have been too big, and her ring flickered like a disco ball after tapping the glass.

"What about your last name?"

"What's that?"

"By the look of that ring on your finger, it seems like you must've changed your last name."

"Well, that doesn't count," Mary Alice said, sinking into her stool with a squeak.

"A name's a name. Doesn't matter where you put it. In some countries they even put the last name first, so if you took a man's name, it would be front and center," she said. Mary Alice knew that but nodded as though she didn't. "What's your husband's name?"

"Last or first?"

"Dealer's choice."

"Samuel. Samuel Roth."

"And where's Samuel this fine evening, Mary Alice Roth?"

"He's home."

"Taking care of the little one," she said with playful disdain before taking another sip of her bourbon.

"No little one. Just him. He lives—" She paused abruptly. "He doesn't live here. I live here. I just moved." Mary Alice didn't mean to say something so personal to someone she just met—she rarely opened up to people she knew well—but didn't regret this particular reveal. Her heart was racing, and she didn't know what to expect from one second to the next, but none of it felt bad. Instead, it was sort of thrilling, like she was ascending to the top of a roller coaster, not knowing when she'd take the drop. It had always been her favorite part, the slow climb.

"Now, I think that's fascinating. Maybe even groundbreaking. A husband you don't ever have to see. Not sure I understand the point, but I must say it's the only version of a marriage I'd show even the slightest bit of interest in."

Mary Alice laughed.

"It's a long story," she said.

"You don't have to tell it."

So she didn't, and for the next two hours they talked about everything but Samuel. She found out Vicky was from Odessa, in the mighty desolation of West Texas, and that she moved to San Antonio right after finishing high school, which she got through by the skin of her teeth. Vicky found out Mary Alice had done quite well in high school, and that she'd followed it up with four years at the University of Texas, a big, exciting school that she was surprised to find Mary Alice found dull and utilitarian. She hardly remembered a thing from her time there, in fact, and those four years passed so quickly she sometimes believed they never happened at all.

For a moment she thought of Samuel; understood the friendships she was always left out of. They talked for so long and with such passion and delight that no one else in the Country dared to butt in. They'd all been there before, having the greatest conversation of their life only to have it ruined by someone who'd had too many whiskey Cokes. So, for the second time in her life, Mary Alice got the best version of a certain kind of moment. Though her memory of the last time, during the party at the old place so long ago, now seemed a little different. She'd been doing more of the talking then, but in the here and now the conversation moseyed from side to side, keeping the steady pace of two people who've somehow known each other their whole lives, who could talk forever.

And then it finally came: last call. Vicky knew better than to invite her over. It was too late and she knew Mary Alice's type too well to attempt locating a crack in the armor. So she wrote her number on a napkin and slid it her way. "It's on me," she said without telling Mary Alice she was enough of a regular to get a friendly discount on nights like this one. "Just head on home and I'll settle up. Nice to meet you, Alice," she said. "You're an Alice, by the way. Just Alice. Not sure if anyone's ever told you that before."

"You're right," Mary Alice said, about to raise her hand for a shake, then nervously shoving it into her pocket. "See you around?"

"I hope so," Vicky said, knowing she wouldn't. And as Mary Alice stumbled out the front door onto St. Mary's Street, the bartender turned to his friend and shook his head.

"I don't know why you waste your time," he said, picking up the last of Vicky's bourbons and wiping the sticky surface underneath.

"That's what you'll never understand," Vicky said, brimming with pride and a hint of regret. "It's never been a waste to me. Not once." She waved goodbye and walked the two blocks to her apartment, the left half of a duplex across from the park.

Her head spinning from the beers and the conversation, it was a wonder that Mary Alice got home at all. As she lay in bed, the piercing wail of Tammy Wynette still echoing in her ears, she knew she would never go back to the Country again. When she returned to Billington the next summer, she behaved as though her departure hadn't been the least bit strange. San Antonio needed a teacher, and she was happy to help, even if it meant sacrificing a year of her life to do so. All the eyebrows that were raised when she left the year before were brought down by midsummer. There aren't many things more distracting than a pregnancy, except maybe a newborn. Michael was born the next spring.

19

JOSIE SLAMMED HER FINGER ON THE ALARM BEFORE IT could finish its first ring. She didn't want Travis to hear and, after checking his breathing in the darkness, was reassured that he hadn't. This was not his load to bear, just hers. Her plan was to finish the potatoes, get ready, load up the car, and be at the church by 6:55. It shouldn't be too bad, since last night while Travis was enjoying himself at Eric Carlye's birthday party, she'd spent four hours peeling potatoes and chopping vegetables while trying to catch whatever was on the TV in the distance. Per Mary Alice's instructions, all she had to do now was chop the potatoes, boil them across the four stockpots she could fit on her stove, and mix them with the prepared dressing. If everything went perfectly, she could even be the first to arrive, though maybe that would be laying it on a little thick.

Chopping took considerably less time than Josie expected, though her cuts grew less consistent as she made her way through the full forty pounds of potatoes. Bringing all four enormous pots to a boil took almost twenty minutes, then the potatoes took another twelve to cook. Once the potatoes were drained, she returned them to the four giant enameled stockpots along with the mayonnaise mixture, quartered, and stirred. The noise made her wretch, and so did the smell, which wafted up from the pots in a thick, pungent steam. Potato salad was one of those foods that was more enjoyable when you ignored what was in it, and that was impossible when you had to make it yourself. It tasted fine—she confirmed that with a spoonful—but a small part of her wished that it didn't. Yes, it needed to be cold, but that's what the morning was for. There were hours of fridge time before lunch would be served.

After she emerged from the bathroom, showered and dressed in a fitted button-down and blue jeans, Travis stirred in the sliver of light from their en suite. "You leaving already?" he asked.

"I have to," Josie said. "Don't want to get murdered."

Josie carefully placed the pots of potato salad in her car as if they were her children, strapping one in the passenger seat and one directly behind it so she could easily check on them with the turn of her head during the short drive. She was weirdly delighted by the sight of the seat belts wrapped around them so snugly. It was all so absurd, but it was also an accomplishment.

She landed in the parking lot at 6:53 a.m. and relished the thought of two minutes of calm before the day's storm began. From her space, she watched Debbie, Linda, and Linda file in with their own assignments. The beans. The coleslaw. More beans. More coleslaw. Someone else's tradition, unfolding right in front of her. For a moment she felt like an intruder, some kind of parasite sent in from the Northeast to feed off the established relationships other people had spent generations forming. But in the early-morning sun, she decided to give herself some grace. This is just what life is. Everything is built on something else. All she had to do was take care in not demolishing anything as she added. Unless, of course, it needed demolishing. But it was 6:55, and there was no more time for her to spiral into a crisis and get philosophical.

She began with the pot in the passenger seat, the batch she had tasted and approved. It probably tasted identical to the one in the back, but she had formed a kinship with this one, and decided it deserved the most care. As she walked inside, all the women but Mary Alice welcomed her with a chorus of hellos.

"I'll be right back," she said. "The other pot's in the back seat."

No one offered to help, but she couldn't say she expected them to. Everyone else had moved one pot at a time on their own.

But her feeling of triumph, or at least minor satisfaction, evaporated when she walked back in to find Mary Alice hovering over the first pot—her favorite batch—with a spoon.

"It's hot," she said.

"It's been in the fridge," Josie said, still holding the other twenty pounds of potatoes and dressing.

"These potatoes were boiled this morning, weren't they? Didn't you read the sheet?"

Of course Josie read the sheet. She read it at least five times. But the sheet had told her to prepare the potatoes the night before, and she didn't have the fridge space to store that much of Idaho.

"Seeing as how this is your first, and potentially last, year participating in the picnic, changing things around doesn't make much sense, does it? The menu was perfect and the wheels were greased long before you decided to waltz in. I personally find it offensive that you'd show up here and decide you know better than everyone else who's been doing it for years."

"Mary Alice, give her a break. What was she supposed to do if she didn't have space?" one of the Lindas chimed in. "She ain't the first person in here to flub some part of this meal, and guess what, people always eat it anyway. We always make do."

But Mary Alice's eyes never strayed from her target. After talking for hours with Katherine the night before, she hadn't slept a wink, and the weight of the week, and what was to follow it, was pulling her down to the point that she felt as if gravity had gotten stronger. And now here was this new woman, this new her, this pretty import swooping in to stake her claim in this town without even following the rules. From the moment it came to mind she knew it was the wrong move, but that didn't stop her from following her most base instinct and reaching for the blemish-free pot and walking it to the large gray trash can in the corner. She flipped it over and watched the whole of its contents slide out in a single, gelatinous plop.

As she went to grab the second pot out of Josie's hands, Maria pulled her arm and a kerfuffle ensued. "What the hell are you think-ing, woman? Have you lost your goddamned mind?"

But as their arms were thrown up, and as her minions turned on her en masse, Josie stayed in the same place, first keeping her eyes on the newly soiled trash can, and then back on Mary Alice. Pitiful old Mary Alice, being restrained by a bunch of women, some even older than she, under the harsh fluorescent light of a midcentury cafeteria-style kitchen next to a church. Her life had never been so ridiculous, she was sure of that much. So amid the chaos filling the space in front of her, she laughed. What else was there to do? She laughed so hard that she had to excuse herself to the bathroom, directly behind her in the hall.

Inside, she kept laughing, leaning on the sink to prevent herself from tipping over from the combination of sleeplessness and fury. And when she looked in the mirror, she laughed at her own face, covered in tears and splotches of red.

When the door opened, she expected—she hoped—to see Ellie, who might at least offer some comfort. But to her surprise it was Maria, who closed the door behind her softly before twisting the dead bolt to the left.

"I'm not going to kill you," she said.

"You're just worried Mary Alice might."

Maria smiled with the wistful pity of a parent who had just watched their child skin their knee for the first time, broken by witnessing them feel pain, but heartened by the fact that it would no doubt make them stronger. "You know what you don't know about her?"

"Maria, I can't." She shook her head and gripped the sides of the sink, which buckled under her weight. "I can't hear another excuse for this woman. Do you know how much I worried about moving here? How scared I was about fitting in? Meeting people? Making friends? Being respected or at least not despised by my students?"

"I can imagine."

"Yeah, well, you know what? Everything's been fine. It's been sort of wonderful, to tell you the truth. And yet she's been bad enough in the handful of times I've been around her to bring everything else down. To make me feel like this was the biggest mistake I've ever made."

"You can't give someone that much power. Especially her."

"Then why do all of you? Why do people pretend like she isn't the most miserable, awful person in this town? You play her games and go along with her terrible stories, even when you see the truth printed in black-and-white."

"What do you mean, *the truth?*"

Josie felt like she'd crossed a line, and trembled while deciding the best way to step back behind it. "I just mean," she said, her voice stuttering. "I just mean that I don't get it. That's all."

"That's right, you don't. And you never will. So the best thing you can do, or maybe the only thing you can do, is to not think about it. Let everything she says roll off you. That's what we all do. It takes practice. A helluva lot of practice, by the way. But you can do it. She don't mean the harm you think she means. Trust me."

"But do you see why that . . ." she said, sucking in a teary breath. "Do you see why that sucks?"

Maria laughed. "Yes, I can see why that sucks. But I'm gonna tell you what a lot of those ladies ain't gonna say, which is that we put up with her because we feel sorry for her. No one wants to say something like that about a friend behind their back, but sometimes you gotta tell the truth even if it ain't pretty. Some folks are just the way they are and there's nothing you can do about it. We put up with her when she's the way she is today because she usually ain't."

Josie rolled her eyes and nodded.

"I know this won't make you feel better right now, but it will. Just keep it in mind. And I'm sure your potato salad was great. Looked good to me, even on black vinyl." Josie laughed and crumbled into herself when Maria approached with arms outstretched. As they hugged, Josie let herself succumb to the warmth, and felt like she was hugging someone who'd been close to her for all time. The best kind of hugs, like this one, weren't just rare, but generous. They're elegant and unbalanced acts of kindness where one person needs the hug and the other knows exactly how much hug to give in return. A hug like this is an offering, an invitation, an Escherian connection between two people where both sides are guest and host.

"She likes you, you know," Maria said. "Based on everything you've said, I'd say she likes you more than she likes any of us."

"Well, she has a funny way of showing it."

"Don't we all?"

Josie shrugged. "I don't know that I do. I've never been that interesting."

"Then why do I watch you sit on the edge of that hole in your backyard most nights? Seems pretty funny to me."

"You can see that?"

"Honey, we share a property line. And your fence, well, even I could jump right over it."

"God, how embarrassing."

"Naw," Maria said. "Just . . . funny. And maybe one day I'll ask you exactly why you went and did that, and maybe one day you'll tell me. Might take a few years, but you're not going anywhere, are you?"

Josie looked up and wiped her eyes. She felt like herself again. And Maria felt like a friend. She shook her head at the question, and both of them smiled.

"Just cook the potatoes at night next year, K? 'Cause you know you're not getting a different job till you're my age."

They hugged once more and Maria walked back to unlock the door. "You coming back out, or do you need a minute?"

"I think I need a minute," Josie said. "But thanks."

Maria tapped her forehead and returned to the mass of women

in the kitchen, all hunched over and mopping up what didn't even come close to the worst spill that kitchen had ever seen.

Josie felt a buzz in her pocket and removed her cell phone. A text from Travis read: How's it going with the potatoes?

She smiled at the thought of him in bed next to Henry, who had no doubt run in by now to play on his iPad while Travis read the news, and typed out a response.

All good, she wrote. See you in a couple hours.

She took a final deep breath, reaching for confidence and exhaling her shame, then stepped back outside. The others pretended not to notice her, but their awareness was clear, emanating off their bodies. She squeezed through the opening along the counter and into the crime scene.

"Can I help?"

"Actually, yes," Debbie said. "You got a car here or did that husband of yours drop you off?"

"Car. I mean, I drove myself."

"Well, I hate to be the bearer of bad tidings, but someone's gonna need to go buy potato salad at the H-E-B up in Trevino. They sell it premade, small tubs, but if you talk to Ed or Jimmy behind the counter, they'll put em in big ol' buckets. Get as much as you think we, uh, lost."

"Sure thing. I can do that."

"Keep your receipt, and the Altar Society will pay you back."

"In about six months," Loretta hollered from the center of the hall, where she was spreading disposable covers on all the dining tables with the others.

"Don't listen to her. But if you don't mind, it'd be the biggest help."

"No, I don't mind at all," she said, now noticing Mary Alice's absence. "But hey, is Mary Alice OK?"

"Oh, she went outside. Probably to take a walk or find something else to check on outside her purview. She's fine, don't worry about it. Just needs to feel needed, I'm sure."

Josie wondered why she'd never noticed the way people really spoke about Mary Alice, a mix of affection and admonishment. Her in-laws were more unfiltered, but maybe they were the rule, not the exception, and maybe it just took a little bit of distance from the woman herself for everyone's true opinions to come out. The realization suddenly lightened her, and she walked to her car nearly having forgotten that she'd made potato salad at all. Had it been up to her, she would have chosen store-bought to begin with, and wasn't it all just potatoes and mayonnaise?

As she drove to Trevino, she smiled at the rising sun on the horizon. She wouldn't just take her time, she would see it for what it was: a gift. The sort of gift given only by people who have lived your experience, who once longed for exactly what they have given, and she had flashes of imagined memories of these women, her new friends, and the sorts of messes they'd gotten into at her age. She was not the first to mess up at the picnic, and she knew for certain that she wouldn't be the last.

She arrived at the Trevino H-E-B at a quarter after seven. "Those all for you?" the cashier asked with a twang and a laugh while gesturing at the tidal wave of potato salad easing down the conveyer belt. She told him they were, without so much as a smirk, and had the tubs of yellow potato salad in the cooler nudged in front of her back seat by 7:20. By the time she was parked back in the church parking lot, the embarrassment from earlier had fully dissipated. She was in no rush to bring the store-bought sides to the kitchen. Mary Alice owed her some time to decompress, she thought. So she turned the AC to sixty-five, flipped on a podcast, and sat. During the first ad break, she noticed a movement to her left. Another car had parked right beside her. In the driver's seat was a man she didn't recognize, about her age. Handsome but unshaven, with a curl of the mouth she found familiar but couldn't quite place. When he turned to her she waved, but he must have been surprised by the greeting, jumping a little in his seat and offering only the tiniest hint of a smile before turning his eyes back to the windshield.

Much later she would tell the man something he never quite believed, even though it was the God's honest truth: from the moment he pulled up beside her, she knew they would be friends.

20

THE FIRST THING KATHERINE SAW UPON ENTERING THE kitchen Saturday morning was the message Mary Alice positioned precisely so that it would be the first thing her sister would see when she walked in. Written on a pale pink index card clipped to the end of a stiff wire attached to a plastic, flat-bottomed apple—a strange but ingenious contraption Mary Alice had been given by a student years ago—the note hovered right there above the breakfast table, in midair if you squinted. In Mary Alice's perfect script it read: *Kathy, left for the picnic, won't be home until dark. Lunch is from 11:30–2:30. Left you a ticket.* Beneath that, *M.A.*

Katherine unclipped the note and behind it found a small red ticket that read: ADMIT ONE. She smiled at the simplicity of it all, the honor system of using a ticket one could acquire almost anywhere to exchange for a filling, hot meal, complete with a dessert she'd already seen and quietly craved for the past day. Like so many markers of a small town, it was the sort of experience that simply couldn't be scaled up. No such event could be as relaxed in a big city, let alone as good of a deal, and she smiled at the thought of it being tried at her church in Atlanta; how expensive it would all be, how mismanaged and frustrating. Most visitors would consider it a facsimile of a small-town gathering, but only she and the others who knew better would see an event devoid of all the charm of the real thing. Lunch tickets would probably be digital, she thought, laughing at the thought of Eric Carlye being told what a QR code is. Hell, she barely knew what they were herself.

Planning on taking advantage of the free meal, she settled on coffee for breakfast and made an entire pot for herself. When she opened the cabinet, she was confronted with two options: a big red tub and the bag half its size that cost three times as much, the specialty bag she bought by habit at the grocery store her first morning in town. Her hand hovered in front of the bag, and then, realizing there would be no one in the house to show off to, moved to the left and grabbed the tub.

Hours later, as she was in Mary Alice's bathroom getting ready to leave for lunch, she heard a buzz coming from another room. It was the trill of a standard ring, not the custom guitar strumming she'd programmed for Jonathan's calls, and she hopped up to catch it before it was sent to the abyss of her voicemail, which she always hated, even back when they were on tapes.

"Hello, this is Katherine," she said, after cocking her head at the New York City area code.

The deep, worried voice on the other end was dry-mouthed and quiet. "Hi, Aunt Kathy."

"Oh," she said, sitting on the foot of the bed so thoughtlessly she almost expected to fall on the floor. "How are you doing? Is everything all right? Is Jonathan OK? Where are you?" Confronted with silence, she kept going. "Michael? Are you there?"

WHEN LUNCH WAS ready to be served, the number of picnic visitors was at its peak. Children ran between groups of adults, colorful and sometimes sparkling shards from their confetti-filled eggs inevitably finding their way into the plastic cups of beer. People played carnival betting games, spending a dollar for the privilege to win whatever prize a big wheel happened to land on. And Father Warren roamed the grounds, welcoming parishioners he knew well and visitors he couldn't place if he tried with the same glacier-cold, impossibly soft handshake. For all the groaning that preceded it—the old-timers thought it was a day for children and many young adults felt that it was an outdated event for old-timers—the magic of the picnic was that nearly all who attended ended up having a fantastic time despite their sour expectations. It's easy to imagine some lone passerby driving near the church grounds and mulling over a stop, worried they'd be perceived as an unwelcome outsider, only to be drawn in by the kinds of warm smiles and laughter that could only be interpreted as invitations. The picnic really was the best of Billington, but more than that, it was the promise of what it should always be.

Gerald was the fifth in line, and Ellie blushed as he approached her table with a ticket. "You must be hungry," she said, her eyes darting to the side as though merely speaking to him was breaking some sort of rule. But when he leaned over to kiss her, she didn't even flinch.

"I'm very hungry," he said. When she slapped his chest with a laugh, the kitchen erupted with childish "ooohs."

"Can't you take a day off?" Debbie said, flinging a spoonful of beans onto what would be Gerald's plate. "Everyone saw you with your hands all over each other at Carlye's last night."

"We did not have our hands all over each other," Gerald said, following the plate as it went down the line. "She was a perfect lady. I just had *my* hands all over *her.*"

The way everyone laughed, really laughed, nearly brought Ellie to tears. Surrounded by such unquestioned and judgment-free delight, she felt all the worry she'd been weighed down with for months up and vanish, almost as if it had never been there at all. Of course Ellie and Gerald being together wouldn't raise an eyebrow. They made more sense as a couple than just about anyone or anything in this town.

The buffet line ended with Mary Alice, who was dishing out slices of pie with such calm that no one would have believed there had been a scene, or even a mess, in this very room just a few hours before. "Dessert?" she asked, holding up a paper plate on which exactly one-eighth of one store-bought cherry pie was placed.

Gerald squinted at the oozing, flaky triangle and then looked back up at Mary Alice with the puppy eyes of a child begging for one more gift on Christmas. Mary Alice couldn't deny that everything, from the plate to the slice to Ellie herself, looked positively diminutive next to this man, who'd been big and charming for as long as she'd known him, and she scoffed at his less-than-subtle—almost Dickensian—plea for more, as well as her own decision to give in when dropping another slice beside it on the same plate. "To think I bent the rules for you," she said, a glimmer of a smile forcing its way in. "But don't start thinking this has anything to do with you going with my best friend. I just didn't want to listen to you whine."

By a quarter of one, the buffet line was a conveyor belt with no off switch. Tickets were taken, people chose their meat, and Margaret and Dottie dolloped a spoonful of each side in the appropriate molded reservoirs before Mary Alice gave them exactly one slice of pie. The work became monotonous and quieter, with the women working on autopilot as they finally approached the exhaustion that had mysteriously eluded them since waking long before the sun rose. That's why Maria didn't even register the man when he said he didn't care which meat; she just scooped up a pile of chopped brisket and sent his plate down the line, where beans, coleslaw, and potato salad were plopped alongside without Margaret and Dottie so much as looking up. Mary Alice may not have recognized him herself had he not called her Mom, which he did in a whisper just loud enough to bring the entire operation to a stop almost instantly.

She dropped the pie without saying a word, but Michael didn't flinch. The first person to gasp was Dottie. Then Margaret. Both came close to screaming, but were just too exhausted from the toll of a day in food service to put in the effort. Josie, on dish duty beside Ellie, recognized the man from the parking lot but wasn't sure what she was witnessing. Something was clearly wrong, it was impossible not to notice, and she imagined this must be what it felt like for birds who sensed an earthquake hours before it hit. For a few seconds there was complete silence. Even the one person who had every reason to scream didn't; she just walked up to Michael slowly, not even looking at Mary Alice, whose gaze went back and forth between her son and her best friend with the steady beat of a resting heart.

In the face, Michael looked more like his mother than his father, with the same big, close-together eyes, slightly upturned nose, slightly downturned mouth, and wavy brown hair falling to his shoulders in that casual movie star way. He was just as thin as Samuel was, with the toned arms of a former gym rat who eventually decided it wasn't worth all the effort. He was tall and he was handsome, by far the best-looking ghost anyone in the hall had ever seen, not to mention one of the most unnerving.

"Michael," Ellie finally said. Her voice, gentle and nervous, shook his focus away from Mary Alice's unreadable face. "Is that you?"

"Hi, Mrs. Hall," he said. "It's me."

She collapsed into a hug, covering his back with dishwater and soap. It was the best and worst hug either of them had ever been a part of, a sudden jerk from one body into another, squeezed more than held, but with a sort of tightness that could only mean love, like she'd pulled him out of a frozen river and needed to give him every bit of her body heat. She hugged him like she was saving his life, and like Kenny had just lost his again. *Kenny.* The thought of him made Ellie push Michael away, startling everyone in the room. She shook her head and wiped her face, not that it would stop the tears, and looked at Mary Alice, whose hand still floated between them as though she hadn't noticed the pie had fallen long, long ago.

"What did you do?" Ellie said before turning her gaze to Mary Alice. "What did both of you do?"

Mary Alice moved her lips, but no words came out. She swayed in slow motion, trying to find out if she'd died yet or was merely about to. Michael looked from Ellie to his mother, as though she was the only one with answers. "Why did you do this to me?" Ellie said, a clearer question, the question she meant all along.

"I didn't," Mary Alice said.

"You didn't? You didn't? What do you mean, you didn't? If you didn't, then what am I looking at? Who is this if you didn't?"

"I didn't mean to," Mary Alice said, the tears finally falling. "I didn't mean to hurt you. You have no idea what happened that night, you don't. Let me—"

"You told me he was dead. I mourned him with you. All of us did." She pointed at Michael, her skin now crawling. How had she hugged him like a son, when he was a liar just like his mother? "But you're right here. Breathing just like me. Did you tell her to lie? Was this all your idea?"

"I never wanted to lie," he said. "I just left."

"So it was you," Ellie said, turning back to Mary Alice with eyes that almost glowed with heat. "You let me believe it. You let all of us believe it."

"It was never meant to happen like this. It was never meant to happen at all!"

Ellie could have asked every question in the world in that moment, but instead she walked out the side door and marched to her car. For the rest of her life, she thought, there wouldn't be enough answers. So why bother asking? No. She was done with questions. Just like she was done with Mary Alice Roth.

"I shouldn't have come here," Michael whispered, briefly making eye contact with Josie, who couldn't stop staring. He left the hall through the main entrance and marched toward his car. If anyone recognized him as Michael Roth out there on the grass, where word of the incident hadn't yet spread, they didn't say anything. It was too nice of a day, with too many other things to see, too many other places to look.

But back inside, surrounded by piercing stares that made her feel the worst kind of shame and regret, Mary Alice ran out the side door and stopped on the edge of the lawn, where the grass met the gravel. She saw Ellie's car go straight through the intersection at the church, and then a small SUV she didn't recognize peel into a hard left. Just minutes ago they were both in her grasp, and now she'd gone and lost them all over again.

21

AS FAR AS MICHAEL KNEW, HE WAS THE ONLY PERSON ASIDE
from Mary Alice who could get to the old place without directions.
Once he started driving, it's the only place he ever wanted to go, even
if Mary Alice refused to step foot there. "You're more than welcome
to go; it's gonna be yours one day," his mother had told him the first
time he grabbed the rabbit's foot off the wall. "But I'm not going to
take you."

"Fine," he said. "Then give me directions."

She had expected the day would eventually come, but that didn't
make it any easier. To explain the many roads and landmarks to the
old place was like handing Michael a key to her most terrible memories, but he was persistent, and more than that, he was his mother's
son. She had no choice but to give him a place to make memories of
his own.

The summer after his sixteenth birthday, Michael spent most days at the old place. At first, he went alone to swim and read in peace. Some weeks later he invited Kenny, calling it an "escape," even though they had nothing all that dramatic to be escaping from. His friendships were few but fine, and his mother was cold and often sad but mostly harmless. There was never friction between them, despite the gaping hole that was his father, but Mary Alice's allowance of space, the gift of time left alone to get to know himself, created an unintended rift. He'd never felt this happy before, far away from his mother, and decided it could only mean that even more distance would do nothing but make him happier. While floating on their backs in the oppressive summer heat, he and Kenny made plans to move off together, somewhere far away from Billington. The old place quickly became a portal to their potential selves, the place their friendship, and its future, secured its roots. They spent the next two summers there, sometimes swimming with their other friends— Mary Alice's biggest fear was an accident in the water and she reactivated the landline in case of an emergency—but usually alone as a pair, making plans for the future they couldn't bear to admit would likely never come true. They were smart enough to know how things worked out for boys like them. They'd seen this town pull everyone back, sometimes so tightly and so far underwater that they never came back up.

They rarely talked about Samuel's death, and when it did come up, it came in like a breeze, when the two of them sat beside each other after a dip. "Do you remember him?" Kenny asked once.

"Sort of," Michael said. "I tell my mom I do, because I know it makes her happy, but I don't remember much. A few dinners, him in the car, a trip we took to San Antonio."

Kenny nodded. "I'm sorry."

"Don't be," Michael said before jumping back into the water and cutting the conversation short with a splash.

The night of their graduation, the two of them knew they would end up at the old place long before Michael had suggested it. The party was only two miles away, and neither of them liked parties all that much to begin with, so when Michael held a Bud Light to his lips and asked if Kenny wanted to bail the party, he didn't have to explain where he had in mind.

Once both of them parked—they had driven to the party at the Martins' separately—Michael pulled the six-pack they swiped out of his trunk and walked it to the water, where he dropped it between the two chairs. Kenny turned on the light on the corner of the house and brought the stereo outside. They drank beers and talked about how lame the entire day had been—the robes, the hats, the reception, the crying, the party—but eventually ran out of things to say.

And that's when it happened: the first touch. Or the hundredth. Maybe even the thousandth. They'd been best friends for years, that was the thing. They had touched each other when they swam together, they had touched each other when they worked on assignments together, and they had touched each other when they played video games together, but they had never touched like this. So when Kenny's hand slowly rested itself on Michael's leg as they stared out at the darkness, the only sound the chorus of crickets and birds, Michael didn't flinch. After expecting that hand for years, he felt nothing but relief. "We should go inside," he said.

Kenny nodded. "We should."

On the edge of the bed, Michael held Kenny's face in his hand. The only word he got out was "I," before they'd collapsed on each other, kissing delicately, then passionately as the stereo continued to play faintly outside the window.

Michael laughed as he took off his clothes, and Kenny did the same. They laughed because they didn't know what else to do, and they laughed because they were happy. Look at them—naked in bed together, about to have sex—while all their friends were getting drunk in a barn.

"I want to do something," Kenny said before nervously leaning over and taking Michael into his mouth. "Is that OK?" he asked, looking up at his friend.

"Yes," Michael said. "It's OK. I mean, it's good."

When Kenny came back up, Michael bent down and did the same, quietly relieved he hadn't been the one to start. Neither of them had known exactly what to expect on their drive there that night, but when they were finished, lying together above the sheets, they felt they had done it all mostly right. Even better, they were eager to try again.

When Michael woke up, Kenny was putting on his clothes. "Oh, are you embarrassed?" he said coyly.

"Ha-ha," Kenny said. "I just thought it wouldn't look great if we got home at the same time. So I'm going to head out now, but trust me when I say it's not because I want to." He walked back to the bed, where Michael lay with his arms propped behind him. A sort of victorious pose, a performance for the man he was starting to think he could love, if such a thing were even possible. "I'm going to kiss you right now," Kenny said.

"I'm going to let you." And he did.

When Kenny had one foot out the door, he turned back to his friend. "I think this is going to be a hell of a summer," he said with a wink. Michael laughed. Kenny had never winked at Michael in his life. Maybe he'd been saving it for this moment all along.

WHEN KATHERINE SLAMMED on the brakes in the church parking lot, she could see her sister on the edge of the lawn staring out at something that wasn't there, and knew she was too late. She jumped out and ran to her.

"Mary Alice, was he here? Did you talk to him?"

"He's gone."

"What did he say? Where did he go?"

Mary Alice was frozen, wholly stuck between memories. "The old place. He must have gone to the old place." Katherine grabbed on to her sister and walked her toward the rental car. "Get inside," she said, easing her into the passenger seat. "I'll drive, but you'll have to tell me how to get there."

"Give me your keys," Mary Alice said, swiping them from her sister's hands. "I'm going alone."

Katherine didn't protest. She didn't even speak. She just watched her rental car slowly pull out of the parking space, and drive out of view at the most normal speed imaginable, easing its way into the distance in no hurry at all, confident as could be that it would make it to its destination.

Michael had been everywhere in Mary Alice's life since the night he left, less a ghost than a gas, floating invisibly alongside the nitrogen and oxygen and carbon dioxide, everywhere there was something for her to breathe. But the moment she laid eyes on him in line at the picnic, back in Billington, home at last, he'd never felt more distant. The version of her son she had spent twelve years imagining was destroyed the second he walked into her peripheral vision, replaced with something bursting with angry, overwhelming life. But even though, to Mary Alice, he was a refraction of himself, tiny reflections filtered to pieces of glass to create the illusion of a grown man, Michael looked like the son she remembered. The son who told her he loved her every day of his life, even that final summer spent at the old place, when he didn't have time for much else.

It was twelve years before, and they had just returned from the funeral. The clear, bright heat of summer had finally crept in after a few mild May weeks, and they broke a sweat seconds after stepping from the roaring air-conditioning of Mary Alice's car into the sticky garage. Kenny's funeral had been an hours-long affair, moving slowly from the church to the cemetery, three slow-moving miles away, and then back to the hall, where Mary Alice marveled at Ellie's composure. *This is how a grieving mother should behave at her child's funeral,* she thought. *With sturdy grace and respectful appreciation.*

When Michael suggested that they stand beside their grieving friend and hold her hand, Mary Alice shook her head. "It would only make it harder," she said in a pitiful whisper. "Just let her get through this day."

His resentment over what he considered his mother's callousness grew as they went through the motions of the funeral, and he coped by sneaking swigs of whiskey in the bathroom, and behind the hall, and, daringly, in the passenger seat of his mother's car while she was talking with Maria and Dottie after the burial. He withheld his tears as much as he could, out of an abundance of paranoid caution, but had to channel his excess mental energy somewhere. He was on the verge of breaking, so instead of focusing on his secret sadness, he gave in to the whiskey's advances and turned to anger. His mother was ruining this day. His mother was making it impossible to grieve. His mother would never understand his pain, and for some reason she wouldn't even try. After she told him the news, he spent hours crying alone, staring at the door and hoping she would barge in and tell him everything would be OK. But she didn't. She stayed downstairs and wallowed in her own shame instead of making certain her son wouldn't feel any of his own. So when they were finally home and the door to the garage closed and Mary Alice let out a big what-a-day kind of sigh, Michael decided his mother was going to learn.

"Aren't you going to ask how that was for me?" he said, standing beside the breakfast table with his hands in his pockets.

"I know how it was for you. It was the same as it was for me. It was awful when your father . . ." she said with a surprising bite before stopping herself and slowing down. "When your father died I was a complete mess. You'll never understand why, and I hope you never do, but it can be worse. You're lucky."

"I'm lucky? Lucky?!" Michael was screaming now, and the smell of whiskey finally hit his mother's nose. "Are you hearing yourself? He was my best friend, Mom, and you haven't said you were sorry. You haven't asked how I'm feeling. You haven't seemed to figure out that this is hell for me, and instead somehow think it's all fine because it could have been worse."

"His mother was my best friend, too."

"She still is. So congratulations, your best friend is alive."

She walked to him and grabbed his arms, pulling them down to his side and looking at him from head to toe. When did he grow into such a handsome man? she wondered. When did he start looking just like Samuel? She shoved those questions aside and cleared her throat. "I'm sorry. But I'm trying to process this, too, right alongside you. We can talk. We can talk right now. For as long as you want. I'm sure it will help us both."

A tear fell down each of his cheeks but with Mary Alice still clutching his hands, he couldn't wipe them away. "Mom, I was," he said, gasping for air. "I didn't fall asleep at the Martins' that night."

Her grip loosened. "What do you mean?"

"I was lying," he said. "We both, Kenny and I, left the Martins' that night and went to the old place."

"Just the two of you?" she asked, already knowing the answer.

They exchanged nods, and Mary Alice touched a finger to her brow, an impulse she couldn't explain even at that moment. Maybe it was just something to do besides considering her son's admission—that's what it was, right, an admission—a way to use her body for literally anything else. But he kept talking, refusing to let her ignore the truth.

"The party wasn't fun, too many people, too loud, too much happening. You know I've never liked parties, neither of us did. So we wanted to leave, and the old place was only ten minutes away."

"So you both spent the night there."

"Mom, I was the last person to see him alive. He left, and then," he said, shrugging helplessly.

"Michael, do you realize what this means? Kenny's accident happened after he left *my* property. Where he was drinking beer with *my* son. Who else knows about this?"

"Just you."

"When were you going to say something to me?"

"I didn't know. I just can't hold it in anymore. We didn't want to leave at the same time because we didn't want anyone to see us drive back together, so I told him to go first and that I'd clean up and leave a little later. It wasn't supposed to be a big deal. And he wasn't even drunk at that point. They checked that."

"You and your daddy," she whispered into the space between them before her head fell into her hands.

Michael stood motionless apart from subtle tremors of his quiet sobbing. "It's not my fault, is it?"

She didn't stir.

"Mom? Tell me it's not my fault."

The debris of his revelations and her own grief swirled together like a funnel cloud inside her: Samuel and Kenny and Michael and all their secrets darkening the sky above the old place. Even her own, there they were, too. When she finally looked up at him, she took a deep breath. She would not be rash. She would not say something she didn't mean. So it surprised both of them when she said, "I can't."

Michael could let out only one word, and it left his mouth with a squeak. "What?"

"I don't think he would have died if not for you."

Michael would never know if she had meant Kenny or his father, but it didn't matter because the words should never have been spoken at all. In neither case were they true; they were an exaggeration, a product of raw, unfocused grief. But they set off something in Michael that had been stewing for a long time: a primal, instinctive rage at his mother, his life, this town. And when he threatened to leave—for good, he swore—Mary Alice called his bluff. The seconds or minutes or even hours that followed were so dark and blurry in both their memories that they may as well not have even existed. All that remained of that time is that at one point Mary Alice simply looked up and Michael was gone. Then, of course, the obituary. Ellie saw it first, and when she banged on the door, already in tears, Mary

Alice couldn't find the words to tell her it wasn't true, or that she didn't write it, or that she suspected Michael sent it himself out of anger. She couldn't even find the words to tell herself, so she gave Ellie a shoulder and let her cry. She let everyone cry, all summer long, but kept her own tears to herself. And when Michael sent Mary Alice a letter apologizing for the cruel stunt six months later, just before Christmas, she kept his confession to herself, too. He wrote her every month, always with an ever-changing Manhattan return address so that the checks she sent would be delivered promptly, and within a year began sending empty envelopes just so she would know he was alive. She never wrote him back, but she always wrote a check. And there lay her biggest regret: not killing him, exactly, but letting him stay dead.

Samuel's life insurance policy paid for his son's tuition at New York University, where he had secretly applied and received a decent grant. When he graduated, it paid his rent. And when Michael got a decent job, his father's money went toward excessive bar tabs and car rides home. There were so many empty exchanges between them, so many checks made out to cash, that she always figured their relationship would get discovered somehow, but it never did. Maybe no one cared. Maybe no one even looked. Maybe they thought it was all too sad to investigate.

In New York, where Michael quickly thrived, he only opened up to a handful of friends. But everyone who came to New York from somewhere else was escaping at least a sliver of their past, so perhaps they never felt it urgent enough for them to scrutinize; Michael was just like the rest of them. There was one friend, though, who gave his story a second look. Leslye was also escaping a family of her own, and when, one night, she asked if he would ever consider reconciliation, Michael responded as though nothing could be more unthinkable. "Why would I go back?" he answered without even taking a beat. They had been drinking—drinking was what they had in common—and he collapsed into her shoulder sitting in their favorite booth half an hour before last call.

"I don't know," she finally said after giving it an honest thought. Some mothers were just toxic, she guessed, quietly thankful hers wasn't. "Maybe you shouldn't." Like so many of his friendships, their relationship was short, intense, and built on the backs of bars with good happy hours. That's how Michael was with people: he would get so close to someone that he passed right through them, always moving in the same direction, never even looking back. It kept him from pain, until it caused someone else's.

Hitting rock bottom was preceded by less of a downward spiral than the circling of a drain. Around and around he went, not getting worse but not getting better. Self-destruction wasn't just an inevitability, it was his life-force, it's what kept him going, until the day it finally took hold and sucked him under in a sudden gulp. He shouldn't have been driving at all that day, but he didn't want to pay for someone else's parking ticket. The car, a months-old BMW coupe, was a coworker's, and he'd been tasked with moving it while the owner was away for the summer. He had taken it on trips to the Berkshires and Provincetown without incident, but there's no terror like driving in Manhattan, and when he slammed into the cyclist on the corner of Seventh Avenue and Bleecker, he thought the man was dead. It's what he told the 911 operator, slurring his words so dramatically that the voice on the other end of the line didn't even hide their judgment when asking if he had been drinking. "Yes," Michael said, sobbing into his phone while watching a small crowd grow around the delivery person whose body and bicycle he still hadn't seen.

The cyclist, in a helmet and big black gloves to protect him from windburn, waved away the passersby checking him for injuries, and was long gone by the time two officers put Michael in the back of a police car. "You may have knocked that delivery driver on his ass," his court-appointed attorney told him some days later, "but he saved yours."

When his head stopped spinning, so too did his life. The judge didn't exactly throw the book at Michael, but he came close. His fine was one thousand dollars, the maximum for a first-time offender in New York, and he served two months in jail without explaining his absence to friends or his employer, emerging with a crumbling social life and no job at all. His most reliable friends enabled his bad behavior, and his most caring friends had long run out of patience to keep caring. And though it had once helped to have rich, trusting acquaintances who spent nine months out of every year in Beijing, when he emerged from jail to find all their plants dead, he knew he wouldn't get the privilege again. With the little money he had left, he abandoned his mutually abusive relationship with New York City and flew to the only person in his life who he believed might still answer the door. He didn't remember much about Katherine, just that his mother never hid her hatred for her. And that was all it took to deem her a kindred spirit.

AFTER PARKING THE CAR in the dirt driveway of the old place and slowly climbing out, Mary Alice crept toward her son as though he were a wild animal who wouldn't budge if she moved silently, but he turned to her with a matching sluggishness. He'd expected her to come, Mary Alice realized, and that made her feel even worse.

"Tell me what happened," he said, eyes still hovering above the stagnant water. "What happened here? What happened to Dad? Was I wrong to think there was something weird about the way people talked about him?"

"No," Mary Alice said, taking one more step toward her son. "I'm sorry you ever had to question it; I'm sorry people whispered around you, but I . . ." she said with a sharp inhalation. "But most of all I'm sorry that I never told you the truth."

"Then tell me now," he said.

"When he drowned, it wasn't an accident."

"How do you know?" Michael said, the tone of his voice unchanged.

"Because he left a note."

"And you never told anyone?"

"Who would I have told but you? And you were only a child."

"But why would he?" Michael said. His forearms were so tense Mary Alice figured he could break a table with a single blow if he tried. "What happened?"

"Mikey, your dad was gay," she said, wiping her hands and raising them up like some kind of surrender. "And it was not easy back then. I mean, it was harder than it is now."

"How long did you know?"

"Before we were married. He had a . . . there was a man. His name was Brian. We were all friends in college, but they were, well, they were more than that. But back then we didn't, or he didn't, think it was the sort of thing he could be. So he chose me over Brian, and we were happy. Most of the time. Then we had you, and he loved you more than he'd ever loved anything. Mikey, I promise you that. But at one point, I don't know, Brian came back into the picture. And then he got sick."

"Dad?"

"Brian did."

"Mom, who is this person? Why haven't I ever heard of him?"

"This isn't easy to talk about, sweetie," Mary Alice said, her face falling back to the ground.

"No shit. So instead of sucking it up and having the hard conversation you just didn't say a fucking word?"

"Michael."

"When Kenny died all I wanted was to tell you everything, but you never wanted to listen. When all I had left in this town was you, you made me feel more alone than ever."

"I messed up then. I messed up long before then, too. But I'm trying to fix it, Michael, sweetie. I'm trying to fix it now."

"Then tell me everything. Why didn't I ever hear about Brian before?"

"He died when you were little."

Michael's face dropped. "AIDS?"

"Yes. It was a terrible time for us. Your father especially."

His combativeness had melted away, leaving nothing but ache and distress. "So Dad had it, too?"

Mary Alice shook her head. "No. He was fine. They checked. After."

"So why did he do this?"

"Not long before he went to the old place that last time," Mary Alice said. "Do you remember when we all went to San Antonio? The trip to SeaWorld?"

"Yeah. First and only time."

"Well, SeaWorld was actually secondary. We went up to pay our respects to Brian's family, but we were told we weren't welcome. They even stopped us from getting out of the car. We talked to his mother through a cracked window. Can you imagine that? In any case, we couldn't explain a drive to nowhere to you, you were so young, but the park was nearby and so we went. We knew we'd hate it but never expected you to also. Do you remember how miserable you were? Oh, you were a stinker. Groaning and moaning so much we finally just went back to the car after that poor man got hurt at the Shamu show."

"And then we went to lunch," Michael said. "At the place with the gift shop. I remember that."

"Yeah. Well. Your dad was never quite the same after that, and then by the end of the summer, he was gone."

"Why didn't you tell me?"

"Baby, I didn't tell anyone. I couldn't."

"You told me I killed him."

"I'm sorry," Mary Alice said. "Not a day goes by I don't regret saying that. I never meant it. I think I was just . . ." she said, stopping short of saying what really mattered. Michael didn't pounce on her, as much as she deserved it. He let her think, take her time, breathe. "Sometimes I think I wanted you to hate me. I wanted you to hate me so much in that moment that you'd never consider coming back. But I never thought you would."

"So it's my fault now?"

"No! No. It's all my fault. Every last bit of it," she said, wiping her eyes. "And you know what's worse? When I missed you and your father the most, when I remembered how much this place meant to him and you, and even Kenny, I couldn't even bring myself to come here."

"Why?"

"Because it felt like a graveyard."

Michael took his eyes from the water's edge to his mother, whose arms were crossed tightly beside him, and curled his lips into the faintest of smiles, the first she'd seen on his face in twelve years. "It's the only place I feel like I'm alive."

"Then you should have it," Mary Alice said.

Michael didn't thank her, or even say a word. He just fell to his side, confident that Mary Alice would keep him from hitting the ground, catching him in a hug that she would hold as long as he wanted. As long as it could possibly take.

22

THOUGH IT CONNECTED BOTH THEIR PIECES OF PROPERTY, the summer had made the sixty yards or so between her and Ellie's houses feel like they no longer belonged to Mary Alice at all. And as she walked them Sunday morning, after staying up most of the night talking to Michael and Katherine about the years they'd all missed, she felt almost as though she were trespassing. As though she should be arrested. If she paused and really listened, maybe she could even hear sirens. But they never came, and after knocking, neither did Ellie.

"Good morning, Mary Alice," Gerald said in heavy voice that might have intimidated her if she hadn't known him all his life.

He must have seen her walking up and watched as she built up the courage to talk to a friend who clearly wanted nothing to do with her. She couldn't see past him, his tall body filling the doorway. The

pity and judgment on his face sparred with the overwhelming friend-
liness of his usual outfit, a bright red polo tucked into a pair of blue
jeans. It was the outfit of a man who enjoys routine and hates sleeping in. The outfit of an accountant; the perfect man for Ellie. "She
doesn't want to see you," Gerald said. "And to be perfectly honest,
neither do I."

But in the twitch of his jaw, Mary Alice knew this was hard for
him, too, and that he could be swayed. Gerald was not an angry man,
just fiercely loyal, and though Ellie outranked Mary Alice, she knew
that a lifetime of friendship must account for something. "Gerald,"
she said, "I know you're looking out for her, and I know she told you
not to let me in, but not talking is what got us into this mess and it
isn't going to make anything better for any of us now."

He didn't move aside, but he didn't argue, either, which Mary
Alice took as a win. She was doing something right, finally, and
would keep on doing it until he let her inside. "I need to let her know
what happened. I need to tell her the whole story. I don't expect her
to want anything to do with me once I'm finished, but at least give
me the chance to tell her the truth."

A voice from behind Gerald saved him from having to respond.
"The truth would be nice," Ellie said, her voice somehow focused and
amplified by the doorway. Gerald stepped outside and let the two of
them meet, face-to-face.

"I'll give you two some privacy," he said, shuffling around to let
her in.

Mary Alice walked inside and shut the door behind her, then followed Ellie as she calmly entered the kitchen. Ellie took a seat at the
breakfast table, the same one where they'd met so long ago, and
waited for her friend to do the same. As Mary Alice inhaled, prepar-

ing to finally unload her side of the story, Ellie cut her off at the pass. "Before you get started, I need to know first and foremost why you're here. Is it to make yourself feel better, or to apologize for all this time you spent lying? And don't say a little bit of both. I won't be able to stand that."

"I'm here to tell you exactly what happened, and to apologize for not telling you sooner. If that happens to make *you* feel better, great. But as for me feeling better," she said, almost laughing, "that's never going to happen."

"Do you want a glass of water? Tea? Gerry just made coffee."

"No, I'm fine," Mary Alice said. The most wonderful woman she'd ever known, offering a drink to a woman who didn't even deserve dirt. "Ellie, Kenny died after spending the night with Michael."

"I know."

"No, they left the graduation party at the Martins' place early. They spent that night alone. At the old place."

"Your old place?"

"Is there another one?"

Ellie nodded, then took a sip from her glass of water. She let it sit in her mouth a bit before swallowing, as if too exhausted to make even the simplest of moves. "So now we know that for sure. About the two of them."

Mary Alice nodded back. "Yes. Now we do."

"Then what?"

"He left that morning, early, so you or I wouldn't see them drive up together. Michael stayed behind and by the time he left, the accident had already happened."

"So Michael was the last person to see him alive?" She paused and looked up at Mary Alice, peering at her with a crooked head.

"But that doesn't explain anything about now. Why is he here now? Why did he *leave*?"

"He told me the truth the day of Kenny's funeral, broke down at home. We had a fight. And I suggested that he leave."

"Suggested."

"I kicked him out."

"For what? For falling for some boy?"

"Ellie, you're only the third person I've ever told this to and I didn't tell the first two till yesterday, but Samuel was gay," Mary Alice said. The rest of the truth came tumbling out of her, and once she started she couldn't even slow it down. "I knew it from the first night we spent together. He knew it well before then. And his death at the old place? That wasn't an accident. I'm sure everyone started whispering about it when the body was still warm, but now you know." She paused to shut her eyes and will the tears away, but they didn't relent. "I didn't want to lose Michael, too. So when he left, I had to let him go."

"But then why did you let us believe he was dead?"

"It was easier. That's all. No questions. Less judgment. Who'd second-guess a grieving mother?"

"Easier?" Ellie pushed her seat back with a squeak, anger coiling inside her. "Are you telling me it's easier to have a son die than to know he's alive somewhere else?"

"No, I—"

"Are you telling me it's *easy* to look at a dead body on a rack, covered in blood and bruises? To watch your friends lower it in the ground? Are you telling me I had it *easier* with Kenny dead than I would have had he gone off to some other place—some *real* place—like Michael? In secret? Living some wonderful, exciting life far away?"

314

"All I'm saying is that it was easier to lie than to tell the truth," Mary Alice snapped. After a deep breath, her body relaxed and she cowered in shame. "I shouldn't have, but I took the easy way out. And I've regretted it ever since."

"Do you really believe that? Look at yourself right now. Look at the two of us. Is any of this *easy*? Was twelve years of guilt *easy*?"

"You're right, and I'm sorry. I am sorry for hurting you. It's the last thing I would ever want, believe me," Mary Alice said. "You mean more to me than I mean to myself, and that's got to be the truth because I'm done lying. I love you, Ellie. I have always loved you."

Ellie twisted her mouth and turned away, composing herself to an audience of tall, cedar cabinets. When she turned back, she was crying anyway, having succumbed to the very emotions she had told herself not to feel. "Oh Mary Alice," she said, falling into her on the chair for a hug. "How in the hell could I not love you right back."

Gerald stepped back from the corner where he was eavesdropping and let them finish their talk alone. As he crept up the stairs to the bedroom he had only recently begun to share, he looked proudly at the walls surrounding him. Life really did feel so much better with Ellie in it.

A GUST OF wind made all the cornstalks in the distance sway, shifting together with some invisible rhythm that almost made them forget time was moving, that everything they had ever seen or known was moving, that nothing ever really stopped. Katherine was wearing the nicest blouse she'd worn the whole trip, a pale pink thing that had never seen a wrinkle, and black slacks draped around her like liquid. Without asking, Mary Alice knew this was her usual traveling outfit, something as flattering as it was comfortable, something chosen with the utmost care and hundreds of dollars. Mary Alice looked down at her own outfit for the trip to Atlanta, jeans and tennis shoes, and wondered if she ought to switch to something that was easier to take off. Something without laces, like her sister's flats.

"So it's straight to Atlanta? No stopovers?"

"No stopovers."

"And they make you take off your shoes at the airport now?"

"Well, that depends," Katherine said with a shrug.

"On what?"

"If they let you come in line with me."

"So you don't have to take off your shoes?"

"No."

"Why's that, exactly? You slip someone some cash?"

Katherine groaned and shot her sister something between a scowl and a smile. "No, because I have a special sticker on my ticket."

"How'd you get that?"

"I paid for it."

"I see," Mary Alice said. She was smiling now.

"When's the last time you were on a plane?"

"Oh, twenty-five years. Maybe more."

"How is that possible?"

"Didn't have anywhere to go," she said as her hand reached down to squeeze her sister's. "And nobody ever bought me a ticket."

They finished their coffee at the same time, and Katherine split the remnants in the carafe between the two mugs.

"You know you're *always* welcome at our house," Katherine said.

"I do now," Mary Alice said, a slight smile appearing on her face.

"Good."

Katherine flinched when she heard a creak coming from inside.

"That's just Michael," Mary Alice said, instantly recognizing the sound of his weight on the floorboards.

"Think he'll join us?"

The door slid open and Michael's voice filled the porch. "Morning." He sounded so much like Samuel that Mary Alice didn't know whether to laugh or cry.

"Good morning."

"Mind if I join you?"

"Do you want some coffee?"

"Sure, but just one cup. Josie Kerr invited me over for breakfast. I told her we were leaving this morning but she insisted, so I'm going to walk over in a few."

"Well, let's make another pot anyway. Ellie's coming over, too."

Michael stepped barefoot onto the concrete slab and grabbed the pot, then headed back for the door.

"You know how many scoops?"

"Yes, Mom, I know how many scoops," he said. She could hear his eyes rolling.

"Just checking."

"We're leaving at eleven, right?"

"Ten-forty-five if we can manage," Katherine said. "I need to drop off the car at the rental place and don't know what the line will be like."

"Ten-forty-five. Got it."

When the door closed, Katherine turned back to her sister and squinted at the sight of her. There was a lightness to her now, a smile that felt like part of her, not something painted to cover a crack.

"You should move, you know," she said.

"Where?"

Katherine shrugged. "San Antonio? Dallas? My guest room?"

The question felt impossible to conceive of, let alone answer, so Mary Alice just shook her head. "Everyone I know is here."

Katherine turned to her sister, her glance lingering long enough that Mary Alice returned it. "But what about everyone you don't?"

Mary Alice looked back at the horizon and tried to imagine her next life. Her second try. All she could see were the people she would have to leave behind, though the future looked good on them, didn't it? Of course it did. It had to. As the sun rose over the scraggly silhouettes of mesquite, she finally allowed herself to come into focus. *There I am*, she thought, squinting into the distance. *I'm right there.*

EPILOGUE

WHEN HIS MOTHER LEFT, NOT LONG AFTER RETURNING FROM Atlanta, she split the proceeds from the speedy sale of her old house right down the middle. Not because she needed the entire half—she would never grow out of her frugality—but because he wouldn't accept a penny more. There were no arguments over her leaving, and only a few tears. Mary Alice had made up her mind, and though living through yet another departure made him ache, he knew this time was different. It's not abandonment if both sides have the chance to say goodbye. This time they sent each other letters, not just empty envelopes. This time they talked on the phone, sometimes so often it made their new friends gently groan. One afternoon, hundreds of miles apart, they were both asked the same question ("Do you two talk once a day?") and gave the same response ("At least").

Michael changed so much of the old place once it was all his, but he didn't knock down any walls. The bones, as they say, were strong, and he thought it disrespectful to break something that had done such an admirable job of holding on. With Josie's help, from her design prowess to her surprising familiarity with every contractor and technician in the area, he finished the renovations in just under a year. When the trucks filled with pipes and wood and paint finally pulled away after months spent kicking up clouds of dust on the roads, parking at worrying angles on the lawn, and moving piles of dirt from one spot to another, Michael studied the view from a few yards away. It was exactly what he wanted, but still felt incomplete. Then it came to him. People. What the old place was missing was people.

He started attending church, even though he would never believe. He spent one night a week chatting with regulars at the Buckhorn, even though he would never drink. He became an English teacher when Mrs. Cowan had a stroke, even though he said he would never follow in his mother's footsteps. For the first time, taking chances was paying off, and by the time he met Taylor, he was only a little surprised by how happy their relationship made him.

Mary Alice always drove down for his birthday, as the party was the most efficient way to catch up with everyone in town, but some months before his fortieth she died suddenly in her sleep. Taylor gently suggested he cancel the party, but grief made Michael even more dedicated to a celebration—a workaround to her will's explicit prohibition of a funeral. The party would fall on his birthday, but they would celebrate her life. There would be more lights. There would be more music. There would be so much food and drink that he felt wasteful buying it all.

When one of Henry Kerr's classmates threw him into the lake, dozens of heads jerked in the direction of the splash, only to slowly turn back after hearing the subsequent laughter. "Oh God, Mrs. Hall, I'm so sorry," Henry said while bobbing in the center of the pond.

"Oh, I'll be fine," Ellie said from her chair on the pond's edge, wiping her now-soaked legs and shaking her head as Gerald stifled a laugh beside her. "Those Kerrs always find the water, don't they."

The two of them were smiling at the sight of Henry's friends following him into the water when Josie put a hand on both of their shoulders. "Sorry about the mess," she said.

"Oh, don't you dare apologize. It's a party."

"Can I get you two anything?" Josie asked. "I'm headed back inside."

"I'm fine," Ellie said.

"I'll follow you in," Gerald said, rising from his seat with a grunt. "Gotta use the facilities. Maybe get another plate of food if there's some left."

"Oh, there's plenty," Josie said, gesturing for him to walk ahead.

Ellie sighed as she looked at the now-empty chair beside her and wished Mary Alice would make a surprise appearance as the second ghost in her family to come back to life. But she knew it was impossible. She'd seen the body. She'd watched Michael sprinkle the ashes in the very pond she sat beside. It had been months since she was able to call Mary Alice and catch her up on everything happening in her life, and for Mary Alice to reveal everything happening in her own, but the urge came anyway. With no number to dial, Ellie just kept her eyes on the sky, her smile still holding on tight.

When Michael took a seat in the empty chair, he could read Ellie's gaze like he'd written it himself. "I wish they were here, too," he finally said, resting his hand on her shoulder and giving it an almost imperceptible rub.

Ellie kept her eyes on the stars. "Is it strange that I think they are?"

From above, the party was a shimmering dot of noise and commotion in an expanse of dark, rugged beauty. On the ground, it was one of those impossibly joyful moments that's gone in an instant and feels like a dream. The sort of night you soak up with intention, one you can feel yourself committing to memory. It was only when Ellie had stopped expecting an answer to her question that Michael grabbed her hand and gave her one. No, he told her, it wasn't strange at all.

ACKNOWLEDGMENTS

Thank you to Kate McKean, my agent, for taking me seriously. That you were so quick to say, "Yes, you will write this book," still surprises me. That you were actually *right* still feels like a dream. I still read your (essential) newsletter as if I'm just there to learn from someone I admire, as if you aren't directly responsible for this story turning into a novel. To Gabriella Mongelli, editor of my dreams, whose love for the characters in *The Old Place* often seemed to exceed my own. Thank you for seeing the value in the residents of Billington and for helping me shape their stories into the novel they all deserved. To everyone at Putnam and Penguin Random House for your support, especially Kristen Bianco, Brennin Cummings, Katie Grinch, Sally Kim, Christopher Lin, Vi-An Nguyen, Anthony Ramondo, Lara Robbins, Andrea St. Aubin, Alexis Welby, and Ashley McClay. From the very first call, I knew I would be in good hands.

ACKNOWLEDGMENTS

This novel was written during the darkest days of the pandemic, and I found a life-saving solace in spending time with these characters. Immersing myself in Billington for a few hours a day—thanks in no small part to the momentum-building of Jami Attenberg's 1000 Words of Summer project—was a way of escaping not just the cramped one-bedroom apartment I shared with my husband and two cats, but the grim, unsettling version of a city that was typically so joyful and inviting. To all those who kept me company when I wasn't at my desk, whose presence meant so much to me despite being merely digital, I could not have made it through without having faith in your friendship. To everyone who kept me sane throughout those two years (and who will keep doing so for the rest of my life, if I'm lucky), but especially Steven Avalos, LaLa Thompson, Rae Votta, Kelly Reeves, Jeff Baum, Aminatou Sow, Shani Hilton, Patrick Sullivan, Dan D'Addario, Benjamin Lee, and Richard Lawson. Though nothing beats being face to face, seeing your names light up my phone screen can still make even the emptiest moments of my life feel full.

Thank you to Emma Carmichael, for pulling me away from an office churning out advertising copy and giving me the chance to write for *Jezebel*, where I was surrounded by the funniest and most talented people I'll ever write blogs and eat gummy worms with. It was a privilege to be edited by Kate Dries, Stassa Edwards, Clover Hope, Julianne Escobedo Shepherd, and Jia Tolentino, and to publish my silly little stories about celebrities alongside essential writing by Kara Brown, Clio Chang, Hazel Cills, Madeleine Davies, Kelly Faircloth, Rich Juzwiak, Anna Merlan, Megan Reynolds, Joanna Rothkopf, Ellie Shechet, and Kelly Stout. All of you made me a better writer, a better thinker, a better person, and all of you still do. Working with you was an honor; being your friend is a gift.

ACKNOWLEDGMENTS

To Amanda Millwee and Matt Nall, for pulling me to New York and changing the trajectory of my life, and to Rachel Humphrey, Delia Sarich, Rebecca Kwan Sutter, Alicia Valle, Hera Yeung, Lauren Zaffaroni, for being anchors when I wanted nothing more than to float away. Your homes will always be my home, whether you like it or not.

To Lindsey Weber, for using and sharing your brilliance to help create the greatest/stupidest job of all time, for taking risks when I choose not to, and most importantly, for answering emails I ignore. I couldn't have written this book without having the utmost trust in you as a professional partner, and more importantly, as a friend.

To my siblings, Mike Finger and Val Finger, thank you for your unbridled enthusiasm. I've looked up to you both my entire life, and that kind of admiration is something I'll never outgrow. It still blows my mind that you give me the time of day, and that after three decades you still haven't revealed what your little inside joke means. I am so lucky to have ya'll.

Thank you to the educators I will never forget—Mrs. Mills, Madame Taylor, Professor Rivera—but especially Mr. and Mrs. Finger. Countless students had the good fortune to have the two of you as unforgettable and unparalleled educators in their school lives, but only three were fortunate enough to have your love and support follow them all the way home. Thank you for everything. There would be no *Old Place* without the old place.

And to Joshua, "Thank you" doesn't cut it. You're last on the list because when it comes to you I always seem to run out of words. You'll always be my place, and I'll always be yours.